The rottie yanked the youth against the wire

Other arms reached out to entangle him, their blackened nails clawing at his flesh. Despite his frenzied thrashing, he couldn't break free.

Several of the ville folk darted forward to try to help him.

"Don't get close!" Ryan shouted. "Chop their arms off!"

His friends tried pulling the youth away, but it did no good. Then he screamed, and blood spurted from the side of his head as a rottie bit deep into his ear.

Ryan stepped into a Weaver stance, his left arm crooked to support his blaster hand, and fired a single round. The trapped boy's head jerked, and he slumped.

His friends stared at Ryan in shock and fury.

"If you're bit, you're one of them!" Ryan growled. "Now learn from that stupe and stay back!"

**Other titles in the
Deathlands saga:**

Demons of Eden
The Mars Arena
Watersleep
Nightmare Passage
Freedom Lost
Way of the Wolf
Dark Emblem
Crucible of Time
Starfall
Encounter:
    Collector's Edition
Gemini Rising
Gaia's Demise
Dark Reckoning
Shadow World
Pandora's Redoubt
Rat King
Zero City
Savage Armada
Judas Strike
Shadow Fortress
Sunchild
Breakthrough
Salvation Road
Amazon Gate
Destiny's Truth
Skydark Spawn
Damnation Road Show
Devil Riders
Bloodfire
Hellbenders
Separation
Death Hunt
Shaking Earth
Black Harvest
Vengeance Trail

Ritual Chill
Atlantis Reprise
Labyrinth
Strontium Swamp
Shatter Zone
Perdition Valley
Cannibal Moon
Sky Raider
Remember Tomorrow
Sunspot
Desert Kings
Apocalypse Unborn
Thunder Road
Plague Lords
    (Empire of Xibalba Book I)
Dark Resurrection
    (Empire of Xibalba Book II)
Eden's Twilight
Desolation Crossing
Alpha Wave
Time Castaways
Prophecy
Blood Harvest
Arcadian's Asylum
Baptism of Rage
Doom Helix
Moonfeast
Downrigger Drift
Playfair's Axiom
Tainted Cascade
Perception Fault
Prodigal's Return
Lost Gates
Haven's Blight
Hell Road Warriors
Palaces of Light

JAMES AXLER

DEATH LANDS®

Wretched Earth

A GOLD EAGLE BOOK FROM
WORLDWIDE®

TORONTO • NEW YORK • LONDON
AMSTERDAM • PARIS • SYDNEY • HAMBURG
STOCKHOLM • ATHENS • TOKYO • MILAN
MADRID • WARSAW • BUDAPEST • AUCKLAND

Recycling programs
for this product may
not exist in your area.

First edition July 2012

ISBN-13: 978-0-373-62615-1

WRETCHED EARTH

Copyright © 2012 by Worldwide Library

Printed in U.S.A.

There are more dead people than living. And their numbers are increasing. The living are getting rarer.
—Eugene Ionesco
1909-1994
Rhinoceros

THE DEATHLANDS SAGA

This world is their legacy, a world born in the violent nuclear spasm of 2001 that was the bitter outcome of a struggle for global dominance.

There is no real escape from this shockscape where life always hangs in the balance, vulnerable to newly demonic nature, barbarism, lawlessness.

But they are the warrior survivalists, and they endure—in the way of the lion, the hawk and the tiger, true to nature's heart despite its ruination.

Ryan Cawdor: The privileged son of an East Coast baron. Acquainted with betrayal from a tender age, he is a master of the hard realities.

Krysty Wroth: Harmony ville's own Titian-haired beauty, a woman with the strength of tempered steel. Her premonitions and Gaia powers have been fostered by her Mother Sonja.

J. B. Dix, the Armorer: Weapons master and Ryan's close ally, he, too, honed his skills traversing the Deathlands with the legendary Trader.

Doctor Theophilus Tanner: Torn from his family and a gentler life in 1896, Doc has been thrown into a future he couldn't have imagined.

Dr. Mildred Wyeth: Her father was killed by the Ku Klux Klan, but her fate is not much lighter. Restored from pre-dark cryogenic suspension, she brings twentieth-century healing skills to a nightmare.

Jak Lauren: A true child of the wastelands, reared on adversity, loss and danger, the albino teenager is a fierce fighter and loyal friend.

Dean Cawdor: Ryan's young son by Sharona accepts the only world he knows, and yet he is the seedling bearing the promise of tomorrow.

In a world where all was lost, they are humanity's last hope....

Prologue

The four of them stood in the darkened vanadium-steel room in the guts of the shattered redoubt: a tall rangy man in a tattered greatcoat; a well-built woman whose hair showed auburn highlights in the backsplash from their lamps off gleaming metal walls; a youth with a mane of long black hair hanging past his shoulders; another youth only a bit older, wearing a patched bomber jacket and glasses.

The woman played the bluish gleam of her solar-charging flash on the walls of what he took to be a hexagonal chamber. To the kid with glasses the walls looked like glass. What feeble illumination the quartet was able to muster wasn't enough to let his weak eyes see anything beyond the glass.

"Shit," the tall man said. "Nothing in this place. No food, no ammo, no meds. It's been looted out. I feel like smashing those fancy windows."

"What good'll that do?" the woman asked.

The tall man shrugged. "Make me feel better."

"You can't," the youth said.

The others looked at him, their eyes glinting faintly. He quailed a little under the pressure of their gaze. His own light, a dingy yellow at best, faded to thirsty-man-piss color as he momentarily forgot to keep pumping the little flywheel generator with the palm of his hand, which ached from the constant squeezing.

The tall man raised a fist as if to backhand him.

"Step back, Drygulch. He may know something," the woman said.

"Yeah," the tall man said, sneering. "He knows a lot of crap. It's all he's good for."

The youth in the glasses actually rallied at that. He did know stuff. He was endlessly curious, always seeking to learn more. And he had a memory like a miser's fist.

"Let him talk," the woman said. She wore a homemade leather jacket, the collar of which was lined with silver wolf hide. A belt held up her khaki trousers and the flapped holster for her remade .45 handblaster. "He *does* know stuff."

"Whatever you say, Lariat," Drygulch agreed, scratching at his cap of hair, which looked like short, tight curls of silver-frosted copper wire. "What's on your mind, Hamster?"

"It's *Reno*," he insisted. He didn't even know how the older man had gotten hold of his hated childhood nickname.

"Whatever," Drygulch said. He wasn't a bad type. He didn't dislike Reno so much as he liked poking at him.

Reno swelled inside with the warmth that came from Lariat's acknowledgment of his value to them. To *her*. He held on desperately to the hope that someday the auburn-haired adventuress would realize his real worth, and return the fiercely burning love he harbored for her.

"That's some kind of armored glass," he said. "Your wrecking bar'd just bounce off. So would bullets, so forget all about shooting at the walls."

Drygulch's badlands face crumpled even more than it had to start with. But he lowered the revolver in his right hand. His left held up a kerosene lantern whose smoke filled the room with an oily smell.

"This is a triple-bust," the tall man growled. "We're wastin' our time."

"No, my friends," said the young man who was the party's fourth member. He wore a long, plaid flannel shirt over holey jeans. The soles of his ancient, pointy-toed cowboy boots were held on by thin pieces of leather, sewed around when wet and allowed to tighten into place as they dried. He carried a well-worn M-1 carbine. "There is treasure down here, I tell you. I have seen it with my own eyes."

"Then why didn't you lead us right to it without dicking around?" Drygulch asked.

The black-haired kid's name was Johnny Hueco. He wasn't one of them. He was a local who'd fast-talked the trio into hiring him to guide them into the busted-open redoubt, where he claimed he knew where to lay hands on a baron's ransom in prime scavvie.

"Because we wanted to make sure nothing was going to jump on our backs when we walked all fat, dumb and happy past doors without checking what was behind 'em," Lariat said. "Also because we wanted to make sure we didn't miss anything worth hauling out of here. So step back off the trigger, Drygulch."

"We got to hurry," Johnny Hueco said, shifting his weight uneasily from foot to foot. "Things come out at night. Or in."

That was why the bunch he'd been with when they'd stumbled onto this place, in what once was western Kansas and was now triple hard core Deathlands, hadn't stripped the redoubt of its fabulous treasure. So he said. Something had jumped them in the dark. Only Johnny got out alive, and only because he was closest to the door.

And because whatever it was had been too busy eating his friends, his new companions reckoned. Not that they held it against him. Loyalty was as good as jack or ammo in the Deathlands. Because it was so rare.

When muties or monsters attacked, sometimes all you could do was bug out, and stickies take the slow. Like jack or ammo or white lightning, loyalty could run out.

"Lead on, then," Lariat said.

Johnny led them back out into the broad main corridor. Their footsteps chased each other up and down the bare metal walls like small frightened creatures.

"Shouldn't there be some kind of padding on the floors?" Reno asked. Their boot soles crunched on drifted dirt leavened with some kind of coarse material that didn't seem quite like rock.

"Rats ate it," Johnny said. "Hate rats."

"I dunno," Drygulch said. "Roast 'em just right, they can be mighty tasty. If they ain't been eatin' too much fresh shit or old chills."

Reno licked his lips, suddenly remembering how ravenous he was. He hadn't eaten since they broke camp in the watery, greenish-orange light of dawn.

It wasn't just his wits and his packrat memory that had sustained him through a brutal childhood. There were the rats, too. Where people were, rats thrived. To the perpetually starving Hamster, the ones that had been feasting off shit and dead people tasted just fine.

"Here, what's this?" Lariat said. She strode up beside Johnny.

They stopped. Lariat shone her flashlight at the wall, where a large white sign with red lettering had been bolted: Danger—Restricted Area—Authorized Laboratory Personnel Only.

Drygulch read the sign slowly. "Okay, what's that mean?"

"It means we're not supposed to be here," Johnny said.

"I know that, ass face. I'm not stupe. I mean, what's it mean *here?*"

"It means there's valuable stuff inside," Lariat said.

"What if there's something living in there?" Reno asked, hustling to catch up. He didn't think his friends would cut him out on any ace scavvie they found. He just didn't like to leave too much to chance.

It was cold in here—as above, so below. Topside, the plains were dusted with light dry snow that eddied in the wind. Despite that, Reno's skin prickled as if sunburned.

He hoped it wasn't caused by rads from fallout from the old ground-burst crater a few miles west, drifting in through the cracks in the installation's immensely thick concrete containment shell. They had no way of telling. Unless your skin started getting all mottled and your hair began falling out in clumps. Or you just went straight to the convulsions-and-bloody-shits stage.

With the first you might not die. With the second, you might not die soon *enough.* He'd seen both.

Drygulch held up his kerosene lantern. Next to the sign was a door that had been jammed partway open.

"Strike," Lariat said. She poked her head through and shone her own flashlight around. "Looks like some kind of lab, all right."

"I don't know," Drygulch said. "I don't feel triple-good fucking with whitecoat stuff. Especially not from old days."

"You think we're in here scuffling like rats for rations and ammo?" the woman scoffed.

"Well, yeah. That and meds. Mebbe some blasters. Boots. I could use me some new boots."

"Small-time. Mebbe you're satisfied with that. Not me."

Reno caught up. "I don't think we'll find much of that kinda stuff, anyway," he said. "Place has seemed picked pretty clean so far."

But Johnny Hueco was dancing from one disintegrating boot to another. "This is it!" he said. "It's what I told you about."

"No shit?" Drygulch said dubiously.

"Doesn't look touched in here," Lariat said, backing out.

"If there really was anything worthwhile in there, wouldn't somebody have gotten to it by now?" Drygulch asked.

"Mebbe not," Reno said. "Mebbe the door hasn't been open long."

"Why'd it be open now, Reno?" Lariat asked.

"Earthquakes," he said. "Get a lot of seismic activity in this area. Some big quakes. Mighta shaken it open."

Lariat studied him a moment longer. Her auburn hair hung to just above the wolf-fur-trimmed collar of her jacket, framing wide cheekbones and dark eyes with a touch of the Orient to them. Mebbe she wasn't a beauty, Reno thought. Most men found her good-looking. She was queen of Reno's world.

She'd made it clear early and emphatically that she was too good for the likes of Drygulch and Reno. They might be trail mates and partners, but no touchy-feely stuff.

Lariat nodded now. "Could be it. I'm going in. Who's with me?"

"Might be bad animals in there, Lariat," Drygulch said. "Muties even."

She drew her .45 handblaster, pinching back the slide to confirm she had a round chambered.

"So, might be animals," she said. "Right. I'm ready. Who wants to live forever?"

"Um, just a sec," Reno said. The others turned, then followed his flywheel flashlight beam upward. The ceiling, higher in here than in the corridor, had buckled sharply downward. "So, if the concrete's seriously cracked, the whole fucking thing might cave in on our heads at any minute."

"It hasn't fallen yet," Lariat said blithely, and went in.

Eager as a hound pup, Johnny followed her. Drygulch sent an eye roll Reno's way before he went on through.

Reno carried a Winchester Model 1897 12-gauge scattergun on a rope sling over his shoulder. A pump model with a hammer and a 5-round tube magazine, it had been old, Reno had read somewhere in an old scavvied magazine, even before the Big Nuke lit the skies with hell's own light. At some point in the weapon's long history the barrel had been sawed off a few inches past the end of the mag.

Transferring the flywheel flashlight from his right hand, which had seriously begun to cramp, Reno took the best hold he could on the shotgun's grip and swung the barrel up. What possible good the weapon could do against a potential cave-in, the young man had no clue. He only knew holding it made him feel better.

"Okay, what's 'prions' mean?" Drygulch was asking suspiciously when Reno entered the lab. He was peering at a cabinet stenciled prominently with that word, plus numerous danger symbols and scary messages. "I never heard of prions."

There was a smell in there Reno couldn't name. More than just cold metal and dust. Not like anything that had crept inside recently and died. And he knew that if anybody had died down here during the Big Nuke, in the hundred years and more that had passed, they'd have got their stinking done long since. But still, *something* made him think of death.

Then again, he reminded himself, that's an occupational hazard for a scavvie. They were basically all about stealing dead people's stuff, and trying not to join them in the process.

"Hamster," Drygulch said, "you're the one with your rat nose always buried in a book. What's it mean?"

Reno frowned and scratched his brow. Questions he couldn't answer tickled. "No idea," he said.

"Call him Reno," said Lariat, who didn't look up from flicking through random debris on a countertop with hands encased in fingerless leather gloves. "Anyway, it means 'the goods.' Means we struck black gold."

"You know this how?" Drygulch asked.

"Whatever prions are," the woman said with an air of tested patience, "the whitecoats back before Fire Day thought they were worth squirreling away under that million tons of concrete and steel that's got Reno's panties in a bunch. *And* a sealed heavy door inside of that. I'd say that's valuable whatever the fuck it is, wouldn't you?"

"Cabinet's locked," Drygulch complained.

"Well, open it," Lariat said. "Use your pry bar. Reno, guard the door."

Johnny prowled the room. Lariat stood watching as Drygulch drew the four-foot pry bar from its scabbard fastened to his big rucksack. They all carried empty packs. Their possessions were cached a half mile from the installation's entrance.

The metal cabinet marked Prions wasn't all that sturdy. A little poking for purchase, a grunt and heave and a squeal of tormented metal, and the door popped open.

Drygulch resheathed the bar, picked up his lantern and hunkered down to peer inside.

"Little vials in here," he said.

"Load 'em in your pack," Lariat said.

Their guide walked to a door at the back of the room. It looked as if it opened by sliding sideways into the alloy wall.

"There's more through here," he said.

"Can we open it?" Reno asked dubiously. "Looks a little hefty for Drygulch's bar."

"It was open when I was here before," Johnny said. "I swear it."

As if to prove his point, he began to pull on it, as if hoping to open it using nothing more than the friction of his fingertips.

Amazingly, it worked. The door slid open with only a token squeal of protest.

"Watch it—" Reno began.

He had no idea what made him voice the aborted warning. Before it finished leaving his mouth a dark shape shot from the blackness beyond the door and hit the kneeling Drygulch as he shouldered his pack. The tall man went over with a crunch that horrified Reno, until he realized it was likely some of the small, seemingly sturdy vials Drygulch had just stuffed in his pack breaking, not his bones.

Then Reno had something to be really horrified about, as he swung his flashlight on target. Its feeble shine revealed what looked to be a spiky-furred gray rat the size of a large dog, but with a snoutful of sharp teeth instead of incisors. And an extra set of appendages like a mantis's clawed forelimbs jutting from just behind its shoulders, three feet long and covered in gleaming black chitin.

Drygulch had somehow got a hand under the mutie's lower jaw and was fending off its fangs. For the moment. Reno stepped up so his shotgun's muzzle was about six inches from where thick neck met misshapen torso, and fired.

The noise was like two cast-iron pans being clapped together either side of his head. Muzzle-flame splashed against the creature's body. The sickening reek of burned hair went right up Reno's nostrils like barbs. The charge of scavenged number 4 buck tore the fanged head halfway from the body.

Reno kicked it aside, where it lay with its legs twitching, jaws still snapping, and those awful insectile claws scratching futilely at a synthetic-tiled floor.

Another figure darted from the door. Lariat's .45 bucked and roared and vomited yellow flame three times, fast. The horror squealed and tumbled into a forward roll that carried it into the far wall.

Johnny stood with his back to the doorway. His lean, handsome face stretched to accommodate a mouth that had become a yawning oval of fear. He held his little carbine halfway to his shoulder as if to shoot at the second creature that had come through.

Then his expression grew strangely curious. Reno heard a sound like somebody stepping on a ripe gourd.

A claw like the first mutie's suddenly burst through Johnny's chest. Blood fountained out around it, but didn't hide the fact that it was way bigger than the one the other rat thing sported. The clawed arm lifted Johnny off the floor. He screamed and flailed his limbs mindlessly. The M-1 carbine cracked with deafening shots, sending ricochets howling around the adventurers.

"Time to go!" Lariat yelled, as a tumbling round glanced off Reno's shoulder.

Drygulch jumped up and ran. Lariat raced after him, firing her handblaster back into the infinite blackness of the inner doorway. Backpedaling into the corridor, Reno started to warn his boss that she might hit their guide.

Then he asked himself why that would be a bad thing.

"LET ME LOOK AT IT," Reno said.

Drygulch held his wounded arm away. "No. It's fine. Leave me 'lone."

The last of their jackrabbit stew boiled in a cast-iron kettle on a little break-down aluminum tripod over a campfire of driftwood and dried weeds. Some flakes of what Lariat claimed was sage bubbled in the mix.

The stew smelled to Reno like stinkbug ass. He guessed it would taste worse. But after this day a good case of the running shits would only be appropriate. Anyway, he was hungry enough to *eat* a stinkbug's ass. A whole pot of stinkbug asses.

But by the sick yellow light of the flames, he made out something disturbing. Reddish inflammation, shot through with nasty dark discoloration, crept up the man's lanky arm from his bandaged hand.

Lariat pronounced the stew done. Drygulch refused any, which right there showed he was in bad shape. Reno ate his share with relish. It was definitely better than stinkbug ass. If not much else.

When nothing remained that his spoon could catch, Reno licked his bowl. Then he scrubbed it with dirt and a handful of crackly, dry bunchgrass. As he stuffed his hobo tool and bowl in his pack, Lariat motioned him aside.

The night sky was full of stars. An orange moon hung near the western horizon. Wind quested restlessly through sere grass. Most of the light snow that had fallen earlier had melted away.

"So what do you think he's got?" she asked.

Reno shrugged. "Dunno. Won't let me look at it."

"I can hear you," Drygulch said. "Got no call talking about me in the third person like I was a…a rock or somethin'. Insultin'."

"Well, if some damn fool hadn't gone and stuck his hand in his pack and gotten cut to shit on broken glass, we wouldn't be having this conversation," Lariat said.

"I was tryin' to find out if them prion vials was okay after I landed on 'em!"

"And found out the hard way you'd busted most of them."

"We got a few intact, Lariat," Reno said. He hated disputes. He knew how quickly *nasty* could erupt. When that happened it was usually him who wound up getting the bad end of the ass-wiping stick. "Oughta be able to get something for them, if we find the right whitecoats."

"I can do that," she said. Then, taking Reno by the arm, she urged him a little farther outside the circle of faint firelight. And more important, out of the aggrieved Drygulch's earshot.

"Could it mebbe be gangrene?" she asked.

"Too soon," Reno said. "Could be blood poisoning, though."

He glanced uneasily back at the tall man, who had slithered into his bedroll and deliberately lain down with his back to his comrades as well as the fire.

"I wonder if those prions have anything to do with his condition," Reno said softly.

"Doesn't much matter if the stupe won't let us look at it," Lariat said in a tone that suggested it didn't much matter to her if he did. "He doesn't wake up in the morning, we'll know something was wrong."

COMMOTION ROUSED RENO from a wondrous dream of soft sheets and blow jobs.

He sat up. By the vagrant red gleam of the low coals they'd kicked the fire into before bedding down, he saw Drygulch thrashing in his sleeping bag. He moaned like an animal in distress.

"Drygulch?" Reno asked tentatively.

Lariat appeared out of the darkness. She'd been on sentry duty. Johnny Hueco's M-1 carbine was tipped back over her shoulder.

"Drygulch?" she said.

He uttered a strangled noise somewhere between a cough and a scream, then spasmed so hard his back arched clear off the ground. His fingers raked frozen soil, then he fell back silent and still.

After he stayed that way for a full minute, Lariat said, "That can't be good."

Reno skinned out of his sleeping bag and started pulling on jeans encrusted with dirt.

"Lariat, be careful," he said.

"Why?" she asked. "Poor slagger's chilled."

She prodded Drygulch with the toe of a boot.

With an inhuman snarl he sat up. His face was a strange gray in the ember light, cheeks sunken, the lips drawn back from his teeth. A network of dark lines spread across his face as if his veins were right beneath the skin and filled with ink. His eyes burned like coals in black-painted cups.

Lariat jumped back in alarm. "Drygulch?" she whispered.

He thrashed, as if the bedroll were a mutie monster whose clutches he was trying to escape.

"Get back!" Reno shouted. "Get away from him! He isn't right!"

"Drygulch, you're scaring me—"

Bursting free at last from the sleeping bag, Drygulch uttered an eerie moan and pounced on Lariat like an angry mountain lion.

Chapter One

"Gig sucks," Jak Lauren complained.

The crowded barroom of Omar's Triple-Fine Caravanserai and Gaudy reeked of spilled beer, spilled sweat and the faint tang of spilled blood.

At least, Ryan Cawdor thought, leaning on the hardwood bar with a protective hand on the handle of a mug of beer, I can't smell puke. Much.

"Reluctant as I am to condone, and thereby encourage, what may be a new nadir of our young associate's articulation, I fear I most heartily concur with the sentiment," Dr. Theophilus Tanner said. He had to shout to make himself heard over the din of drunken conversation, riotous laughter and tinkling of a gap-toothed and out-of-tune upright piano.

The piano, inexplicably painted canary-yellow, was played by a girl of about twelve with freckles, pigtails, a homespun dress and at least a little skill. Those who thought her musical talents deficient were well-advised to keep their opinions behind their teeth, if they liked having teeth. The girl, Sary-Anne, was one of the innumerable children claimed by the tavern keeper and his three wives.

Omar kept a hickory cudgel in a leather holster down his leg to bust the heads of the obstreperous, not to mention the teeth of the hypercritical. A similar holster down the other leg carried a sawed-off, double-barrel scattergun for the especially hard to convince.

As gaunt as a crane, Doc Tanner perched next to Ryan on a bar stool of stout raw planks hammered together, with some sawdust-filled burlap for a "cushion." The tails of his frock coat hung down almost to the loose sawdust that covered the warped wooden floor.

He raised a tumbler of what the bartender sold as "whiskey," and which Ryan was sure was just shine colored brown with he-didn't-want-to-know-what. For a moment Doc studied its contents, which would probably have still been murky had the glass been clean and the light better than the glow of a few kerosene lanterns strung strategically around the crowded barroom. Strategically so that none of the patrons could get too good a look at the goods on tap. Then, with a convulsive heave, the ancient-looking man grabbed the heavy glass in both hands and tossed the shot down his throat. Immediately, his body quivered.

"Mother's milk," Doc said. His long, silver-white hair seemed to have gotten wilder. His seamed face hitched into a sad smile, and his blue eyes took on a faraway look.

"You know it's not like we had a choice," their shorter companion said. The man in the leather jacket and battered fedora adjusted the glasses on the bridge of his nose. "Our point of arrival was picked clean, and we all got a nasty addiction to eating, which we have to tend to."

"Point of arrival" was J. B. Dix's way of saying "redoubt" when unfriendly ears might be listening to their conversation. Located in redoubts, deep beneath the earth, was a network of functioning six-sided matter-transfer units with armaglass walls color-coded for identification. These mat-trans units gave potential access to sites dotted not just all over North America, but the rest of the world, as well.

"Can hunt," Jak said, tossing down his beer. He was a teenager with a mane of long hair as white as snow. The color of his skin matched his hair. He was an albino, and still cranky over the dispute that had met his initial attempt to enter the caravanserai.

The sign over the round arch over the gate through the high mud-brick wall that surrounded the compound read No Muties. Fortunately, Omar himself, eventually summoned by one of his sons, understood that albinism wasn't a mutie trait, and allowed Jak to enter.

Their employer, Boss Tim Plunkett, had complained loudly at the delay the whole while. There were reasons why Jak said the gig sucked.

"That's your answer to everything, Jak," J.B. said, taking off his glasses and wiping them clear of condensation with a shirttail. "We can hunt, yeah. If you don't mind living on about half an irradiated lizard a week, which is all even you could come up with in this sorry-ass place."

"We've done jobs before," Ryan said. "Didn't always care for all of them. But we did them and moved on. Like J.B. says, we have to eat."

"Could leave," Jak said stubbornly. He meant go back to the mat-trans and jump out.

A woman as tall as Ryan and skinny as a chicken bone came up, carrying a tray with empty mugs of grimy glass and chipped ceramic. Despite stringy blond hair and a thin face without much to boast of by way of a chin, she wasn't bad to look at. If he wasn't deeply in love with a gorgeous redhead who was off somewhere with the other member of their party, predark freezie Mildred Wyeth, Ryan might've eyed the blonde with some interest after hard days on the trail. Plenty of the caravanserai customers were doing so— the wag drivers in their leather and weird hairdos, with hard voices and harder eyes, and even the mild-mannered cultists who were traveling west in a green school bus, all wearing scarves over their heads that were tied beneath their chins like bonnets.

As far as Ryan knew, she wasn't available for that kind of service to anyone but Omar himself. That was because she was one of the caravanserai owner's wives, known only and unsurprisingly as the Skinny One. Omar's other wives, the Fat One and the Nuke Red Hot One, were somewhere out of the picture, although Ryan thought he could make out Red's voice, which had a notable edge to it, carving a new bunghole in one of the kitchen help for spilling stew.

The Skinny One had arrived to see if they needed refills. Doc ordered another shot, which made Ryan's already thin lips tighten until they almost vanished. Doc sometimes had a tenuous grip on the here and now. The one-eyed man didn't see that he needed to kill his brain cells with any more rotgut.

But J.B., who was the group's armorer and Ryan's oldest friend, flashed an easy grin. "Lighten up and let a man ease his troubles," he said. Then, as if to pretend he was talking about himself, he ordered another shot, as well.

Ryan studied his own heavy tumbler a moment and decided he didn't need any more. He wasn't normally queasy, but the glass had so many thumbprints on it they appeared to be etched in. Between that and the brown shine eating the lining off his stomach walls like hydrochloric acid, he reckoned he'd feel gut-shot if he kept on. He held a hand over the glass to indicate he didn't need a refill.

The Skinny One bustled off, returning a moment later to fill Doc's and J.B.'s glasses from a bottle.

"Besides," J.B. said, as if he hadn't been interrupted, "we might wind up somewhere worse. It's happened."

A commotion started at the door. A tall, stout man with a florid face and sweeping brown mustache strode in, as proud as a baron. Faces turned to stare.

"Boss Plunkett sure loves to make an entrance," J.B. muttered.

Plunkett was dressed in expensive if tasteless scavenged clothing: a pink shirt, yellow cravat and a matching vest that strained to contain his paunch; overly tight brown flare-bottom trousers; black, pointy-toed boots shiny as lizard eyes. The companions' employer had a woman on either arm, one blonde, one black-haired, both looking pretty good, not too hard or shopworn. They were named Tina and Angela. He called them his secretaries, but as far as Ryan and his friends could tell they were just sluts, companions hired to look good on his arm and perform whatever other duties were required.

Behind the big man and his women came Loomis, his bodyguard. He was middle height, with a dark face like the blade of an ax, black hair cut close to his narrow skull, a mustache almost as extravagant as Plunkett's, and a perpetually unshaved jaw. He wore leather pants and a leather vest, but was shirtless, showing off a chest furred like a black bear's ass. On one side of a silver-studded belt he wore a big survival knife with a saw-back blade. On the other he carried a chromed .44 Magnum Taurus blaster, which looked to be in good condition.

He gave Ryan a quick, hateful stare as soon as he noticed him. He resented the companions' presence. He seemed to think it reflected a lack of confidence on his employer's part, which Ryan reckoned showed Plunkett had more sense than most people would give him credit for.

The fat man immediately began to berate the nearest server, a skinny, pigtailed girl, in a loud voice.

"Stupe," Jak muttered.

"Yeah, well," Ryan said. "It'll be over soon. Soon as we deliver the boss and his mysterious trunks to Sweetwater Junction."

They'd been three days on the road guarding Tim Plunkett's corpulent body, his two "secretaries" and an assortment of other flunkies including Loomis. The companions spent most of their time split up among a Toyota Tundra pickup truck that served as a sec wag, a former RV that carried extra bodies and bags, and occasionally the Land Cruiser that was the boss's personal ride. They'd met Plunkett and his motley crew east of Omar's at a trading post even farther out in the back of beyond, little more than a shack and an outhouse set too close to a watering hole for comfort. Despite Loomis's swaggering assurance that he and his pair of assistant sec men, who doubled as roustabouts, could handle anything the wasteland could throw at them, Plunkett was clearly nervous. He'd offered the friends jobs as extra sec before even introducing himself.

They'd tried not to act too eager. They really were running on fumes, with barely the jack to buy water from the sketchy well. They'd had a run of poor luck of late.

"'Beware yon Cassius,'" Doc quoted sonorously, "'for he has a lean and hungry look.'"

"Plunkett?" J.B. asked in amazement.

"I think he means Loomis," Ryan said.

"I do indeed, my dear Ryan," Doc said. "Our esteemed employer more closely resembles a hog in a silk suit. Though I grant he has a hungry look to him as well, especially when he's tucking into a hearty repast."

Doc shook his head. "Swine. I *hate* swine." Tears brimmed in his blue eyes. "The sows, the sows—whenever I eat a ham sandwich, I feel vindicated. Vindicated!"

"Easy there, Doc," Ryan said.

Although he looked to be on the hard end of his sixties, Dr. Theophilus Algernon Tanner was chronologically only in his thirties. Yet he was enormously old—scary old. He'd been born on Valentine's Day in 1868, then trawled out of his own time by twentieth-century whitecoats. Doc proved to be a difficult subject, so he was trawled forward in time to the Deathlands. The result, along with premature aging, was that his mind wasn't clamped down any too hard, and tended to wander at times.

"It was under an evil star that we signed on with Plunkett," he said now, suddenly focusing.

Ryan scratched his shaggy head. "Not my favorite thing, either," he admitted. "I don't know whether it's something he did, something he's got in his brain or something he's got in one of those trunks. But he's triple-scared somebody's going to make a play for it, whatever it is."

"Folks don't pay like he pays us if they aren't scared, Ryan," J.B. said. "You're right. We've done tough jobs before, and always come through ace. Or at least alive, which amounts to the same thing."

"Any landing you can walk away from is a good landing," Doc announced. "Eddie Rickenbacker told me that. He was a good lad, if rather on the reckless side."

Ryan had no idea what Doc was talking about. He decided to let it slide. It wasn't that he lacked curiosity. But whenever Doc launched into one of his tortured explanations, Ryan's head hurt.

Just then, with a gust of cold evening air, somebody poked his head through the door and shouted, "Hey, everybody! That big-tit redhead and the black woman are dustin' it up with a pack of caravaneers!"

Ryan wished he hadn't passed on that refill. "Time to go."

A HARD SHOVE between the breasts sat Mildred Wyeth down hard on her tailbone. The impact sent white sparks shooting up in her brain, and raised tears in her eyes.

How'd I get myself into this? she wondered.

It was a question with several possible answers. In one, she'd been a physician and cryogenics researcher in America at the end of the twentieth century. Complications following routine abdominal surgery had resulted in Mildred being frozen in an experimental cryogenic unit, with the hopes of reviving her in the future.

Then the world ended.

Several years earlier Ryan Cawdor and the others had stumbled across her cryopod and thawed her. She'd been with them since, trapped in a future she definitely hadn't volunteered for.

But, more immediately...

She and Krysty Wroth had been walking back from where the wags were parked across the compound.

"You know, Krysty," Mildred said, "it's weird. Usually these storage places were built in or real near a town of at least some size. So they'd have, like, *customers,* you know?"

Krysty nodded and smiled absently. Mildred stifled a sigh. Sometimes her companions had little curiosity about the history of their kind and their continent, except insofar as it might lead to plunder or some other more or less tangible advantage. Not even the tall, statuesque woman with the flame-red hair and the emerald green eyes, who had a lively intelligence, imagination and general thirst for knowledge about the world. She, too, was mostly fixed on the present.

Of course, Mildred reminded herself, if you wake up every morning with no way to be sure there'll be food to eat or water to drink, and that terrible muties aren't going to kill you or coldhearts rape and enslave you, you might find the concerns of the moment a lot more pressing than some past, so long dead it isn't even moldy anymore.

"I guess the war or the quakes knocked down whatever

town lay nearby, and storms and scavengers took care of the rest," Mildred said.

Screw it, she thought. Sometimes it feels good to connect to my own past. Krysty was a genuinely generous person as well as a friend. Mildred would just take advantage of her good nature and impose.

"Of course, most of the storage units must've gotten wiped out, too," she continued. "Only a few dozen are left."

Those were arranged around three sides of a wide square. The fourth was occupied by the three-story, wooden gaudy house itself, along with a combination water- and watchtower, thirty feet high, beside the dirt road to the main gate beyond. The earth around was stamped flat by generations of feet, tires and hooves, but Mildred guessed the open space had once been a paved parking lot. The gaudy probably stood where the office had been. The storage sheds were still being rented, but mostly by the night—or the hour—as cribs and temporary shelters for wayfarers across the desolate, acid-rain-racked wasteland that had once been the Great Plains.

A fair number of wags were parked in the big open space: Plunkett's RV, big cargo trucks from the trade caravans and the old school bus, its bright green paint job faded the color of asparagus.

A pair of people appeared in front of them. Krysty tensed at Mildred's side. Strangers moving to intercept wasn't a comforting nor a welcoming thing in the Deathlands, but these were nondescript people, a man and a woman dressed in the usual postskydark shabby clothing, but with dark green handkerchiefs knotted over their heads.

"Cthulhu wants you," the woman said, smiling angelically.

Mildred shuddered. "He can't have me."

"He'll have us all someday, friend," the tall, skinny man

said, beaming. "Come to him now and know the peace of his love."

"Why do you all wear those green scarves?" Krysty asked. She had instantly relaxed upon recognizing the pair from the twenty or thirty cultists overnighting in the caravanserai.

They seemed harmless, but Mildred said, "Don't talk to them, Krysty! It only encourages them."

"Why not?" she asked. "I'm interested in the paths people walk to the truth. Anyway, I want to know."

"Why, sister," the woman said, "it represents seaweed."

"Seaweed?" asked Mildred despite herself. *"Seaweed?"*

"Why, certainly," the man said, nodding. "The seaweed that covers our lord Cthulhu's head as he waits, dead and dreaming, in lost R'lyeh!"

"Praise Cthulhu!" the woman declared, raising fervent eyes toward a sky banded with purple, orange, red and indigo. It was just sunset, though, not any kind of terrible storm coming in. "Cthulhu *fhtagn!*"

"Dead?" Krysty asked, seeming a bit stunned.

"Dead," they both said, nodding in unison. "Dead to rise someday."

Declining the offer of a handout, which seemed to consist of woodcuts on God—or Cthulhu—the two women walked on.

"What an odd belief system," Krysty said.

Mildred shook her head. "Dang. I never realized just how similar the whole Cthulhu thing was to the Christian mythology."

"You mean the sect existed during your earlier life?"

"Sort of. Only then they were called the science fiction fans." She rolled her eyes. "My daddy'd go upside my head, he heard me comparing the two."

Some of Omar's staff, or children—to the extent there

was a difference—were circling the central yard, lighting torches as darkness fell.

"What's happening over there?" Krysty asked, pointing.

By the flaring orange torchlight that flickered in a chill, rising breeze, Mildred saw a skinny guy being bounced like a pinball among a group of dusty, mean-looking wag drivers. They were hooting derisively as they thrust him from one to the next. He reeled, unable to get his balance.

Mildred scowled. "They hadn't ought to do that to a little guy. With glasses."

Squaring her shoulders, she marched toward the fracas. It didn't even occur to her to wonder whether Krysty would follow or not. Mildred didn't care. She hated injustice.

As the little guy was pushed from pillar to post, a bald wag driver stuck out a boot. The victim went sprawling, his glasses flying off his face. Desperately, he shoved himself up onto all fours to scuttle after them.

They'd landed near another knot of jeering, laughing wag drivers. One waited until the skinny guy's fingers almost reached the glasses before he stepped on the specs and crushed them with a vindictive ankle twist.

"Well, now, look what I gone and done," he said, showing a gap-toothed grin to his buddies. "Ain't that a shame?"

Evidently deciding his pal was getting too much of the attention, a larger man with a mop of dirty hair took it up a notch. He stepped toward the scrabbling victim, clearly getting ready to put the boot in.

Mildred grabbed his shoulder. "Here, you got no call to do that," she said, spinning him.

The predark doctor was a sturdily built woman. In her time she'd been an avid hiker, not to mention an Olympic-class pistol shooter. Since reawakening into the Deathlands she hadn't exactly slacked off at either pursuit.

But the guy was a head taller than she was, and what

little wits he had were fuddled by advanced testosterone poisoning. As he turned, he snarled and punched her hard between the breasts. She reeled backward three steps and sat down hard.

So there she was. And the dirty-haired guy was winding up as if to deliver to *her* the kick she'd stymied.

Chapter Two

The burly wag driver, who turned out to have a rat's-nest beard to go along with the hair, did a little stutter step to kick the sitting Mildred. She gave him a hard heel thrust in the nuts. He sat down not far away from her, bent over and clutching himself.

Mildred jumped up. The whole rowdy group converged on her, the little dude with the crushed glasses forgotten.

Suddenly Krysty stood shoulder-to-shoulder with her friend. Her prehensile hair swished around her shoulders, betraying her agitation. It also betrayed the fact that, however beautiful she was, Krysty Wroth was a mutie. Given the sign above the gateway, not to mention the temper of the mob closing in on them, Mildred hoped onlookers would think it was just the breeze stirring her scarlet locks.

"Wait!" Krysty said, holding up her hands. "What's all this about?"

"Thanks, Krysty," Mildred said from the corner of her mouth. "But you probably should have stood clear."

Krysty just smiled at her. That wasn't the way of any of them, to stand by and watch a friend get stomped. Mildred felt sick at what she might have gotten her friend into.

A wag driver with a Mohawk like a dead squirrel atop his head backhanded Krysty. "Clear out, bitch, or you'll get what we give her."

The force of the blow snapped Krysty's head around. She came back with an overhand right that flattened the man's long nose against his face with a crunch of breaking bone and cartilage, and blood squirting out each nostril. His eyes rolled up in his skull and he folded to the yard.

With a vicious collective snarl, the man pack closed in around the two embattled women.

Hard arms enveloped Krysty from behind. Hot breath washed down her neck and back. It stank like an overflowed shitter.

"Gotcha!" her captor grunted triumphantly as he tried to hoist her off her feet.

He got more than he bargained for. Krysty brought her knees up and drove a double-booted kick to the jaw of a short, wide wag driver with a faded bandanna tied around his head, hurling him into the crowd. Then she slammed her head back into the face of the man who held her.

Krysty's skull was stronger than his jaw was. She felt something crunch at the impact, and he squalled and let her go. She gripped her hands together and turned into him fast, driving the point of her elbow into the pit of his stomach. The air burst out of him.

As he jackknifed, Krysty was already responding to the men rushing in on her. She whipped herself upright, bringing her elbow under the chin of one of them. His jaws clacked together, then he screamed, revealing red teeth that had bitten deeply into his tongue.

She caught a glimpse of Mildred. Surrounded, the stocky black woman had turned into a whirling dervish of fists, boots and elbows. She was peaceful by nature but could fight when she had to. And years of Deathlands living had taught her to hold nothing back. She was giving her attackers all they wanted and a double load more.

Krysty didn't regret stepping in to help Mildred. The woman was too softhearted and shouldn't have intervened. Krysty understood intellectually that Ryan was right about the need to keep out of fights that weren't theirs, no matter how her own compassionate nature rebelled. But there were times when bad behavior had to be resisted.

Whatever the cost.

Her arms were grabbed from both sides. She sagged toward the closer assailant, who had caught her right arm. Cocking her knee, she turned and fired her left leg back in a powerful kick that caught the man who held her other arm between navel and crotch. It knocked his legs out from under him, and he slammed into the merciless ground face-first.

Krysty swung back around, driving her left knee toward the groin of the man who still held her arm. He twisted his own hips. And her knee drove hard into the big muscle of his thigh. It had to have hurt like rad fire, but he grinned in triumph that she'd missed pulping his balls, and made to grab her with his other hand.

She got her foot down, turned back and, grounding her powerful legs, pistoned a blow against his ribs. Bone cracked like a pistol shot. He gasped and sagged.

Another man was already closing in from behind. Krysty snapped her left leg straight back, then whipped it up and around. Her heel thwacked the new attacker's left cheek and spun him away.

There were too many of them; she and Mildred could never win. But Krysty put that knowledge from her mind and gave herself totally over to fighting.

A TALL MAN IN A JACKET with tarnished silver studs and frayed gray patches spun toward Ryan, and away from an ill-considered attack on Krysty, which had earned him a wheel kick in the cheek.

He almost stumbled into Ryan. "I'm gonna teach that bitch," he said. "Get my back!"

He wheeled to charge the flailing, fighting redhead. Re-calling a lesson from Trader, back in the day, Ryan folded his right hand into what the cagey old man had called a "phoenix-eye fist," with the forefinger knuckle protruding, braced by the thumb. It wasn't a shot Ryan had had many opportunities to make. He was interested to see how it would pan out.

It panned out ace. Grabbing the wag driver's shoulder, Ryan dug a brutal uppercut into the man's right kidney, putting plenty of hip twist and leg drive into the short, sweet, savage stroke. The guy squeaked like a stepped-on deer mouse and slumped to the ground. There he curled up into a knot of pain and lay mewling and drooling into the hardscrabble dirt.

"What seems to be the problem here?" Ryan said, raising his voice.

Nobody paid any attention. Instead, peristaltic waves of mob closed in and over the two women. Setting his jaw, Ryan prepared to wade in.

A colossal boom roared out behind him, and a garish yellow-white flash lit the whole courtyard.

Everybody froze, then pale, surprised faces turned in Ryan's direction.

But they weren't gazing at him. He looked around to see Doc standing tall in his frock coat, grinning hugely. Bluish smoke trailed from the shotgun tube fixed beneath the barrel of his enormous LeMat wheel gun.

"Now that I have your attention, boys," Doc called in a surprisingly hearty voice, "I yield the floor to Ryan Caw-dor."

To Ryan's left, Jak stood with his .357 Magnum Colt Python revolver aimed at the mob. J.B. had checked his Smith & Wesson M-4000 shotgun at the gaudy door, as

Omar's rules required. But he'd drawn the mini-Uzi from beneath his leather jacket, and held it leveled from his hip.

Several wag drivers yipped in alarm and danced as hot buckshot rained down on them. Doc's shotgun had enough punch to take off a man's face or chop up his guts at arm's length. But fired straight up it didn't throw the double-0 balls high enough to do more than give a whack when gravity inevitably brought them back down.

Ryan didn't draw his own SIG-Sauer handblaster. He didn't want to escalate the situation.

All the wag drivers started talking at once. The Le-Mat's volcanic roar had knocked the fight out of them. Now they were all tripping over one another to explain how they were just having themselves some fun with this skinny kid for talking crazy, and then these bitches came and jumped them....

Krysty moved forward to help Mildred, who in turn was helping the skinny little dude holding a well-crushed pair of specs in one hand. He was the worse for wear.

The wag drivers paid no attention to them. They seemed to have had a bellyful of the two wild women.

"All right," Ryan snapped. "The fun's over. Nobody's chilled yet."

He swept the crowd with his lone ice-blue eye. "What do you say we keep it that way?"

The wag drivers looked at one another. He could read their thoughts plainly on their faces and in the set of their shoulders, without need of any mutie mind powers, which he surely didn't possess. This wasn't fun anymore. He suspected for those who'd come to grips with Mildred and Krysty, it had stopped being fun considerably earlier.

He frowned at Mildred. "This was your doing."

It wasn't a question.

Though she was bent over from the exertion and a fair

amount of pummeling, she straightened and braced her shoulders. "They were beating up this poor skinny kid for no reason. Kicking him around like a soccer ball."

Ryan shrugged. "Not our business. Minding other people's is a good way to wind up staring at the sky."

"Fine. You didn't have to back me up, anyway."

"Yes, we did, Millie," J.B. said mildly. He still had his Uzi out, in case some of the mag drivers got frisky again. "You know we've got to back each other's plays. That's why Ryan doesn't want you jumping into every swollen river to save every stranded calf. You know what I mean."

"Why, John," the stocky woman said, her deep brown eyes lighting, "that's almost poetic!"

Ryan raised a brow and looked at Krysty, who shook back her scarlet hair.

"She did what she thought was right, Ryan. So did I."

He felt a hand pat his shoulder, and glanced back to see Doc's prematurely aged face hanging over him.

"Give it over, Ryan," the old man said. "This is a fight you can only lose. Especially if you win."

Ryan was about to retort that the statement made no sense, then it hit him that it made total sense.

"All right," he said. "That bullet's out of the muzzle of the blaster, anyway. Say goodbye to your stray and let's head back inside. No point freezing our asses off in this wind when the stove's hot inside."

"Can't he come with us?" Mildred asked.

The kid hung back. His narrow face was puffy and turning color. "Truth is," he said, "I'm not even supposed to be here. Me and my friends were attacked. Lost everything."

"That why those slaggers were thundering on you?" J.B. asked.

The kid shook his head. He had a shock of dark hair

like an untended garden, and prominent ears. "No. I was trying to warn them."

"Warn?" Jak asked. "What about?"

The youth shook his head again. "You'll just start hitting me, too. And anyway, I better go."

"I say we bring him inside with us," Mildred said. "I'll pay for him out of my share of what we got for the job."

Ryan frowned. As was standard practice, Boss Plunkett had given them half their pay in advance. Nobody was going to do bodyguard work on credit; nobody was going to hire guards and give them all their jack before they'd guarded their share of body. People who did either weren't even triple-stupe, they were chills. And it was handsome pay. Handsome enough that Ryan and the others came close to taking for granted Plunkett would try to stiff them at trail's end. But they'd burn that bridge after they crossed it.

It wouldn't be the first time a boss had tried to stiff them. But if Ryan had anything to say about it, it'd be the last time this particular one tried.

"Millie, you—"

"Don't 'Millie' me, John! It's my share, and I can do with it what I choose!"

"Three days ago we were almost down to boiling the straps of our packs for sweat soup!"

"That's about where I find myself now," the newcomer said. "Sorry. I'm Reno."

"Yeah," Ryan said.

"I will kick in," Doc said. "We are flush for the moment. I for one am willing to pay for the entertainment of a good tale, if nothing else."

"Pay too," Jak said. "Want warning."

"Shouldn't he be happy enough to take the fact we saved his life as payment?"

"He's in a hard place," Mildred said. "We've been there ourselves. Recently."

"I know," Ryan said. "That's why we're working for that fat bastard Plunkett, in case you forgot."

"Anyway," she went on, "hasn't the notion ever occurred to you that if you help a stranger down on his luck, someday when you're down on your luck a stranger might help *you?*"

Ryan stared at her. So did J.B. and Jak.

"Drawing a blank here," the Armorer said after a moment.

"That a stranger might help another out of kindness, or even deferred self-interest," Doc said gently to the black woman, "is a concept alien to our friends' experience."

As a usual thing, the two got along like cats and dogs. But there were times when refugees from their own times stuck together against their thoroughly modern comrades.

"It's a good practice, Ryan," Krysty said, "even if it's hard for you to see."

"Oh, for shit's sake," Ryan said, throwing his hands up in the air. "When did we become a rolling charity? Fuck it. Bring the bastard."

He turned—and ran into a barrier: yet another skinny girl, this one on the cusp of puberty, in a long shapeless frock, with red pigtails and an excess of freckles.

"My daddy sent me out," Loretta said. "Ain't no shooting allowed in the caravanserai."

"Tell your daddy it was an accident," Ryan said. "We're…sorry."

The girl bobbed her pigtails and vanished inside.

Krysty patted Ryan's shoulder. "There, now," she said, smiling. "That didn't hurt, did it?"

Ryan rubbed his bristly jaw. "Kinda."

Another figure moved to intercept them by the door.

"Cthulhu saves," said a roly-poly man with a green hankie tied around his head, extending a woodblock leaflet.

"Best step back, son," J.B. told him in a not unfriendly way. "He's not on hand to save *you*."

Chapter Three

"So let me get this straight," Doc said across the barroom table. "There is an infestation of these strange creatures that is coming this way. And they eat people."

"Cannie muties," Jak said. He was turning one of his throwing knives across the back of a white hand, knuckle to knuckle. "No big."

The kid Mildred had rescued from the mob shook his head. "Not muties," he said. "They're...sick. And you can catch what they got."

"What do you mean?" J.B. asked.

"They're not mutants. They're normal people who have changed. They've turned into mindless, soulless monsters who hunger for human meat. For us. There are hundreds, man. And they're following right behind me!"

He was getting worked up. He stood half out of his chair. "You've got to believe me! Somebody's got to do something!"

Sitting protectively beside him, Mildred took the tattered sleeve of his plaid shirt and tugged him back down. Though she never would've admitted it to her friends, she was trying her damnedest not to laugh. The poor crazy kid talked like somebody from a B horror movie.

"So, not muties," Jak said. "Just cannies. Seen cannies. Killed cannies."

"You don't understand," Reno said. His face worked as if the muscles were trying to pull themselves apart beneath his grayish skin. "They're worse than any cannies you've seen. Worse than you can imagine."

"We've seen some pretty rough ones," J.B. said.

"And our imaginations are quite expansive," Doc added, though not unkindly.

He might be half out of his mind some of the time, and lots of his attitudes struck Mildred as more neolithic than Victorian, but overall he was closer to her conception of what a normal human being was like than these born Deathlanders. Krysty showed at least flashes of compassion. But even she, with her unquestionably big heart and spirit, could surprise Mildred.

"They're triple-hard to kill," Reno said. "At least as bad as stickies. They don't feel pain, see. It's like they're... dead. Walking chills. They even start to rot. But it doesn't slow them down. Oh, no. They move like lubed-up lightning, some of 'em."

Mildred looked at her friends. She could tell they were thinking the caravaneers were right. This was crazy talk. She wasn't so sure. The young man had clearly seen something that frightened him terribly.

"And here's the worst part," the youth went on. "If they bite you, you become one of them. If they chill you, you rise again as one of them. Unless you're lucky enough they just eat you alive. Once somebody gets bitten, you have to chill them right away. Right now. Because it's only a matter of time before they change, too!"

The little bubble of silence that surrounded the table after that pronouncement seemed to repel the raucous chatter that filled the saloon. At a breath of cold, relatively fresh air from outside, Mildred turned to look at the door, relieved for the break.

The leader of the Cthulhu cultists, Brother Ha'ahrd, swept in. She was sure the name was really Howard, but that was how the ever-ebullient prophet introduced himself, and how his followers reverently pronounced his name. He was of middle height, a tad taller than J.B. His face had clearly been broad even before age started to turn it shapeless and run it down over his neck. Iron-gray hair hung down the back of his dark green robe. He alone of the believers wore no headcloth.

He smiled and loudly greeted the Nuke Red Hot One, who was seating customers at the moment. She smiled back. The Fat One was bustling to the kitchen with a big galvanized metal tub full of dirty crockery. The Skinny One still worked the bar. Omar himself was nowhere to be seen.

Mildred took advantage of the break to study Ryan for his reaction to all this.

Frowning slightly, he turned to Reno, who was fumbling in a little sorry-ass backpack that, judging by its shape, held mostly nothing. The kid unfolded a fresh pair of eyeglasses, these with bat-wing frames, and fitted them experimentally in front of his watery blue eyes.

"Where'd you get those, Reno?" Mildred asked.

He shrugged. "When I'm scavvying, I always keep my eyes peeled for unbusted pairs that're close to what I need," he said, smiling shyly and half-apologetically. "Only way I can see anything."

"So how do you come to know all this about these… rotties?" Ryan asked.

Reno shook his head. "Don't know all about them. Sorry. I know way too much. But not all. We were scavvies, like I said. My friends Lariat and Drygulch and I. A few nights ago they hit us where we were camped."

"So you were the only one who got away?" J.B. asked.

Mildred looked at the Armorer narrowly, trying to divine whether he was trying to equate the kid's survival to cowardice. It was a fine line in the Deathlands. Nobody liked somebody who'd run out on his partners when the shit hit. Yet nobody survived any length of time without being ready to just run when the odds got too bad. She still had little idea where the line lay. She suspected it was pretty subjective.

But Reno shook his head. "No. We all got away. But one of my friends got bit. That night while we were sleeping, Drygulch changed. He jumped on Lariat and bit her. That's when I ran. And came within a hair of running right into the rest of these—what'd you call them? Rotties?"

He grimaced. Mildred reckoned he was trying to smile. "Good a name as any, I suppose." She wondered why nicknames for muties in Deathlands all ended with *ie*.

"Pardon my asking," Doc said. "But how do they come by these numbers? These are desolate lands, barely inhabited."

Far away from reality as the old man could wander, he could be as focused as a microscope. Usually he stayed here and now when danger threatened. Or when, as now, his curiosity was aroused.

"It's a big country, Doctor," Reno said. "Look around. There's fifty, sixty people staying here tonight, and mebbe twenty live and work here full-time. If you shake out all the folks who live in a hundred-mile radius you can get a mighty crowd, even in hard core Deathlands like these."

Ryan's lips tightened, as if he didn't like the way the skinny kid's words tasted. Mildred thought she detected something a little off about the tale herself.

And so what? she asked herself. In the Deathlands, everybody has secrets. *We* have secrets.

Back in her day they used to talk about how valuable information was. Talk about the information economy replacing the economy of everyday physical things. In the end physical reality had reasserted itself with a bloody vengeance. Yet information or its lack could get you chilled. Like any other resource.

She wanted to remind Ryan of that. She suspected it would only make things worse.

"Sounds crazy," Jak said. But Mildred could see white around his ruby irises, and his fine nostrils were flared like a winded horse's. He was spooked by talk about the walking dead. He had been raised in the bayous of the South, steeped in superstition. Except who could say what was superstitious these days when so many fantastic—and horrible—things stalked the land?

"Please," Reno said hollowly. "You have to believe me. We need to either get ready to defend this place, or get out of here while we still can!"

That seemed to make an impression even on Ryan. Before Mildred could more than catch his eye, a fresh commotion came from the direction of the stairs.

Boss Plunkett and some of his retinue lumbered down from the upper stories, where the luxury accommodations were located, and where the gaudy house part of the caravanserai's trade was carried out. The boss had changed into a satiny purple dressing gown that looked suspiciously as if it had started life more than a century before as a bedsheet. He had a bottle in one hand, a cigar in the other, and his arms draped like beef boughs over the necks of his "secretaries." Two of the gaudy sluts accompanied them. Loomis followed close behind, glaring around at the other bar customers as if ready to take a bite out of anyone who got within range. As always, he put Mildred in mind of a Village People wannabe.

Plunkett swept his boiled-ham face around the room. It reddened slightly when he caught sight of Ryan and friends. He turned to mutter something to his personal sec man.

As the Nuke Red Hot One squired Plunkett and his female satellites to a table, which she cleared of caravaneers with one flinty look, Loomis swaggered over to the companions' table. He was hitching at his tight black leather pants as he came. Mildred didn't even want to *think* about what that might imply about what had just been going on in the boss's private room above.

Loomis stopped a few feet away and thrust his unshaved face at Ryan like a challenging canine. "Boss says he wants to talk to you, Cawdor," he said. He jabbed a thumb back over his shoulder. *"Now."*

Behind the round lenses of his glasses, J.B. narrowed his eyes at the man. For him that was about as good as cussing Loomis out loudly. Mildred squeezed his leg under the table.

"Be back," Ryan said laconically, rising. He turned and looked at Loomis. The sec man stood glaring up at him for half a minute. Then, realizing he wasn't going to win any staring contests with the taller man, he turned and led the way back to their boss's table.

"WHAT THE HELL are you playing at, Cawdor?" Plunkett bellowed as Ryan came up. "You ain't gettin' paid to sit on your asses listenin' to fairy stories. Get out there and guard my shit, before these convoy scum steal me blind!"

Ryan took his time answering. He and his friends had taken Plunkett's jack. The one-eyed man felt bound to see a job through once accepted, if it was at all possible without throwing away the lives of his companions. He was tempted to give their current boss a second mouth to bellow through, between, say, chins two and three. But it was bad form, and he didn't want to do it unless he really had no choice.

Anyway, it wasn't as though the boss's abusive bluster was news.

Besides, there was an off chance the fat man would pay the balance owed at the end of the trail, just as he said he would. That in itself was worth keeping him alive. For now.

"Right," Ryan said. "We'll do that." He glanced at Loomis. "Startin' to smell bad in here, anyway."

He turned back to his party. He doubted the sec man had the stones to jump him. And if he did, Ryan was certain he'd read it in the faces of his friends, all of which were turned to watch him.

He got back to the table without incident, noticing the caravaneers drinking in the bar seemed to let their eyes slide away from him like oil drops on a hot pan. The cultists, too.

Fine, he thought. It saved complications if they were afraid of him. Omar had a strict rule against anyone who wasn't Omar chilling anybody inside the adobe outer walls of the compound.

"Let's go," Ryan said. "Boss says it's time to get back to work."

"Ryan—" Mildred started.

"Yeah, okay," he said. "He can stay with us."

"Thank you!" Reno said. "You won't regret this."

"Don't get ideas," Ryan said. "We'll probably chill you in the morning."

RYAN CAME AWAKE all at once, as he usually did.

He was instantly aware of a presence leaning over him in the cold darkness of the cinder-block hut. Something was tickling his upturned face.

It was Krysty's hair.

"There's something going on," she said as soon as his eye opened.

Ryan sat up. He slept in the shed where Plunkett's sec wag was parked. Krysty would've slept alongside, but had her turn on watch. J.B. and Mildred had the shed with the boss's personal wag. The RV was parked outside the structures. Jak and Doc slept in it.

"What?" Ryan asked as he picked up his 9 mm SIG-Sauer P-226 handblaster and his eighteen-inch panga from where he had them laid close to hand. He tucked them away in appropriate places and started to pull his boots on. Apart from them he slept in his clothes.

"Guards have been reporting movement out in the night," Krysty said. The land lay clear for anywhere from fifty to a hundred yards all around the perimeter wall. Omar's crew kept it swept of brush or anything else unwelcome visitors could hide behind. Or use as cover from blasterfire. "They think they're human."

"Could be starting at shadows," Ryan said, grunting as he hauled on a boot. "Mebbe they heard your pal Reno's scary stories."

The skinny bespectacled guy had pitched his bedroll next door with J.B. and Mildred. If Mildred was going to take in strays, she was going to have to take care of them herself. And J.B. would have to deal; Ryan grinned a little at the thought.

Krysty shook her head. She squatted next to him, ready to spring into action at an eye blink's notice.

"Don't think so, lover."

From outside they heard voices raised. She looked around.

"Now what?" Ryan said.

Krysty shook her head. She straightened, and they both walked out the open bay door into the yard.

The first thing they saw was eight or ten of the wag drivers. They were roaring drunk, standing in a ring passing bottles around. Fortuitously, they were on the far side of the compound from where Boss Plunkett's wags were parked. They seemed to be engaged in some kind of roughhousing.

From over by the gate they heard voices raised. "But Maw," a male voice, high and near cracking with adolescence, called in protest. "She was just a little girl, wandering out there all alone in the dark. Leon said weren't no harm in letting her in."

The bucktoothed kid was a twig of about thirteen, all nose and Adam's apple. Omar's wives had dropped uncountable girl children—at least, Ryan hadn't been able to count them all. But they seemed to have produced only two boys—this one, Locke, and eight-year-old Paco.

Leon was one of Omar's guards. The Fat One looked at the big man, who shrugged. "She acted scared," he said.

"Little girl?" asked J.B., emerging from the neighboring shed. "What's going on?"

"Probably nothing," Ryan said.

"Nothing?" Reno echoed, fumbling to adjust his glasses on his nose. "They didn't let anyone in, did they?"

"Appears that they did."

"They're crazy! It could be one of them!"

"Where is this little girl?" Mildred asked, hugging herself tightly beneath her generous breasts and not looking thrilled at being rousted out of a relatively warm bedroll. Her breath came in puffs of condensation.

"Ryan," Krysty said, "those men again—"

The wag drivers were hooting in rising merriment. Only the fact the Fat One was busy reading Locke the riot act prevented her from jumping on them for making noise at this hour, Ryan reckoned. That was against Omar's rules, too.

Then the circle opened a bit and Ryan saw that the wag drivers were pushing around a girl with pigtails. For a moment he thought it was one of the host's daughters. But he quickly dismissed that; if they could stand up, the wag drivers weren't *that* drunk. He remembered how Locke claimed he and Leon had admitted a lone little girl.

Now the wag drivers were bouncing her around the way they had Reno earlier in the evening.

"What is it with these assholes?" Ryan asked.

"Ryan," Krysty said, "we've got to do something."

"No," he amended, "no, we don't. We've got our hands full now. Let Omar's people deal with it. What we have to do is get back to sleep. Plunkett's going to want us hustling tomorrow."

Jak was frowning. "Girl not look right."

"What?" Ryan said. He had headed back to bed. Now he turned to look once more.

The sky was clear overhead, but the pitiless stars didn't cast enough light to see by. Nor did the lantern light seeping through the gaudy house windows. Still, it struck Ryan that the little girl did move strangely, as if she were stiff, somehow. And was it a trick of the light, or did her face appear gray?

"What's going on out here?" Omar himself, shaved-headed, ferociously mustached, stood in the doorway to the barroom. He wore his inevitable apron and held his sawed-off scattergun in his big blunt hands. He wasn't shy about raising his voice regardless of the hour.

The wag drivers ignored him. One of them blew kisses at the teetering, silent child, then he leaned toward her, puckering his lips.

"Gimme a kiss, little girl," he said.

As if shot from a catapult, she sprang at him. Her arms flew around his neck. She pressed her mouth to his in what looked like a kiss.

"Jesus God! That's plain wrong," Mildred said. "Get him away from her!"

The wag driver screamed. He reared up, batting frantically at the child, who continued to cling like a pigtailed monkey.

She turned her head to look at Ryan and his companions. Her eyes were sunken pits. A dark stain was smeared all around her mouth, and dark liquid ran freely down her chin.

The wag driver's lips dangled from her teeth like a limp onion ring.

Chapter Four

Stiff-legged in horror, the wag drivers backed away from their stricken friend. They weren't quick enough. The little girl jumped on the nearest man's back and sank her teeth in the side of his neck.

"Shit!" Reno shrieked. "She's one of them!"

"What the fuck?" Ryan said.

Someone was hollering from the watchtower. "Stand back! Stand away from the gate there or I'll shoot!"

Wag drivers pried the little girl off their second stricken buddy and dashed her to the ground. Omar was striding toward them, shotgun in his fist. His body language suggested he wasn't sure who to shoot first.

"Start the wags," Ryan told his companions. "It's time to go."

"What about Plunkett?" J.B. asked.

"I'll get him," Ryan said grimly.

He'd scarcely started walking toward the gaudy when Krysty screamed, *"Ryan!"*

Instinct made him look left, away from where the warning cry had come from. A man lurched toward him from the shadows between sheds.

He moved hunched over, his face thrusting forward, his arms dangling. One cheek had been torn off, exposing teeth on his upper jaw. The wound didn't bleed. His skin was gray in the faint light, his eyes white marbles.

At Krysty's cry Ryan had drawn his handblaster. Bracing it with both hands, he fired two quick shots through the center of the man's chest.

They were good hits. He saw them hit, punching through ragged plaid flannel over the sternum. One or both had to have penetrated the man's heart. But rather than slowing, he put on a surprising burst of speed.

"Don't let it bite you!" Reno screamed.

Ryan gave the onrushing thing a front thrust-kick to the sternum. The creature reeled back three steps, then with unwavering determination charged forward again.

As much from habit as anything else, Ryan punched a third bullet through its forehead. The creature folded obediently as a dead man should, and lay still.

"Head shots work!" Ryan shouted as he sprinted toward the main building.

Around him people spilled from the sheds and the gaudy house itself. The yard was filling with bodies, confusion and noise. People screamed. Shots popped.

At the front gate the Fat One didn't seem to quite grasp what was going on. With Locke and Leon trailing behind, she walked toward the center of the yard, waving her flabby arms and shouting for everyone to cease firing.

The little girl, the lower half her face painted with the blood of her victims, jumped up, apparently unhurt. She darted toward the large woman. The Fat One saw her and dropped to her knees. Holding her arms wide, she cried, "Come to me, child! Run!"

The girl did. When she was ten feet from the kneeling woman her head exploded. The decapitated body flopped forward almost to the horrified woman's feet.

Stopping by the door to let a knot of panicky people out, Ryan looked back over his shoulder. Mildred was lowering her blocky ZKR 551 target revolver from a one-armed shooting stance. He caught a gleam of torchlight on tears streaming down her cheeks.

The Fat One squalled in outrage and jumped to her feet. "That wasn't a little girl anymore!" Reno yelled, jumping in front of Mildred as if to shield her from the wrath of Omar's heftiest wife.

From somewhere came the cry "They're over the wall!"

More of those creatures, men and women but not men or women, moved with unnatural hitching gaits through the crowd in the yard. Ryan thrust his way into the gaudy house, breasting a stream of half-naked sluts screaming as they raced out.

The first thing that hit him when he entered was an eye-searing stink of smoke. It was more than the potbellied stove could possibly account for unless the chimney had gotten blocked. He took a wild flying guess that wasn't the case.

Behind the bar the Thin One flailed vigorously at three no-longer-human opponents with an aluminum baseball bat. It made musical thunking sounds as it bounced off bone lightly padded by muscle or skin, off joints and skulls. Family members, employees and patrons wrestled with enemies whose skin, bluish in the lantern light, was cratered with running open sores. Some were missing big chunks from their bodies, even arms.

A wag driver grabbed the arm of an elderly man to try to pull the oldie off a comrade. The arm came off in his hands. He stared at it in comic amazement as the changed oldie sank his few remaining teeth into the second wag driver's neck.

Plunkett and crew were nowhere in sight. Fleeing sluts, guards and customers were blocking the stairs. Ryan began shoving them bodily out of the way. As strong as he was, their fear was stronger. He didn't make much progress.

Smoke began rolling along the hollows of the ceiling between the beams. The gaudy house was well and truly on fire.

Loomis tumbled down the wooden stairs, wearing only his shiny, black leather pants. "They're already changing!" he screamed, catching himself on all fours.

Buck-naked and baby-pink, Boss Tim Plunkett lurched down the stairs behind his sec chief. His hairy, fish-pale belly hung low, obscuring his genitals. Blood gushed from his torn-out throat. His voice box and airway were apparently still intact, or mostly so. As he banged from rail to wall and back, clutching his blood-gouting wound with one hand, he kept croaking, "Help me!"

He toppled, to land on his gut with a massive crash.

SHUDDERING ORANGE FIRE erupted from the combined watch-and water tower, followed a beat later by a roar of full-auto blasterfire. Pressing the hand that held the pistol grip of his M-4000 scattergun to pin his battered hat against his head, J.B. reached with his free hand to snag the back of the man's flannel shirt Krysty Wroth wore. He dragged her to the ground.

Bullets cracked right over their heads, where their bodies had been an eye blink earlier. Headlights popped as the burst raked the Tundra's front.

The burst went on, sweeping the length of the big RV. Metal flexed musically.

"Shit!" Krysty exclaimed. That startled J.B. The red-head normally didn't use bad language.

Then he smelled gasoline and understood why she cussed. Krysty threw herself over him, grabbing him so they both rolled sideways over the cold, trampled earth, away from the fuel-leaking RV. It also took them out of the dubious cover of the wag's thin-gauge metal walls.

The burst hammered on. Good way to burn out a barrel fast, the armorer in J.B. noted. Inevitably, the bullets struck a spark. The big wag lit up with a fat pillow of blue fire and a low but loud *whump*.

J.B. felt a wave of heat wash over him as he came to rest on top of Krysty, looking down into her green eyes. He grinned.

"I better climb off," he said. "Don't want any misunderstandings with Ryan."

"Reckon he'd understand," she said.

The machine gun lashed back across the crowded yard. J.B. could tell humans were getting hit. They fell and stayed down. The triple-strange creatures—the rotties—kept shambling along despite repeated torso strikes.

"Look out!" Krysty gritted. J.B. tipped his face to the ground as bullets stitched right to left not two feet in front of him. Ricochets whined over him, gouts of dirt tapping the front brim of his hat.

"That stupe in the tower's gonna chill us before the rotties do," he said.

He heard the bark of a .38 from his left. The muzzle-flare from the tower was cut off. J.B. looked to where the single gunshot had come from.

Mildred knelt on the dirt, her left elbow braced on one knee, her left hand cradling her handblaster.

"You chill the dude, Millie?" he called.

She shook her head. "Like you said, J.B. He was a bigger danger."

"Wags fucked," Jak said, coming out of the shed behind J.B. "Tundra chilled. Other—"

He shook his white-maned head in irritation. The burning cargo wag blocked the third vehicle in the shed. It blazed too vigorously for anyone to try to push the big vehicle clear.

Krysty sat up beside J.B. She suddenly whipped her upper body left and shot twice with her snub-nosed Smith & Wesson. Right toward Mildred.

Spinning around, J.B. saw a man with a black pit where one eye should be reel back from where he'd been about to blindside the sturdy woman. Apparently Krysty had hit him in the body, not the head, and he lunged for Mildred.

"Shit!" J.B. yelped. He rolled fast right, trying to clear his own scattergun for a shot at the rottie. It'd be dangerous with Mildred in the way. But if it was really true that if you got bitten by one of these hoodoos, it turned you into one of them...

There weren't many things in this world that J. B. Dix shied away from. He'd seen his share of scary shit and then some. But he couldn't stand to think of that happening to Mildred. To any of his friends.

But he wouldn't make it in time. Seconds slowed as he watched the rottie close in on Mildred, who was lining up a shot on another target and still unaware of her danger. He shouted a warning he knew would come too late.

With a crunch a thin steel blade poked through the man's head from right temple to left. The rottie went to his knees.

"Touché," Doc cried. He put a boot to the side of the slack-skinned, veined face and pushed. The creature flopped to its side and lay unmoving.

J.B. scrambled to his feet. A man with an arm swinging from his elbow like a busted gate loomed in front of him, a vomitous reek of rotting flesh.

Whipping up the M-4000, J.B. jabbed the steel-shod butt into the creature's face. It lurched back two steps, then its head exploded as J.B. reversed the scattergun and fired, eight inches from the bridge of its nose.

"You guys hold them off," Krysty shouted, stuffing a

speed-loader into her snub-nosed handblaster. It held only five shots, a triple-rough disadvantage in a fight like this. "Mildred, come help me get the packs."

"What do you plan?" Doc asked. He fended off a short-haired changed woman with his rapier and stabbed her deftly through the eye.

"We've got to get out of here, fast!" Krysty said. "That's my plan!"

She and Mildred ducked into the shed.

AN EYE BLINK before his boss's nude, bleeding bulk crashed down on him, Loomis took off like a sprinter, almost knocking down Ryan in his mad desire to get out the door.

Two naked women came down the stairway. By their hair Ryan guessed they were the boss's "secretaries," Tina and Angela. Their faces were hard to recognize, gray and distorted with some unimaginable passion behind liberal smears of gore. Bottle-blonde Angela's belly had been cut or ripped open. Purple lengths of intestine trailed out the red, gaping cavity. They were short, their ends ragged, as if the loops had been bitten through.

Black hair flying, Tina flung herself on her boss's wide, hairy white back. He thrashed feebly. It amazed Ryan he could move at all, at the rate he was bleeding out. Tina grabbed his head and, despite the thickness of his bull-like neck, began to bang his head against a stout square stair post. Angela, not inconvenienced in the least by her missing viscera, joined right in, gnawing her boss's head as her partner rhythmically pounded it into the wood.

A hellish light showed through the boards of the ceiling over the barroom. Sparks fell like glowing rain. A bald man stumbled toward Ryan, extending a clawed hand from which the little finger had been bitten. The wound had stopped bleeding. Ryan shot him in the face almost casually, so horribly fascinated was he by what was happening on the stairs.

He felt no strong urge to try to rescue his employer. The big man was a sure chill anyway, with that neck wound. Not to mention that Reno's crazy talk about victims rising again as one of the changed if the rotties chilled them was looking pretty plausible here.

With a sound like a melon being dropped, Boss Plunkett's head split open. Amazingly, his naked limbs continued to twitch, and he moaned in dismay. Tina clawed briefly, then peeled back a section of skull with scalp attached.

With a superhuman effort the huge man reared to his knees, reaching a pudgy arm toward Ryan.

"Help me," he mouthed.

Then he stiffened and his eyes rolled up in his beet-red face. Tina had plunged a long-nailed hand into his opened cranium and scooped up a juicy handful from his until-then-living brain. She mashed it against her wide-open mouth, getting as much blood and dough-colored brains on her face as inside.

Plunkett plopped forward, unmoving.

Chewing, Tina looked at Ryan. Her eyes were as white as milky marbles, yet had a terrifying intensity. Without thinking, he raised his SIG-Sauer, swiftly braced and flash-aimed, and shot her through the forehead.

She slumped. Her partner stayed astride Plunkett's pale fat back and began to greedily stuff fistfuls of brains into her mouth.

With a roar, the ceiling caved in over the bar.

"Time to go," Ryan said. He turned and dashed back into the night's cold but welcoming embrace.

Chapter Five

The caravanserai yard was a hell full of the struggling damned. Bodies thrashed. The doomed screamed as rotties bit great chunks out of living human flesh. Across the yard Ryan saw the former Boss Plunkett's big RV burning merrily. He made for it at a run, as if it were a beacon.

He shot a woman covered in human blood when she lunged from his right to bite him. A skinny adolescent boy, not Locke or anyone Ryan had seen before, blocked his path. He drew his panga and hacked at the youth's head. The kid fell. Whether he stayed down or not Ryan never knew. He wasn't about to hang around to watch.

He reached his friends. J.B. was holding a tall man's head and shoulders against the side of the burning wag, where yellow flames enveloped them. The man continued to paw at the Armorer as if nothing unusual was happening, his sleeves yellow wings of flame.

Ryan shot the man through the head. He collapsed into a flaming, stinking heap as J.B. leaped clear.

"Quit fucking around, J.B.," Ryan said. "We got to shake off the dust of this place."

Krysty had her back to a shed, fending off an attacker with a trenching shovel from a wag's emergency kit. Ryan hacked the rottie across the back of the neck. He folded.

Doc stuck the tip of his rapier through the eyeball of an approaching rottie. Behind him, Mildred held a baseball bat cocked should anyone get past him. Jak danced around with a big trench knife in his hand, easily evading swipes from a bearlike foe and awaiting an opening to dart past and stab him in the back of the head.

"We need a ride out, and fast," Ryan said.

"Easier said than done, Ryan," J.B. answered. "Seeing as how our wags are either in flames or blocked in."

Krysty ran to Ryan and gave him a quick hug. She had been rooting around inside the wag with the shot-up engine block. The ax handle she held was stained with blood at the tip. He kissed her quickly on the cheek, then pulled free to point back across the yard.

"There's our ride," he said. "Right there."

"That's those damn Cthulhu cultists' bus," Mildred said. "They might have something to say about our hitching a lift."

Planting the blade of his panga under his right arm, Ryan switched magazines in his SIG. He didn't much worry about getting gore on his coat. It wasn't the first time and wouldn't be the last.

"Doesn't mean we got to listen," he said. "Follow me. Wedge formation."

Without looking to see if his companions would follow—because he knew from long experience they would—he set off at a trot for the battered, faded-green bus. It had a snowplow blade up front and chicken wire over the windows, most of which lacked glass.

Cultists surrounded the school bus, trying to hold off the moaning horde by pushing at them with their bare hands. They were determined and vigorous enough to manage it for now.

The concentration of warm food drew the changed.

Ryan passed Brother Ha'ahrd, who was surrounded by a phalanx of followers, including a few former wag drivers that seemed to have undergone a last-minute conversion in the face of overwhelming, mind-frying horror. He was loudly preaching a doctrine of love and forbearance and waiting on the will of the Great Old Ones. The rotties didn't seem to be listening. They were more interested in eating his head.

Which meant most of the shambling freaks were focused on something other than the approach of Ryan and friends from the rear. He heard a couple shots pop off behind him, and the thwack of stout ash wood on a skull, accompanied by a grunt of effort and triumph from Mildred. Apparently a few of the freaks still tracked them.

Ryan didn't look back. Unless somebody screamed for his help, his job was clearing the way.

He waded into the mob of rotties surging toward the bus door, where three cultists had linked arms to keep them out. Ryan hacked at the backs of necks and skulls as if the changed were a stand of brush he was trying to cut a trail through.

A woman turned a blood mask to snarl at him and he shot her between the eyes. He sensed a presence on his right and whipped the butt of his SIG around to squash a changed man's nose in a spray of dark fluid. The rottie staggered back. An eye blink later Doc's slim rapier impaled the creature through both temples like an apple on a skewer.

A burly rottie, obviously a changed wag driver, barechested and with a short Mohawk, spun to bare his teeth and spread his arms to seize the one-eyed man. Ryan hammered him between the eyes with the SIG's butt, then shot him in the forehead as he staggered back.

The rotties pulled down the two women and one man barring the door. As the cultists futilely screamed and thrashed, the rotties homed in on them. Ryan kicked at the flailing tangle until the way was clear, then rushed into the school bus with his friends at his heels.

A stout woman in a robe sewn together from burlap bags barred their way. "Stop! There's no room in here for anyone but believers!"

Ryan was about to rebut her with a copper-jacketed 9 mm bullet where it would do the most good when Krysty grabbed his arm from behind.

"Wait!" she yelled. "She's right!"

The cultist was. Ryan looked around the bus to see the seats and aisles jammed with refugees. Not all of them looked as if they belonged to Brother Ha'ahrd's flock, or at least had started the day that way. Still, the practical puzzle was insoluble: even shooting the reticent wasn't likely to drive these people out into the blood-smeared rottie mob.

"Up!" he heard Jak call.

"Say what?" Ryan turned to see Jak disappearing up the first window behind the door.

Ryan jumped back outside. After even momentary exposure to the relative warmth inside the bus, generated by close-packed bodies and humid panting breath, the chill hit him like a slap. As did the stench of burning petrocarbons, human flesh and hair, and spilled intestines.

"Follow Jak!" Ryan yelled. He stooped to grab one of Krysty's calves. J.B. grabbed the other, and the two men boosted the woman high enough to scramble onto the roof after the albino youth.

Stabbing, slashing, shooting only when utterly necessary, Ryan and Doc helped the cultists stave off the rotties while Mildred and J.B. quickly passed the packs up to Krysty and Jak atop the bus. Then Ryan and J.B. gave Mildred a boost, and Doc. Finally, Ryan stood facing out, while J.B. scaled him like a monkey and clambered up.

The changed surged forward. Unfeeling hands reached out for Ryan, blood-spilling mouths gaping wide to consume his flesh.

MILDRED HAD BARELY got her bearings atop the ice-cold metal roof of the bus when another stout woman wearing the Cthulhu cult's flowing robes and head scarf came bustling up alongside the baggage that had been strapped onto a rickety roof rack.

"You can't come up here!" she snapped. "This is for believers only—"

"Gaia forgive me," Krysty said. She kicked the stout woman off the roof.

Mildred felt her brows climb up her forehead. Krysty looked back at her and shrugged.

"Move your broad butt, woman!" yelled a familiar voice from behind. Mildred turned a furious glare on J.B., whose head popped up over the roof edge like a curious prairie dog's.

"John," she said, "you and me are going to *talk*."

But she shifted aside to make way for him as a great cry went up from the cultists below.

"Brother Ha'ahrd!" a voice screamed.

Ryan looked past the rotties closing in on him to see the long-haired prophet knocked off his feet by a surge of creatures who had overwhelmed his guards. Cultists stampeded off the bus, bowling over the rotties in their path in their zeal to rescue their guru.

Ryan had caught a break.

Not a man to waste an opportunity, Ryan holstered his panga and handblaster, spun around and jumped as high as he could. Krysty and J.B. caught hold of his outstretched arms and hauled him up on top of the bus as if he were a child.

"After all this trouble we could ride inside now," Mildred said peevishly. She knelt on the heaped baggage, making fast their own packs. Doc squatted to one side, reloading his revolver as calmly as if he were out for a morning stroll outside his home in nineteenth-century Vermont.

Ryan shook his head emphatically. "Just as glad to ride up here," he said. "Rotties get inside—"

Screams pealed out the door. "Shit!" J.B. said, leaning out to peer over. "They are!"

"Grab legs!" Jak called. Without waiting to see if anybody responded, he got down on his knees at the front end of the bus roof. While the few cultists and other refugees who had also sought safety up there looked on dumbly, Krysty and Mildred jumped to grab the youth's ankles as he let himself topple forward.

An instant later Ryan heard the roar of Jak's .357 Magnum Colt Python.

FEELING KRYSTY'S AND Mildred's grips strong on his ankles, Jak let himself almost smack face-first into the cold windshield of the bus, using his right palm at the last moment to keep from breaking his nose.

Beyond the glass, which remained unfogged due to the icy air streaming in the open door, he saw the look of terror on the driver's face, rendered more comic by being upside down: the saucer eyes, the mouth a screaming O below a bearded chin.

The driver had good reason to scream. He was trying to hang on to the wheel, probably to keep from getting pulled out of his seat, and batting with his right arm at a rottie who was trying to bite his head. Other rotties had got themselves jammed in the door in their lust for human flesh and hot blood.

Jak pressed the vented muzzle of his blaster against the

glass near the first rottie's head and pulled the trigger. The Magnum blaster kicked itself away from the windshield as the glass collapsed inward. He let his arm straighten to ride out the recoil; he hadn't been able to brace properly, and expected the reaction.

Inside, the bus driver stared in even greater horror at his attacker. The back of the changed woman's head had been blown off. The guy was staring through her mouth at the other rotties still struggling to break free and get at him.

The half-headed rottie collapsed. People in the bus were screaming and leaning over at least one person who'd been hit by the 125-grain hollowpoint slug, which hadn't expended all its energy blowing the rottie's head apart. Jak took in the fact without emotional reaction. These were no friends of his, nor enemies, either. So why care?

With the window glass gone he had clear shots at the rotties in the door. Grabbing the Python's grips with both hands, he fired three shots as fast as he could. Two of the creatures went down at once, shot through the forehead. The third reeled back with her lower jaw torn away. Instantly, hands grabbed her from behind and threw her to the ground as furious cultists surged in, bearing their injured leader.

Jak turned to the driver. "Drive," he said, gesturing with his Python for emphasis.

Eyes all but popping free of his lean, ashen face, the driver put the wag in gear and hit the gas.

A BLOOD-STREAKED GRAY head appeared over the rear end of the bus roof as the vehicle took off with a jerk. Kneeling on the cool metal, Ryan had unstrapped his Steyr from the top of his backpack and cracked the bolt to make sure the weapon was loaded. He put a hand down briefly to steady himself against the sudden acceleration, then whipped the longblaster's butt to his shoulder and fired.

The head disappeared. Whether he'd destroyed the brain or not Ryan didn't know. The 7.62 mm bullet might have caught the creature in the shoulder. It didn't matter as long as the thing didn't get up here.

"Everybody all right?" Ryan shouted, hanging on to the jury-built luggage rack as the bus wheeled in as tight an arc as it could toward the compound exit. "Sing out."

"Yes," Krysty called.

"I'm here," J.B. said.

"Capital, Ryan!" Doc declared.

"Ace," Mildred said sourly, as she and Krysty stood up together, hoisting Jak back up with his white hair swinging wildly. "Jak's here, too."

The albino youth jackknifed up between the two women and popped to his feet.

"Holy shit!" Ryan saw Mildred pointing straight ahead.

The caravanserai gate was shut. It was also on fire.

Chapter Six

Yellow flames danced against the backdrop of the snow-dusted prairie beyond.

The bus driver never slowed. "Brace yourselves!" Ryan shouted. He saw Krysty and Mildred turn away from the front of the bus and throw themselves on the mounded baggage. He did likewise.

The snowplow blade hit the gate. Whether more weakly constructed than it appeared, or weakened by the flames, it flew apart, sending flaming planks and posts spiraling away like pinwheels.

The bus took off down the dirt road, which was basically a pair of ever-deepening ruts running northeast to southwest.

"Tie on!" Ryan shouted over his shoulder to his companions. As far as he could see, the six of them now had the roof to themselves. The handful of cultists who had climbed up here, presumably not as keenly honed to a survival edge as the companions, either had been tossed off by the wag's wild maneuvering, or had bailed voluntarily.

A mob tottered in slow pursuit of the wag, black figures silhouetted against yellow flame. They faded rapidly as the school bus jounced off across the countryside.

Lying on his belly, Ryan used his belt to fasten himself to the steel rail of the roof rack. His companions chimed in with shouts as they finished making themselves fast.

"Weapons out!" he called when Doc called the last acknowledgment.

"The rotties can't catch us on foot," Mildred said.

"Do you know there's not a hundred of 'em waiting out here?"

"Weapon out," Mildred said.

THE GREAT PLAINS were never as flat as they appeared, Mildred thought. The dark land scrolling past them mostly looked like the top of a billiard table. Yet she ached in elbows and thighs and breasts from being slammed on the metal roof every time the bus bounced over an unseen obstacle or crashed down onto ground as hard as a baron's heart, each time threatening destruction to its ancient suspension. Meanwhile the back of her was freezing through from the ice-blast wind of passage, especially her legs, covered only by the thin fabric of her camo pants.

Every bounce also reminded her that the dark country abounded with hiding places for lurking foes. Not just the changed, either. Lethal predators abounded in the Deathlands, animal, mutie and human.

Shadows seemed to flit across the shadowed land. A score of times Mildred opened her mouth to cry an alarm, or slipped her gloved finger into the trigger guard of her Czech-made .38-caliber target revolver. Each time she held herself back from screaming or shooting. And each time no attack came.

She was horribly aware that didn't mean the threats she thought she saw in the shadows *weren't* real.

The bus picked up speed, trading the occasional bone-slamming jolt for a constant rattle that felt as if it might detach Mildred's retinas. But she gritted her teeth and hung on.

Because one thing she'd learned, more than a century before she'd ever opened her eyes to this terrible new world, was to endure.

AN HOUR LATER the bus rumbled to a stop in a sandy wash next to a slowly moving stream. Steam rolled from under the hood. The engine hissed and pinged as it cooled.

"What's happening?" Ryan called.

"Driver says he thinks we're far enough away to take a break." Krysty called back. "He says we've come about thirty miles."

"Great," J.B. said. "I could stand to try to winch my bones straight again. The knots in my muscles're getting knots in them."

"All right," Ryan said. "Everybody cut loose. Keep eyes skinned and blasters ready."

"Really, friend Ryan," Doc croaked, "sometimes you belabor the obvious."

Ryan stood and stretched. He felt about the same way J.B. did—as if some triple-size mutie had grabbed his ankles and tried to bust boulders using Ryan as a hammer.

The door opened and passengers spilled out onto drifted sand. Some fell weakly to hands and knees. Somebody puked noisily.

A woman with a hood pulled up over her head scarf stopped after several paces and turned to look up at Ryan.

"Any of our brothers and sisters up there with you?"

"No," he said.

She gazed up at him for a spell, then turned and walked off.

"What that about?" Jak asked, walking up to Ryan. He moved with his customary youthful-predator swagger. Ryan shrugged in response. He reckoned Jak didn't feel much better than anybody else, but had enough resilience to hide it better.

The one-eyed man already knew none of his party was injured. It had been hard to make himself heard above the bus's clatter, but he'd confirmed that nobody had caught any grief beyond scrapes and bruises.

And, most importantly, no bites.

The companions moved off to the side. The cultists and other refugees showed no interest in mingling with them, and they were just as glad not to have to answer any uncomfortable questions about the manner in which they'd hitched a ride. Not to mention the fates of the cultists who'd been atop the bus with them.

"A fire would be welcome," Doc said, rubbing his hands together. "Restore warmth to chilled bones."

In lieu of that they squatted in the lee of the bus. An east wind had risen during their uncomfortable ride. It came whistling beneath the wag's swaybacked undercarriage, cutting through Ryan's clothes and skin like a knife.

"What do you plan to burn for fuel, you old coot?" Mildred asked. "Your extra long johns from your pack?"

They had unloaded their backpacks from the luggage rack, just in case they needed to make their own way out of there in a hurry. Or in case some of the cultists unexpectedly drove off.

"What are those rad-blasted creatures?" Ryan said, ignoring the byplay. He stood with his back to the wag and his Steyr slung over his shoulder.

"Triple-pain in the hindquarters, is what," J.B. said.

"They have me feeling the creepies all over," Krysty said.

Ryan looked at her. "How come they don't feel pain? How come a wound that would drop any normal man doesn't slow them down? How can they even move? And why do they need to eat, anyway? Far as I can tell, they're chills, or next thing to it. What do they need food for?"

"Why, my dear Ryan," Doc said, "you seem to have taken an unusually empirical turn of mind."

"Didn't think you went in much for abstract curiosity," Mildred said.

"Nothing abstract about it. 'Know your enemy like you know yourself,' Trader always said."

"I don't want to know these things," Krysty said. "They're not part of Gaia's nature."

"Worse than muties?" J.B. asked.

"Yes," the redhead said emphatically. "There's a wrongness about them I've never felt from the most horrible mutie. Ryan, they're *dead*. They really are. Just like those hogs in Canada."

Ryan nodded. "That's why I want to know about them, Krysty. How do you fight what's already dead?"

"Shoot head," Jak said. "Works."

"Yeah," Ryan said. "Why?"

"You really aren't succumbing to curiosity for its own sake?" Doc asked.

"Fireblast, no. If I know why that chills them, I may be able to find something else that does it, too. At least waste less time and ammo doing stuff that doesn't faze the bastards."

"Chopping their heads off should work," Krysty suggested.

"Yeah," Ryan said. "I hacked one or two through the back of the neck, too. That seemed to drop them, and made them stay down."

"Their central nervous system appears to retain some function," Mildred said. She squatted with her arms crossed tightly beneath her breasts. Her big chocolate eyes stared intently at nothing in particular as she wrestled with the questions.

"Or perhaps something else makes use of their nervous system," Doc said.

"You talking crazy, Doc? Don't need you losing it, just now," Ryan said.

But Mildred had raised her head and was looking hard at her customary antagonist. "What are you getting at, old man?"

"Clearly, or at least so far as we can tell, life has fled these poor unfortunates that Ryan dubbed 'rotties.' Yet they move. And we saw none of those horrid worms from the north."

"You channeling Galileo?" Mildred asked. *"Eppur si muove."*

Doc laughed, a soundless, head-bobbing motion.

"What are you two rambling on about?" Ryan demanded.

"Ancient history," Mildred said. "You wouldn't be interested."

"Perhaps these unfortunates have been taken over by some kind of organism, not the worms of Canada, which we haven't seen."

"Well, we definitely know that's a possibility," Ryan said.

"When I was held captive by the vile whitecoats," Doc said, "my captors often spoke of artificial organisms that they could program to do their bidding. Like living steel, but so small the finest optical microscope could not see them."

"You talking about nanotechnology, Doc?" Mildred asked.

He blinked. A light snow had begun to fall, swirling

on the side of the bus away from the wind. White crystals crusted the long lashes above his intense blue eyes.

"I believe that was the term they used, yes."

"We've heard about that before," Krysty said. "But how could this nanotechnology be involved here? These are people. Or rather, creatures that *were* people."

"Perhaps the nanotechnological machines permeate the bodies of their victims," Doc said slowly, clearly speaking thoughts as they formed in his mind. "Somehow they animate the limbs and impart some measure of direction to their actions."

"That almost sounds like demonic possession you're talking about, old man," Mildred said.

Doc frowned at her, seeming to chew over the concept mentally rather than take offense.

"Aside from arising from an agency not strictly supernatural," he said slowly, "how is this possession not aptly described as demonic?"

"So why does shooting their heads chill them?" J.B. asked.

"Obviously, the organisms, or whatever they are, require their victims' bodies to sustain and reproduce themselves. Like disease germs. Perhaps they also make use of the human nervous system to control their stolen bodies."

"Ugh." Krysty shivered.

"Drive us," Jak said. "Like bus."

J.B. turned to him, his eyes squinted behind the round lenses of his glasses. "That's cold-blooded even for you, Jak."

The albino teen just shrugged.

"If the pathogens are nanoscale robots," Mildred said, "that might explain why the, uh, the *change* is infectious."

"There's something I don't understand," Ryan said. "Or mebbe I should say, something else I don't understand.

From what that skinny kid told us back in the 'serai, it took his friend hours to 'change' after he got bitten. But Plunkett's gaudy sluts were already rotties when he came screaming down the stairs, when I went in to get him. They couldn't have been bitten more than a few minutes before."

"That reinforces the idea the change works like a sickness," Krysty said.

"How would that happen?" Ryan asked.

"Different people show different reactions to disease," Mildred said. "Some die quickly, some just get sick. Some are even immune."

Ryan felt his lips peel back from his teeth, which instantly sent spikes of pain up the bones of his face from the cold.

"So they're plaguers?" he said.

Mildred nodded.

"All right," he said. "So we know blowing their brains out drops them. So does cutting the spinal cord, at least in the neck. Shooting them anywhere else is pretty much a waste, unless it gets them to back off long enough to get in a head shot. Or bash their skulls in."

"Cutting off their arms and legs should do it, too," Mildred said. "Eliminate them as threats, anyway."

"Long as you're careful not to get close enough they can bite you," Dix said.

"Always the charmer, John," Mildred said. He flashed her a grin.

For a while they squatted, or in Ryan's case stood, in silence, listening to the wind boom and sigh across the plains.

"I feel kinda bad we lost the body we were supposed to be guarding," Mildred said. "Plunkett did pay us up front to protect him and his people."

"It happens," Ryan said. "Not even the first time it happened to us."

"We could never be accused of failing to do everything within our power to carry out our charge," Doc said. "These were circumstances as unforeseeable as they were beyond our control."

"Boss Plunkett," Jak said. He spit, carefully aiming downwind of himself and his companions. "Was dick."

Mildred shrugged. "And there you have it."

J.B. rubbed the stubble on his chin. "So what now, Ryan?"

"Continue on to Sweetwater Junction, I reckon. We got some jack and supplies from Plunkett up front, but we burned a triple-lot of ammo getting away. Mebbe we can buy more there."

"And water," J.B. said. "That ammo will command some serious jack, though."

"Right." Though it lay in the midst of some of the worst, most desolate Deathlands, the ville of Sweetwater Junction was relatively large and prosperous, owing to its location on a trade crossroad, as well as the aquifer that gave it its name. "Our canteens'll be dry as neutron bones by the time we get there. Mebbe we can even find work for a while, stock up."

Krysty looked up at that, her emerald eyes big and her red hair starting to uncurl a bit. Ryan knew what she was thinking. She never gave up hope that they'd find a place to settle down, rest from their wanderings and make a real life for themselves.

Fireblast, Ryan thought. It's what keeps me going, too. Nothing he'd heard about Sweetwater Junction really screamed out "safe haven" to him. But what the nuke? They wouldn't know until they got there.

"Excuse me."

Everybody's head snapped around at the timid words. The speaker was a thin young cultist woman, shivering in her sackcloth robe.

"We heard that one of you was a healer," she said. "We have wounded."

Mildred got up. Ryan frowned briefly but said nothing. He wasn't thrilled with her helping the cultists, but he had to admit he had no grounds to try to stop her. None of *them* needed her services, and he could see how a little extra goodwill might come in handy out here in the middle of the badlands. Even the goodwill of as sorry a pack of people as the cultists.

"Thank you so much," the thin woman said. "Brother Ha'ahrd is in a mighty sore way."

"Brother Ha'ahrd?" J.B. repeated incredulously. "He's alive?"

She nodded. The wind whipped wisps of blond hair from under her head scarf.

"He's hanging on to life, by the grace of the Great Old Ones," she said. "He was bit something grievous by those monsters. As were a number of our brothers and sisters. But the faithful rescued him and brought him back aboard the bus, and we were carried here to safety."

Mildred was nodding, her mind already switched to the mode of assessing the task ahead of her. She started walking toward the clump of moaning cultists.

Ryan caught her arm.

"What?" she demanded, turning back.

The others had gone still, as if they'd finally been frozen in place by the merciless late-winter wind. Ryan felt as if his skin was stretched over an ice sculpture himself.

"Did you say bitten?" Krysty asked.

Chapter Seven

"Yes." The young woman nodded. "Some were shot, or cut or burned pretty bad. But most of our injured were bitten and scratched by those horrible things."

"Let go of me, Ryan," Mildred said. "I've got to—"

"Got to what, Millie?" J.B. asked. His normally soft voice was edged like a blade. "Get bitten and changed yourself?"

"I— Oh. *Oh*." Her face acquired a greenish-gray tinge.

"Time to go," Jak said.

Ryan heard an exclamation, more an awed mass exhalation, from the direction of the cultists. He turned and looked.

Brother Ha'ahrd had stood straight up from amid his adoring followers. It was as if he'd been miraculously healed.

Or…something decidedly else.

For a moment the huddled believers stared up at their prophet in worshipful awe. The thin blonde who had spoken to Mildred ran toward him, crying, "Brother Ha'ahrd! You've returned to us!"

The others shifted aside to let her through. Brother Ha'ahrd's big baggy head turned toward her as she ran up, her arms spread to hug him. For an instant Ryan thought he saw a red glow as of reflected firelight in his sunken eyes.

He grabbed her shoulders and bit a chunk out of her cheek.

"Fuck me," J.B. said matter-of-factly.

"No," Ryan said. "Fuck these stupes. We're leaving."

The crowd had shrunk away in horror when their beloved prophet sank his teeth into his acolyte. Now she screamed and thrashed impotently as he gnawed at her skull. Around them other figures grappled wildly, silhouetted against the feeble bluish flames of the fire.

One broke free and sprinted for the companions. It was a small, slight man whose scarf had fallen back to reveal a balding head. One side of his face looked as if it had been chewed off. The eyeball bounced around wildly on the stalk of its nerve.

Mildred turned sideways, raised her ZKR 551 one-handed and fired once. His head snapped back, a hole in the center of his high forehead. He collapsed, to roll bonelessly across the frozen ground for several feet.

"Some of these bastards're fast," she said.

"Leave how?" Krysty asked.

"Isn't it obvious?" J.B. asked. "Why flee across the landscape on foot like bare-ass hillies when we can ride in style?"

"Get the gear on the bus," Ryan commanded. "Also your asses. Time to move."

"But it's not our bus!" Mildred protested.

"It is now," he said, hefting his own pack.

Mildred looked distressed, but she holstered her handblaster, picked up her own backpack and was second on the bus after Doc.

"Snap it up," Ryan said. Most of the cultists were still preoccupied dealing with their comrades who hadn't exactly survived, but refused to stay dead. But one woman spotted the companions piling into the wag, and raised a cry of protest.

It rose to a shriek as another woman chomped the side of her neck from behind.

"Don't know how many of these people're going to have use for a wag, anyway," Ryan said as Krysty and Jak piled aboard.

People started running for the bus. At this point, which were normal and which were rotties didn't much matter. Ryan sprang quickly up the steps inside.

J.B. was ensconced in the driver's seat.

"No key!" Jak called.

"Have some faith, Jak," the Armorer said. He already had a multitool in action, digging a bundle of colored wiring out from beneath the steering wheel. A moment, a spark, a smell of ozone, and the bus's engine blatted and growled to life.

Still in the step well, Ryan pivoted and slammed the door shut, leaning on the bar. A heartbeat later a cultist crashed into it. He hammered desperately on the glass with his fists.

"Let me in!" he pleaded, his voice muted by the glass. His breath made a smear of condensation that blurred the look of sheer fear on his face.

Other figures came up from behind. Hands seized him, and he howled as fingernails dug into his cheek.

"Go," Ryan said. "Now. Time really is blood here, J.B. Ours."

The bus accelerated. The screaming cultist and his changed companions bumped along the steel flank and were left behind.

"Old girl just needed to warm up a moment," J.B. sang out.

"Old bitch nearly got us chilled," Ryan grumbled, hanging on to the steel post by the first seat as the ancient wag bounced overland.

"People are running after us," Mildred reported from the rear of the bus. She sounded upset about it. "I don't think they're all rotties."

"Good for them," Ryan said. "If they're not stupes, they'll keep on running."

BUT THE OLD CLATTERY BUS had something to say about carrying them all the way to their goal, Sweetwater Junction. Namely, that nobody had topped up its fuel at Omar's before their unceremonious departure, and the tank ran dry.

It stopped in the middle of a featureless nowhere. Ryan opened the door and stepped outside into a blast of cold wind freighted with tiny ice particles that stung his face.

"Damn," he said, and went back inside.

They slept the rest of the night in the bus. It wasn't warm, but it protected them from the wind.

In the thin gray light of dawn they ate a cold breakfast of jerky and dried fruit from their stores. Then Ryan had them bring the cultists' packs down from the roof to be rifled for items of use or value.

"I feel like a grave robber," Mildred said.

Ryan and Jak kept watch from the emptied roof. Ryan occasionally swept the horizon with his rifle shouldered and his eye to the scope. He could easily hear the conversation on the ground below despite the rushing wind.

"We don't know if all the folks whose packs these were are dead, Millie," J.B. said.

Uh-oh, Ryan thought. He and Jak looked at each other.

J.B. was Ryan's best friend. There was nobody handier with a gun or a gadget, and nobody he'd rather have at his back—except maybe Krysty. There was no harm or malice in the little armorer. Unless you were an enemy. In which case, fuck you.

But sometimes he just didn't say the right thing.

"That doesn't exactly make me feel better, John," Mildred said. The tone in her voice was as cold as the prairie wind. "We're robbing people of material they might need to survive."

They had piled meds, canned food, some jerked meat, jack and water bottles in a heap. It was turning into a tidy pile. To Ryan's annoyance there were neither weapons nor ammo. These cultists were pacifists.

"We're not taking it back to them, Mildred," Krysty said. "No point in letting it go to waste, is there?"

She nodded. "I hear you. Still…"

"Way I see it," J.B. said, "their loss is our gain."

Mildred shot him a look like a burst of machine-gun fire and stalked away. Frowning in puzzlement, J.B. started after her.

Krysty caught his arm and shook her head.

It all rolled off Ryan's shoulders and down his back like rain beading on his coat. Mildred had her spells. She was no different than Doc that way. Only instead of straying from reality, as the old man occasionally did, Mildred sometimes got overwhelmed by how different the world she lived in was from what she'd grown up with. She had come a long way over the years, but she had her moments.

Her squeamishness didn't bother him. Both Mildred and Doc had valuable skills for the group. Neither had much trouble snapping to and doing what needed to be done when the shithammer came down. That was what mattered most to Ryan.

They split the proceeds among their own packs. Mildred accepted her share without comment, although she was still tight-lipped. J.B. shot the sun with his minisextant and confirmed their position was a two to three days' walk out of Sweetwater Junction. They set out west for the ville.

They walked for a day beneath skies filled with clouds

the color of spilled brains, bent over to reduce the impact of the wind. They were near enough the main route to the Junction, a predark road with two cracked but mostly intact lanes of pavement, to catch sight of it every now and again. Ryan decided to stay clear. The going wasn't too bad with the ground frozen, and he didn't feel eager to encounter any fellow wayfarers just now. If any of the companions didn't like that decision, they didn't say so.

As sunset cast diffused shadows across the plain to the east, they saw smoke drifting from the far side of a rise a mile or two ahead.

"Coldhearts," J.B. said.

"Mebbe," Ryan said. "But Baron Sharp of Sweetwater's got a rep for wide-ranging and frequent patrols. And not much sense of mercy."

"You thinking of signing on for that, lover?" Krysty asked.

Ryan shrugged. "Like to keep the option open."

"Careless, letting smoke seen," Jak said, squatting on his heels and looking like a red-eyed white wolf. "Double-stupe."

"Mebbe, mebbe not," Ryan said. "They might just be confident they can handle any grief the smoke draws to 'em. Anyway, we're not looking to sign on with them. Not sight unseen."

"We could use some information," Krysty said. "Especially if they're just out of Sweetwater Junction."

"Yeah," Ryan said. "Jak, you head on out front. Creepy-crawl their camp, see what they look like. We'll come on after you."

"Shouldn't we try to set up some kind of rendezvous point?" Mildred asked.

Jak laughed. "Day can't find friends in open," he said, "day to die."

AN HOUR LATER, the nighttime landing on the Deathlands like a geological stratum of coal brought the party to a sudden halt.

"Don't need to go stumbling into any sentries in the dark," Ryan said. They were no more than a quarter mile from the camp. Its fire could be seen as a little dome of yellow glowing atop a long slow rise.

The wind in the grass made a sound like six billion soldier ants on the march.

The companions hunkered down with their backs to the cut of an arroyo to shelter them from the freezing wind. They'd hardly done so when Ryan heard nine soft hoots float on the cold night air, fading away at the end. They sounded almost like words "who cooks for you, who cooks for you all...."

It was the call of the barred owl, a species with a wide range, including the densely wooded bayous of the Gulf Coast. But a bird whose range did *not* include a land as treeless as this.

Ryan stood up. The wind ran icy fingers through his hair, and the chill went right through his scalp, seemingly into his brain.

"Head on in, Jak," he called softly. "We won't shoot at you."

Even Ryan jumped when Jak suddenly landed on the soft sand of the dry stream bed right at his side. The youth laughed noiselessly.

"You can be such a dick, Jak," said Mildred, who'd been half dozing with her arms around her knees.

"What'd you find?" J.B. asked. "Do we fight or flee?"

"Or mebbe even talk to them," Krysty said with gentle irony.

"Not look like coldhearts."

"Ah, but Jak, what do coldhearts look like?" Doc asked.

"Shave heads. Big mustaches. Tattoos. Too many weps."

Hard as it was at first to try to envision "too many weps" in the Deathlands, Ryan quickly caught the point. A peaceful party would be well armed if it wanted to stay alive, unrobbed and unraped. But it couldn't afford to load itself down with blasters and knives. Those things were heavy and unwieldy, and interfered with carrying trifles like food and water. So a party that bristled with armament meant coldhearts.

"So what do our friends out there actually look like?" Ryan asked.

Jak shrugged. He had bitten into a strip of dried fish scavvied from the pilgrims' packs, and was crunching on it. The stuff was so horrible even his Deathlands-born companions, J.B., Krysty and Ryan, who had been known to eat day-dead coyote with relish, couldn't stomach it. But the albino teen loved it.

"Traders," he said, little bits of fishy vileness falling from his pale lips. "Talk like. Look like had to leave someplace in hurry."

"How can you tell that, Jak?" Krysty asked.

"No wags. Just drag pole, mebbe two."

"Even conveyances so crude would constitute a genuine rarity out here," Doc said, "given the paucity of trees."

J.B. swapped looks with Ryan. "Be the sort of thing traders might grab on their way out of a ville in a rush, though," the Armorer said.

"And the nearest ville that way is Sweetwater Junction," Mildred commented.

"Right," Ryan said with a decisive nod. He stooped to collect his backpack, which he'd dumped as soon as they'd sheltered in the wash. "Let's go see if they want to talk."

FROM TWENTY FEET AWAY Ryan could actually feel the warmth of the fire on his face. It was that cold out there.

"Evening, friends," he said, stepping forward, holding his hands spread out at his sides to show they were empty.

About ten dark figures were huddled around the little buffalo-chip and winter-grass fire. They gave a collective jerk when he spoke.

Heads turned toward him and he heard the mechanical cricket chorus of blaster safeties coming off.

Chapter Eight

"Back off the triggers of your blasters, boys and girls," said a bulky figure in a silver wolf-pelt coat, rising on the far side of the campfire. "Take a look at this specimen. Think he's triple-stupe enough to blunder into an armed camp without longblasters trained on it?"

Actually, the only longblaster on them was Ryan's Steyr Scout Tactical, being aimed by Krysty. But there was a scattergun and three handblasters holding down the group from the darkness. So it was a pretty good call.

"The name's Ryan," he said, as weapons were reluctantly lowered. "I just aim to talk. We got some food and meds to trade."

They had plenty, thanks to the unwitting and unwilling generosity of the Cthulhu cultists. Most would remain cached well away from the campsite. Ryan knew better than to tempt the greed of his fellow man too much.

A woman had stood up next to the man in the wolfskin coat. Even taller than he was, she was dressed in a long quilted coat, with her heavy hair in dark braids. She held a flintlock longblaster in gloved hands. Ryan reckoned she had a lot of Plains Indian blood flowing through her veins.

"Why come sneaking up like that if you're friendly?" she demanded.

"Give it a rest, P.F.," Wolf Coat said. "If they meant to jack us, their blasters would've opened the palaver for them."

He looked hard at Ryan, with his head angled slightly to the side. He was a well-weathered bastard, with silver hair and a black-and-silver beard on wolf-lean cheeks and a thrusting chin. His eyebrows were as black as coal smudges. He might've had some Mex or Indian in him, as well. He looked as if he'd be rangy without the bulky coat.

"So now that we've got the pleasantries out of the way," he said, "why not bring your pals in? There's room by the fire."

Ryan closed his right fist, leaving two fingers stuck out, which he wagged three times.

Almost at once Jak materialized by his side, holstering his big Magnum revolver. Shortly thereafter Krysty and Mildred emerged into the light to Ryan's left, and Doc and J.B. to his right.

Wolf Coat's eyebrows shot up. Plainly, he recognized what the companions had done: arranged themselves to take his party in a crossfire that offered no hope of cover if things went rapidly south, with minimum danger of shooting one another.

"You people know your business," he said, "if your business is chilling. You got any other trade, my friend?"

"What comes along," Ryan said, "we do. Mind telling me who you are?"

"Sorry. Your unexpected arrival put me clean off my manners. I'm Wolfskin Jones. This here's my life partner, Prairie Falcon. P.F. for short."

He indicated the woman in the quilted coat. A dark, boot-leather brown, her face was handsome rather than pretty, with unplucked brows, a beak of nose and a generally fierce expression that strongly suggested her namesake.

"You got to make allowances for P.F. She's Só'taa'e Cheyenne, and culturally inclined to a touch of paranoia."

"Bite me, Wolf Foreskin," she growled.

"We enjoy what you might refer to as a tempestuous relationship," the grizzled man said. "The rest of these hard cases and hard casettes are all that remain of a once mighty trade convoy. And by that I mean six power wags and twenty crew. So not so much mighty as respectable. But I might as well talk 'em up, since they're gone with the new moon."

"What happened?" Krysty asked.

The man turned and looked her up and down with obvious appreciation. Prairie Falcon growled low in her throat, more like her man's namesake than her own.

"Don't get your underwear in a twist, P.F.," Jones said. "I'm not fool enough to cross you. And not triple-stupe like I'd have to be if the one-eyed death machine over there is this one's mate. As I'm guessing, miss?"

"You guess right," Krysty said with a smile that could charm the snarl off a mama cougar. "And you can call me Krysty."

"Pleasure," Jones said. "And in answer to your question, Krysty, Sweetwater bastard Junction happened."

"BEEN A POWER SHIFT in Sweetwater," Ernesto said. He was a burly dude made bulkier by his parka, complete with a fur-lined hood that made his round face look like a dark, stubble-bearded moon reflecting yellow firelight. "Things all went to glowing night shit, triple-sudden-like."

"Heard the boss there was Baron Jeb Sharp," J.B. said. "He get chilled?"

"Some say he did, some say he didn't," said Lita, a gangly woman with red pigtails spilling out from her green knit cap.

"He fell sick, or so the rumor goes," Jones said. He sat by the fire gnawing a haunch of roast coyote. Grease glistened on his beard. P.F. knelt next to him, glowering silently in her blanket robe. "Least that's what we heard right before the shit hit the propeller. Shooting broke out in the palace. Next thing anybody knows the streets are all full of sec goons, popping caps at each other and everything else that moved."

"Heard tell Sharp's sec boss made a power grab," Ernesto said.

"Geither Jacks." Jones turned his head the other way to spit theatrically. "A real bastard. True coldheart. 'Gate to hell,' they call him. As monikers go it's a tad on the unwieldy side, but no one can say it ain't appropriate."

"Mostly they call him Gate," Lita said, "but ever'body knows what's meant."

"But somebody was shooting back," Ryan prompted. Like a lot of Deathlands travelers, this bunch loved outside company, but enjoyed hearing themselves yammer so much it sometimes made it hard for visitors to cram a word in sideways.

"Yeah," Jones said. "Loyalists to the baron, or his wife and his heir, anyway. Some said Miranda was in the thick of the shooting that chased Gate's bunch out of the palace, firing a longblaster like a devil in a black suede skirt. Which'd be just like that Mex-lander she-devil. She's a fiery one, beautiful as the clearest winter night and with a soul twice as dark."

He jumped and turned to glare at his partner. "Ow! Why'd you have to go and gouge me in the rib cage?" he demanded, although Ryan hadn't seen P.F. move a muscle. "You're she-devil enough for me, and probably two or three others beside."

Ryan got the impression a smile flitted across P.F.'s features, which normally looked as if they'd been hacked out of hardwood by the steel-hafted hatchet she wore at her waist.

"So this sec boss made a power play and lost," J.B. said.

"Not exactly," Jones said. "He didn't win. Which ain't the same thing."

"No?" J.B. asked.

"Not hardly. He failed to take over the palace. In fact, he and his blasters got chased clear out of the north half of the ville. But he just grabbed the other. Sweetwater Junction's split down the middle. Each side claims the whole shebang. They're more'n eager to chill to back it up."

"But neither side's strong enough to take on the other," Ryan said.

"That's so," Jones said.

"What about the ville folk?" Mildred asked.

"Keep their heads down and hope nobody notices 'em, if they got any sense," Ernesto said. "Liable to wind up dead or drafted, otherwise. Or both, uh, usually in opposite order."

"They stole our wags," P.F. said, "and grabbed our people to make 'em fight for them. Or just for slave labor."

"We just got out with our hides and what we could manage to run with," Jones said. "Damn shame about our friends. But our getting chilled or enslaved ain't likely to ease their lot appreciably."

"Thanks for the heads-up," Ryan said. "What do you people look to do next?"

"Head east," Jones said. "Away from Sweetwater Junction as fast as our legs will carry us."

"East not good," Jak said.

The traders looked at him blankly.

"We got a story to tell you, too," Ryan said.

RYAN COULD TELL the traders only half believed their story of the rotties.

The companions spent the night in camp alongside the refugee traders, sharing watches. At first Ryan was disturbed by dreams of people dying, and then rising to attack, hands outstretched, mouths gaping with mindless bloodlust, coming on and on despite bullet strikes to the body, even with their own guts tangled around their legs.

But he'd seen things as bad before. Some worse. His body had spent a hard day and his mind was hard. Eventually he fought through the nightmares and slept.

In dawn's ashen light a pair of traders watching the road to Sweetwater Junction reported strangers approaching from the east. Ryan and Jones stepped out into the roadway empty-handed as two goggled riders sped toward them, legs pumping furiously at the pedals of mountain bikes.

"You've done this before, my boy," Jones commented, his wolfskin coat making him look like a mountain man.

Ryan had automatically stopped short of blocking the right-of-way. It was standard protocol of the road: *we're here, we'd like to talk, mebbe trade.* It wasn't always sincerely meant, like anything else in the Deathlands. Except for professions of bloodlust. Those were always sincere.

"Spent a few years as a trader myself," Ryan said.

The riders slowed about fifty paces away. They pushed their goggles up onto their stocking caps. Both were as lean as old coyotes. One was a woman, the other a man. The woman carried what looked like a crossbow slung over her back. They held their hands out to their sides in the recognized gesture of peaceful intent.

"You should be running," the woman called out. She had a nasal Northeastern accent.

"Now, why'd that be?" Jones asked. "You wouldn't be threatening us?"

"Not us," the man said. He had a long and narrow face, as if a giant mutie had clamped his head in a vise and pulled hard on his chin. "Them."

He jerked a thumb over his shoulder.

Jones made an exaggerated show of peering up the narrow road. Dust drifted over it, but fairly regular traffic kept the ancient blacktop from being buried under the dirt of ages.

"Who'd 'they' be?" he asked. "Seeing as you're the only folks on the road."

"Don't be a dick, Wolfskin," P.F. said, sliding down the cut behind her man and Ryan, with her flintlock longblaster cradled in her arms. Standing, she turned out to be bigger than she looked. She stood a good two fingers taller than Ryan. "Ask 'em to join us."

But the riders shook their heads frantically. "We got thirty or forty miles between us and them," the man said. "We'd be happier if it was a hundred and thirty."

"Thirty-four hundred would be better still," the woman said. "You people need to get moving, too. They won't be here for a few days yet. But when they do…"

Ryan could see her shudder.

"Who're these 'they' you keep talking about?" P.F. asked.

More of the refugee traders and Ryan's friends had appeared. He felt a rise in warmth on more than just a physical level as Krysty came up and put an arm around him. A quick glance confirmed what he knew: Jak was lying low, making sure everything stayed on the level. He wasn't much for palavering, to say the least.

"Heard some folk call 'em rotties," the woman said. She shook her head. "If we told you what they were really like, you'd never believe us. But imagine the worst trouble you've ever known. Then triple that."

"And it won't be enough," her partner added.

"Rotties," Jones repeated thoughtfully. He turned his pale wolf eyes to Ryan and Krysty. "Isn't that what you called those unkillable, brain-eating monsters you were telling us about?"

"You've heard of them?" the woman asked. "Then why are you still here? You can't chill 'em unless you shoot 'em in the head. They just keep coming no matter what. They don't feel pain or fear."

"Just hunger," the man said. "For your meat. And your brains in particular."

"And if they bite you, unless they eat all your brains, you rise up as one of them. If they bite you and you die, the same thing happens." She shook her head. "Their numbers just keep growing. There're dozens of them already! And they're heading this way."

"This sounds familiar."

"I told you these people were speaking straight," P.F. said to her man.

"You didn't! You never told me that!"

"You're such a dick."

Jones shrugged. "It's part of my charm. Where are you folks headed?"

"Sweetwater Junction, to spread the word," the man said. "Then on. All the way to the Cific if we have to. And then mebbe we'll catch a boat."

"Might want to change your route," Ernesto called. "The Junction's enjoying itself a nice little civil war. Unless you're willing to sign as mercies for one side or t'other, best give it a wide berth. They look on outlanders as meat on the hoof. They'll chill you or slave you sooner than look at you."

"Thanks for the word," the woman called. "We'll take a detour."

"You could join up with us," Jones said. "Looks like we'll be taking a detour ourselves. Safety in numbers and all."

The two bicyclists looked at each other. "Thanks," the woman called. "But we believe in safety in speed."

Without another word they pulled their goggles back down and began pedaling for all their lean-muscled legs were worth. When they passed Ryan and the rest they were practically flying.

"So," Jones said, watching them fade into the distance, "you were telling us straight all along. Well, that'll teach me to believe there's anything too strange for this triple-crazed world of ours."

Chapter Nine

Dust swirled in a miniature fountain by the side of the road, mixed with hard, dry snow that had been coming down slowly since Ryan and friends had said farewell to Jones and his crew.

The traders had decided to head south. "Where at least it might be warmer," Jones had put it. "Also, if we got to take a boat to keep away from these rotties, Gulf Coast's closer."

The sound of the gunshot reached Ryan where he lay on his belly behind a scrubby bush, peering through his Navy longeyes. His companions hid out of sight in a fold in the flat-looking landscape.

The man running down the road with the loose-limbed stagger of complete desperation coupled to complete exhaustion staggered back into the middle of the right-of-way. Thirty yards behind him was a battered pickup truck, long since gone the color of the plains dirt itself, with a bent-pipe cage welded over the front bumper. Its bed was full of hooting coldhearts.

The human prey was dressed in rags and as skinny as finger bones. He lurched into the road with his hands flopping like flippers. It was obviously the end of the chase for him.

The truck hit the runner. The impact flung him ten feet in the air and forty feet down the roadway. When he landed, he rolled over several times and lay flopping like a beached fish.

"Ryan," Mildred said quietly, through clenched teeth. The one-eyed man said nothing.

"It's not our fight, Millie," J.B. said.

The wag came right up by the flailing, screaming man. It did a quick U-turn, putting its nose toward the ville and its tailgate toward the victim. Men wearing green armbands spilled out of the back.

Laughing and whooping, they tied ropes to both the man's ankles. The volume of their merriment went up as the volume of his shrieks did when they jostled his evidently many broken bones, grinding the ends together in a perfect storm of pain.

They leaped back into the bed. The wag accelerated back toward Sweetwater Junction, just visible as a low brown serration breaking the western horizon. The victim bounced behind on the road like a screaming puppet.

"Wonder which side?" Jak said.

"Does it matter?" J.B. replied.

"One's as likely as the other, I reckon," Ryan said. "It's how barons and sec men act."

"Not where you came from," Krysty said.

"True. Until my brother took over."

"But you set Front Royal right in the end."

He hunched a shoulder. "That bullet's long since left the blaster. Right now we've got to see to our own survival."

"Might that not best be served by following either set of the travelers we parted with today?" Doc asked. "Heading north or south, giving wide berth both to the ville of Sweetwater Junction and its woes and the hapless swarm of the changed?"

"That's how I'd go, I got to admit," J.B. said.

"We already jawed this over," Ryan said. "We go forward with the plan."

"Getting caught in a ville civil war doesn't seem much

better than getting caught by rotties," Mildred told him. "Just a longer way of dying badly. You said it's none of our concern."

Ryan sighed and looked at Jak. "Eyes skinned," he said.

The smooth, snow-colored face wrinkled. Ryan knew Jak thought he might as well remind him to breathe.

Ryan slipped back to settle down out of sight of the road. "Listen, this rottie thing is special. It's different from almost anything we've been up against. At least since that thing up in Canada."

"What does that have to do with getting stuck in Sweetwater?" Mildred demanded.

"You should know, Mildred. You and Doc both said this shit's contagious, right?"

"Evidently so, friend Ryan," Doc said. "It appears to be saliva-borne."

"Or anyway carried by bodily fluids," Mildred added.

"And it's spreading, right?"

"So the information we've received suggests," Doc said. "It may not be altogether reliable."

"What's to stop it spreading? Anything?"

Nobody spoke.

"How will us signing on to help the goons in Sweetwater Junction commit atrocities stop the change spreading?" Mildred asked.

"The rotties are coming to Sweetwater Junction," Ryan said.

"Wait—now you're losing even me," Krysty said. "What makes you so sure? I know the bicyclists said the creatures were heading west. Why would that mean they'd be coming here, specifically."

"Meat."

Everybody looked at Jak. The albino teen squatted with his white hair blowing free in the killing wind, gazing out toward the desolate highway. He seemed to be laughing soundlessly. It made him look even more like what his enemies used to call him down in the bayou country: the White Wolf.

"Gotta eat. Rotties go to food. Country empty. Ville full. Do math."

"The lad does make a compelling point in his unlettered yet concise way," Doc said.

"So how's going into the ville and likely getting ourselves pulled apart by trucks in the town square going to help end the plague?" Mildred asked.

"I'd say Ryan reckons we can fight the rotties better if we got a whole ville to help us," J.B. said.

"Why would you think that'd even work, Ryan?" Mildred asked. "Do you really think you can get this lady baron and her turncoat sec man to just lay aside their differences?"

"If we don't stop the rotties," Ryan said, "what will?"

"Is that really up to us, Ryan?" J.B. asked.

"Who else is going to do it?"

"You're the one who's big on not sticking our noses into other people's business," Mildred said. "For that matter, Sweetwater Junction'll at least slow them down for a while. Why not use the delay to just cruise on our way and forget about these freaks?"

"Cruise where?" Ryan asked.

She frowned and shook her head. "I don't know. Mexico? The Darks? Canada? Someplace far away."

"How long?"

"Huh?"

"What he means, I believe," Doc said, "is how long before the horde catches up to us in those places."

"Why would they?"

"Mildred," Krysty said gently, "you said yourself the

change was catching. And the horde is growing. What's to stop it spreading to overtake us wherever we go?"

The predark physician looked blank for a moment. Then she shook her head again, tightly this time, as if trying to shed water from her plaited hair.

"Maybe we could do what Jones and his friends said they were going to—go the Cific and jump on a boat."

"Cific's big," Krysty said.

"Mebbe rotties sail," Jak said.

"They're mindless," Mildred pointed out.

"Do we know that?" Ryan said. "Most of them act like they're brain-chilled, sure. But they don't all act alike. That stunt using the little girl rottie to get Omar's people to open the gate—that looked like tactics. So did climbing the wall where nobody could see, and storming the gaudy. What if we turn up in China and a boatload of rotties hits the coast twenty, fifty, a hundred miles away?

"Look, people. You know I've got no problem running when running's the way to survive. This isn't trouble we can get away from by running. Sooner or later it'll catch up to us. We have to stop this now."

"How?" Mildred said. "You saw how they overran the caravanserai."

"Omar wasn't prepared," J.B. said. "Nobody's prepared for something like that."

"We can prep the ville," Ryan said. "Rouse the place, fortify, get the locals to fight."

"What if they don't believe us?" Mildred demanded. "Or what if the sides are more interested in fighting each other?"

"Then like I said before," Ryan said. "We got to adjust some attitudes."

"You really think you can adjust people out of wanting to be barons?"

"There're ways, Mildred. Even for that."

"But Ryan, do you think we can end this by fighting?" Krysty asked. "Bullets can stop rotties. Can they stop the change?"

"I don't know. I'm damn sure we can't stop them without fighting. So I say fight 'em as soon as we can. It'll only keep getting harder until it's impossible."

"Just hypothetically, how could fighting stop a plague?" Mildred asked.

"Chilling all the carriers," Ryan said. "Or if we can find out what's behind this whole deal, stop it at the source."

"Those seem like awful slim hopes to pin our survival on," Mildred said. "Even if we can somehow get the warring factions in Sweetwater Junction to cooperate."

Ryan shrugged. "They're hopes. What does running away offer us? Other than delaying the inevitable."

J.B. looked off toward the ville. It was invisible from the little depression they hunkered in.

"I gotta say I don't see much chance of us pulling this one off, Ryan," he said, scratching under his battered fedora.

"The whole idea's plain crazy," Mildred said.

Krysty's beautiful face was pale, drawn taut with emotion.

"Lover," she said hoarsely, "would you really split us up for this?"

"I'll do whatever it takes to survive," Ryan said. "Like always."

Chapter Ten

"Mother," Colton Sharp said. "I wish you wouldn't prance around like that."

He winced as he heard the whine that edged his voice. Way to assert yourself, Colt, he thought.

The woman stood and struck a pose, hand on angled hip, head tipped with long black hair hanging artfully over one shoulder. One naked shoulder. One naked hip.

"Prance around like how, dear?" she asked. Her words had a trace of the accent of her native Mex-land.

As she so often did, Colt's mother, Miranda Sharp—he wasn't clear on whether she was baron in her own right or acting as regent until his own majority—was fluttering about the common room of their quarters on the third floor of the baronial palace in the nude.

Miranda stood there artfully silhouetted in the late-morning sunlight filtering through gauze curtains. It cast a halo around her hair and her still-perfect, olive-skinned body—narrow waist, flaring hips, lean legs. It did nothing to hide her full breasts, although shadows added a bit of mystery to the dark arrowhead tangle between her strong thighs.

She had married Baron Jeb Sharp young, and borne her only child, Colt, to him. She was still in her mid-thirties and religiously kept herself trim.

Colton Sharp was sixteen years old, his young, slightly pudgy body a constant sizzle of hormones.

Buck naked, he wanted to reply. But his tongue would tie itself into knots if he tried to say that to his mother. Instead he settled on waving one hand in a feeble gesture.

"Like, uh—that."

She laughed. "It's not as if you haven't seen me this way before. Who do you think gave birth to you?"

"Well, that was kind of a long time ago. I don't really remember it."

He was babbling. He saw her this way all the time. And far from getting used to it, it was starting to…affect him more and more.

She came swaying up to him, smiling mischievously. She put her hands on either side of his head, against the pink upholstered back of the chair he was sitting in, and leaned in close, so he could smell the freshly bathed feminine scent of her. In fact, almost suffocate in it.

"Pobrecito," she said huskily. Her forehead was tipped almost to touch his. Her heavy, untamable hair hung around his face like a curtain. "Does Mother make you uncomfortable?"

"Umm," he said. He tried to avoid looking at the two perfect breasts hanging inches from his eyes. His face flushed so hot he was surprised her hair didn't start to smolder, not to mention his own blond locks.

She put her lips by his ear. Her hair tickled his cheek and nose. "You need to learn how to handle yourself in the presence of a woman, *mi amor,*" she purred in his ear. "You need to learn how to handle a woman."

"Mom!" he yelped. It was the only thing he could manage to do.

She straightened and moved away with a half-spiteful laugh. "You're a good boy, Colt," she said over her shoulder. "Mama will see you brought up right."

It was double entendre city in here. Colt *had* been well

educated. Miranda had insisted. His late father had figured an iron fist and some reliable henchman were all a man really needed to get by in life. Not that he'd done so well on that second part.

The upshot: Colt knew what a double entendre was. He could read and speak three languages. He could do math. But he'd never learned how to do anything he thought was *real*.

Or, indeed, as his mother said, how to handle a woman. He had a feeling no man would ever really handle his mother. His late father sure hadn't. And her current boy-toy sec boss, Jenkins, couldn't either, that was for damn sure. Not that *he* realized it.

Colt felt suffocatingly hot, even though the potbellied stove on its colorfully painted maroon tiles in the corner wasn't doing more than keeping the chill coming through the window glass at bay. He had to think of something to say to break the mood. Anything.

"I want to learn to shoot," he said. "Dad promised he'd get someone to teach me."

She whipped around. "You'll hurt yourself," she said, frowning.

"Not if I'm taught right."

"But why would you want to use a blaster?"

"To, you know, protect myself and stuff."

Colt recalled the pants-pissing terror of being caught in the middle of the firefight when Gate to Hell Jacks had betrayed the baron and tried to seize control of Sweetwater Junction. Having angry men trying to hurt him was bad. Seeing his old tutor, Marconi, go down with a big chunk blown out of his bald head and his brains spilling out on the throw rug was bad. Seeing his best friend, Anthony, writhing in terminal agony around the two bullets that had pulped his guts was worse. Hearing bullets crack over his own head as he sheltered behind a table and a pair of loyal sec men was unimaginable.

Worst by far, though, was not being able to do anything about it. The sense of utter helplessness. In that awful moment he'd understood as never before that having a blaster wouldn't in any way render him less susceptible to bullets hitting him. But it would let him fight back. Maybe even shoot somebody before that somebody shot him.

It would give him some kind of power over his own life and circumstances. Which, young Colt Sharp had also come to realize on that terrible night of blood and flame and pain, was something he in fact had never had. Despite the fact that both his father and his mother had brought him up hearing constantly how he was born to rule.

His mother was frowning deeper and shaking her head. It made the tip of her nose turn up slightly and her brow furrow.

"You're going to be baron," she said sternly. "Shooting blasters is what you have sec men for. You don't fix your own wag or empty your own pisspot. You leave that to the menials."

"But...but what if the sec men get killed? Or aren't around?"

Or turn on you like rabid dogs after years of apparently loyal and devoted service, with the same savagery they brought to the job of keeping the citizens in their place? he thought.

But he couldn't say that. Not to his mother, not so soon. It would throw her into one of her rages. The fact that her fury would be directed against Brown and the band of traitors—who had tried to kill her and her son, had succeeded in chilling the desperately ill Baron Jeb, and had stolen half her ville out from under her—and not at Colt himself, wouldn't make it easier to take. He knew that from bitter experience. It wouldn't even be much safer, if she got to throwing things.

The way she scowled told him he'd wandered dangerously close to the edge already. Her face got darker and she took a deep breath. Her breasts rose and spread on her rib cage.

Oh, shit, Colt thought. Here it comes. Her throwing one of her epic fits stark naked, with all that entailed, would only make everything twice as freaky.

A knock sounded on the door to the common room. He slumped in the chair, instantly coated in sweat.

"Baron."

It was the voice of Hedders, one of the sec men who had stayed loyal to the Sharp family, his young voice muffled by thick wood. The veneer door that had originally sealed the entryway had, unsurprisingly in retrospect, proved no barrier to bullets. Despite the fact that milled lumber was literally worth its weight in gold out here in this treeless flatland, Miranda had insisted on a solid oak replacement. And gotten it.

"What is it?" she called. She reached for a green satin robe. For all her flouting of her lush naked body in her son's presence she was quite prudish about displaying the same goods to the lessers.

"You got visitors, ma'am."

"Who are they?"

"Three mercies, looking for jobs."

She nodded. "I'll meet them in the parlor downstairs. Tell them to wait."

"Yes, ma'am."

"BARON," THE YOUNG, intense, dark-haired sec man who called himself Hedders said, "this is Dr. Theophilus Tanner, Krysty Wroth and Ryan Cawdor."

The sitting room in the four-story stone structure at the north end of Sweetwater Junction that served as the baron's palace was decorated with salvaged porcelain figurines and fussy-seeming furniture with lace doilies on arms and backs to prevent staining of the fabric. The room smelled of lavender and old, dried sweat. Krysty guessed the new baron had had her way in decorating this room, at least, long before Baron Jeb Sharp reached room temperature. It seemed to fit, somehow, with the structure itself, which was of a look and general solidity that suggested it had been old when the Big Cull hit.

"No such thing anymore," said the tall and extravagantly muscled sec man introduced as Jenkins, biting into a chunk of dried apple. He even had muscular cheeks. "What he's a doctor of? Looking stupe?"

From the corner of her eye Krysty saw Doc give a goofy smile. Sometimes that meant he had slipped his reality tether again. Sometimes it didn't. He seemed, actually, to be more at ease in this setting than he had in a long time. It went to substantiate Krysty's theory that the room's decor was as old-timey as the building itself. Those old times *were* Doc's proper time.

"I had the good fortune to receive a stellar education, my boy," Doc said cheerfully. "And the term 'doctor' was bestowed upon me as a sign of respect for the vast store of knowledge that I acquired over the years." The lie slid smoothly from the old man's lips.

"Huh," the sec man said. He had dark olive skin that glistened as if oiled. His hair was shaved to a Mohawk, a low, dark one that almost looked painted on. For all his air of hypermasculinity, his manner was petulant and surly. "You still look like a stupe."

"Manners, Leroy," the baron said sharply.

Watch it, kid, Krysty mentally warned the surly sec man. You have no idea what this man's capable of.

The Baron's dark eyes widened considerably once they lit on the tall, dark and dangerous form of Ryan Cawdor.

Krysty wasn't much troubled by jealousy. What did concern her about Miranda Sharp's not-at-all-subtle interest in Ryan was the mischief it could cause. Such a woman was used to getting what she wanted, and stepping on rivals like roaches.

Miranda stepped right up to Ryan, hand extended. Krysty felt brief relief. The baron held her hand out vertically, as if expecting a shake, not horizontally, as if expecting a kiss. That'd get things off to all kinds of a wrong start.

"Ryan Cawdor," the baron purred, drawing the syllables out and rolling the *R*s in a Spanish way. "A pleasure to meet you."

"Pleased to meet you," he answered. "And this is Doc Tanner and Krysty Wroth, like the man said."

Ryan nodded firmly at his companions. Krysty bit down on a grin.

"Dr. Tanner," the baron said, gravely taking Doc's hand. "You clearly are a man of the mind. Are you a man of action as well, then?"

After shaking her hand, firmly but gently, Doc did turn it over and kiss the back. Miranda Sharp's eyebrows went up.

"So you are a gentleman of the old school, too," she said.

"I try to be all of those things, madam," Doc said, "as circumstances and chivalry require."

Krysty caught Ryan's eye behind the two and grinned openly. Doc, you sly old dog, she thought. Of course, he really was in his thirties, not terribly older in days actually lived through than the beautiful sex-bomb baron herself. But his aged appearance counted against him.

Still, he could be remarkably suave when focused and properly motivated. If the baron didn't so overtly have her claws out for Ryan—and if the sulky guy with the stripe down the middle of his scalp, who was looking rad death at Ryan, wasn't so obviously her current lover—Krysty thought the professor might actually have a chance. Baron Miranda was clearly a highly sexual being who might just give him a try out of curiosity.

Krysty felt no disdain or hostility toward the woman for such overt sexuality. Her own nature wasn't all that much different. But she'd learned to keep it more tightly controlled. Her life hadn't been the sheltered one of a baron of a powerful ville.

Finally, the raven-haired woman turned to her. They shook hands in a businesslike way. Krysty wasn't surprised to find Miranda's grip had a wiry strength hardly less than a man's. Krysty's arm strength had the potential to be greater than a normal man's, but the baron played nice, without any manlike hand-crushing games. And Krysty always played nice. As long as it was possible to *be* nice.

To her surprise the baron enfolded her in a fervent hug, which she returned belatedly but firmly.

"It is so good to meet a woman of substance," Miranda said, breaking free. For a moment Krysty wondered if the baron was making a crack about Krysty's build, even more voluptuous than her own. But Miranda followed instantly with, "*Claro,* you are a woman of education as well as strength of spirit. I bid you welcome to Sweetwater Junction."

She stepped back. "All of you."

"Thank you, Baron," Ryan said.

"And this is my son, Colton, the future baron of Sweetwater Junction," Miranda said, turning to introduce the somewhat ungainly figure who had appeared in the doorway behind her as if on cue. Which suggested to Krysty that he had been waiting for one.

He was of medium height for a male, somewhat shorter than Krysty herself. His obvious youth suggested he had some growing yet to do. He was fair-complected, unlike his mother, and his eyes were hazel. His hair was blond, curly and tousled. He was a handsome youth, or would've been if not for the baby fat that padded his cheeks and frame.

He stepped up and shook hands with each newcomer in turn. He met Krysty's eye and his gaze lingered for a moment, as did his grip.

"It's a real pleasure to meet you, Ms. Wroth," he said. His handshake was firm if not indicative of great physical strength. When he released her hand, he did so abruptly and almost convulsively.

He seemed almost afraid of Ryan, but after only the briefest hesitation shook his hand and looked him in the eye, as well.

Colt Sharp struck Krysty as a not unintelligent youth trying to break free of chubbiness and uncertainty. Would he be equal to the terror the not-too-distant future seemed to hold for himself and his ville? She saw, sadly, no evidence that he would.

Give him time, he'd learn, she thought. Triple-shame the one thing he didn't have was time.

"So you're mercenaries?" he asked, stepping back to his mother's side. She loomed over him, although much of her height was due to the high heels of the laced-front, knee-high boots she wore.

"You're not ready to handle such matters yourself yet, Colt," Miranda said, with a pleasant smile and just a hint of a whip crack. "Watch and learn, *mijo*."

I see, Krysty thought. I know that story. She recognized a mother who loved her son—perhaps mebbe too much—

but not more than she feared loss of control over him. Or, judging by what they'd heard of events in Sweetwater Junction, over any tiny little element of life in the ville.

"It is true you wished to discuss employment?" the baron asked Ryan.

"We heard you were having a bit of a set-to with your former sec boss," Ryan said. "Thought you might be able to use three more blasters at your side."

Eyebrows arched, Miranda swept the trio with her dark, intense gaze. "You all three are handy with blasters, then?"

"We all know our way around them," Ryan said. "Don't let Doc's appearance fool you. You could do worse than have him at your back when blasters start talking."

"What a bunch of crap," Jenkins said. "I could mop the floor with all three of them at once."

"If you think that, you're a bigger fool than I thought," the baron said without turning. "Now, keep silent. Or I'll force you to try to make good on your empty-headed boast."

The darkly handsome face got a lot darker. If the man had been glaring hot death at Ryan before, now it was a wonder just the side-scatter didn't set the antimacassars ablaze.

Miranda glanced to where the travelers' packs leaned discreetly by the baseboard, behind a china cabinet.

"So, Mr. One-Eyed Stranger," Miranda said. "Do you really know how to use that very big rifle of yours?"

"He's *masterful* with it," Krysty almost purred.

I know it's naughty to say it that way, she thought. But at least I didn't say "and the longblaster, too."

Chapter Eleven

"Ryan," Doc said from behind him. "Krysty's back."

"Ace," Ryan said. As intensely focused as he could be when chilling was at stake, he had had trouble concentrating the whole time Krysty was out on the bitterly contested streets of Sweetwater Junction doing recce.

He sat in an uncomfortable wooden chair beside a heavy wooden table, both of which had been shellacked within an inch of their lives. The varnish had long since started to discolor in shades of yellow and brown, and crack. Perhaps that was why no one had bothered scavvying the furniture from the fourth floor of the ancient redbrick office building on the northern side of Sweetwater Junction's central square. Or perhaps they were just too heavy and uncomfortable to lug down so many stairs. He wasn't sure why they hadn't been broken up for fuel if nothing else, in this timber-poor, fuel-poor desolation.

The room smelled of cold brick, wood, varnish and the dust that floated in the ocher afternoon light coming through the unglazed, south-facing window. The desk was set a yard back from that window. On it rested Ryan's Steyr Scout Tactical longblaster, propped on some water-damaged throw cushions Baron Miranda had donated from the palace for this mission.

Whether scoping out a target or lining up a shot, you didn't do it from the window itself. The target would spot you, sure as stickies loved hurting norms.

By the time they'd sneaked into the old office building and climbed the dusty stairs to the fourth floor, the sun had passed far enough west not to shine directly into the room. The gloom was good cover if you didn't make sudden moves.

Ryan didn't take his eye from the Navy longeyes focused on the five-story wooden tower two hundred yards away across the square. The big scope atop the longblaster would let him look into a man's ear hole at this range. But it was too unwieldy and its field of vision too restricted for him to go to it until he was ready to take a shot or needed to be prepared to do so on an instant's notice.

The same pair of men he'd been watching for two hours were still up there. By the visual evidence they were just smoking and joking and taking regular hits of something Ryan didn't think was water.

Not even in a ville whose prosperity was mostly built on being the only large-scale source of clean, pure water for fifty miles in any direction would they carry it in square-sided glass bottles, he reckoned. Nor that the ville would be called Sweetwater if its namesake was that shade of brown.

He also didn't think for a moment it was predark whiskey the Jacks-faction snipers were tossing down their throats over there. He judged it was most likely Towse Lightning with brown dye or even tobacco spit mixed in for color.

A soft footfall made the bare hardwood floor creak behind him. He lowered the glasses and turned. Krysty stood in the doorway. Even he scarcely recognized her in the bulky quilted jacket and the billed, big-crowned cap that contained her hair and half obscured her face.

"Ace," he said. "You're back."

Below the bill of her green cap her grin was radiant as always. The fresh-air smell of her livened up the room.

"Did you ever doubt, lover?" she asked.

You bet your sweet ass I did, he thought. I worried every second you were out there alone. Just like I wasn't triple-comfortable with moony old Doc being my only sec while I'm lost in the glass.

He longed to have Jak, elusive as a living ghost, doing the scouting. Or at least watching Krysty's back while she scouted the ville around the plaza with its big public fountain. Ryan wished he had the steady, unflappable Armorer keeping guard while he watched their targets. He wished Mildred were there to patch them in case they got shot.

But he had chosen to split the companions. And life had taught him early on he had to live with the choices he made.

"Shall I take up surveillance of yon scapegrace inebriates, Ryan?" Doc asked.

Setting the longeyes on the table next to his Steyr, Ryan shook his head. "No. I've been trying not to look at them too long at a stretch. Man can sense when somebody's staring at him too keenly."

"Surely that's mere superstition."

"No. It's true. Happened to me on both ends, plenty times. And to everybody I ever talked to who's hunted humans, or been hunted himself. You can *feel* eyes on you."

"It's true, Doc," Krysty said. "I've felt it, too."

Ryan got up to catch her in a brief, strong embrace. He didn't want to show how nervous he'd been, for fear she'd take it as evidence he didn't trust her competence. Which wasn't true. She was as solid as they got, smart, shifty and resourceful, and never lost her head. The thing was, what she'd done was nuke-red dangerous for anybody, no matter how expert in skulking. And she was his woman.

But she insisted on carrying her own weight, no matter what. It was one of many reasons he loved her.

He kissed her forehead and cheek. In her dancing emerald eyes he plainly read that he didn't fool her for a millisecond. And that she was fine with his concern as long as he didn't say anything to show her up.

"What'd you find?" he asked.

She shrugged. "Only two people up there at a time. Nobody saw any different today. They got about two hours left on their shift. They'll switch around sunset."

She'd been wandering around trying to talk to the ville folk. Better, trying to find ville folk talking so she could eavesdrop.

"People on the north side of the line say there's just two up there, day and night," Krysty said. "They have longblasters."

"And why do the ville folk keep such close tabs on them?" Doc asked.

"Because they shoot at anyone from the north side of town who tries to get water from the fountain."

"So, it's all just like Miranda told us," Ryan said, sitting down and picking up the longeyes again.

BARON MIRANDA SHARP and her son may have lost their sec boss when Jacks turned his coat, but she retained a core of loyalist sec men, backed up by the palace staff and servants. The quiet people who came and went to do the new baron's bidding had the air of having done so for a spell, Krysty thought.

She also had an adviser in the form of a hard-bitten man on the grizzled side of middle age who went by the name Perico. He was middle height and seemed to be made of burnished hardwood, with steel wool for hair, growing in tufts from the sides of his bald head, on his thick forearms and the backs of his hands, and encasing his wolf-trap jaws.

"When that bastard Jacks, may he suffer, made his play," he was saying as he smoothed a hand-drawn map of contemporary Sweetwater Junction across a round drawing-room table cleared of bric-a-brac for the occasion, "he got most of the sec force, plus some malcontents from the ville, to back it."

Perico put what looked to be a small, ancient iron on one side of the map to hold it in place. On the other side he put a square, cut-crystal dish holding various trade-good candies. Baron Miranda stood by looking competent and forbidding in her tight black pants and lavender silk blouse. Colt hovered by her side, half eager and half scared he might get whipped. Like a mistreated pup, Krysty thought.

Hedders, who seemed nice enough for a sec man, had withdrawn. Jenkins stood by and sneered. Krysty already mostly discounted him. He could be dangerous, like a scorpion in a boot. But he didn't count.

Likely he knew it, too. And it made him angry.

"Geither Jacks favored his goons and toadies. Otherwise he was a pure bully—sucked up to his bosses, rained pain on everyone beneath him."

"Not a new story," Doc murmured.

Perico raised a brow to stare at the old man for a moment. "Be surprised if it was," he said after a moment. "While Jacks got some of the key richies in town, like Morgan the cloth trader and Delgado the spice guy, most of the ville folk supported the old baron, and after they found out he was gone, Baron Miranda and Colt. Got to admit it wasn't so much out of love for the Sharp family as knowing what a vicious stoneheart Jacks is. Your pardon, Baron."

Miranda's flushed face was knotted in anger, but her scarcely checked rage wasn't aimed at her plainspoken adviser.

"Some on this side harbor treachery in their hearts," she said, her voice a hiss of fury. "We'll root them out and destroy them like the snakes they are! Then we'll put an end to this stickie in man's clothing, Jacks."

Ryan raised his unscarred right eyebrow at the baron's display. She was too preoccupied to notice, Krysty saw with relief.

If we held out only for employers who weren't even a little crazy, she reminded herself, we'd've starved to death years ago.

"Now the ville's split pretty much in two," Perico went on in a voice like a heavy wag driving down a gravel road. "There's a no-man's-land runs right through the middle of it. Smack in the center is the big public fountain."

"How does anybody get water?" Krysty asked.

"Every other day there's a two-hour truce. Starts an hour before noon. Anybody with a chit can draw water from the fountain. We still get traders coming through. Even a mad dog like Jacks knows that's gotta continue. Also the ville folk from both sides can draw their water rations."

"That's how you keep the palace supplied?" Ryan asked.

Perico shook his head. "We've got wells dug in a few key buildings," he said. "Here in the palace. Also on the south side, in Sinorice's gaudy, where all the drovers and wag draggers went. When we ran his traitor ass out of here, Jacks took his coldhearts straight there. They chased out poor Brad Sinorice and made his place their headquarters. Sinorice is bunking with his old pal Bill Itomaru the carpenter in no-man's-land west of the square."

"It is forbidden to dig wells for private purposes," Miranda declared. She had recovered her composure and with it her hauteur. "Those who attempt such selfish acts are publicly drowned in glass vats for their crimes."

"Don't get offenders more'n once or twice a generation," Perico said. "There're wells in some other locations. Jacks's headquarters has one."

The sec man rapped the map with hairy knuckles. "Anyway, there's your tactical situation."

"And the gig you want us to do for you?" Ryan asked.

"There's a square wood tower," Perico said, stabbing the middle of the map with a blunt forefinger, "on the south side of the square. Gives a commanding view of the fountain and everything around. They keep a team of snipers up there."

"It is an intolerable provocation," the baron declared. "I want them destroyed."

"They're a royal pain in the ass," Perico said. "If we can seize that tower, it'll be a major coup for our side. Be a long first step toward recovering the whole ville."

"I beg your pardon, Mr. Perico, Baron, young master," Doc said, "but as adept as we are, we are but three. Storming an enemy tower is much to ask of us."

"That's not what we're asking," Perico said. "We just want you to take down the blasters. You do that for us, Jenkins here will lead an assault team to do the rest."

"You will be handsomely compensated if you handle this for us," Miranda said. "Do it well enough, and we shall discuss longer-range employment."

"Fair enough," Ryan said. "When you want it done?"

"Today would be good," Perico replied with a grin.

Ryan polled the others with a glance. Krysty nodded once, while Doc smiled slightly.

"Get your strike team ready," Ryan said. "Give us an hour or two to scout and set up, and we're good to go."

"And we'll do the *hard* work," Jenkins said. "Remember that, money-fighter."

"Keep telling yourself that, son," Ryan said. "Now, what do we have on this side of the line for vantage points?"

Chapter Twelve

"What happens now?" Doc queried.

Ryan looked at the redhead.

"I sent Luke to tell the baron's men that we were ready, so they could take up position to storm the tower," Krysty said. "Luke" was a boy sent with them to be their runner.

"Then," Ryan said, settling back into the comfortless chair and taking up the longeyes again, "all we can do is wait and not get spotted."

He scanned as much of the south side of Sweetwater Junction as he could see from the window without getting too close. The ville had mostly grown up after the nuke war, cobbled together around a core of predark buildings solid-built enough to stand through the nuke attacks, and the great quakes that had resculpted part of the country after the missiles stopped falling. Like many villes, much of it was essentially a shantytown of scavvied parts, including flattened cans painstakingly tacked together and used for inner and outer walls on ramshackle frames of aluminum and PVC pipes, angle iron and precious scraps of wood.

When the survivors crept out beneath the slowly clearing skies following the Long Winter, they'd found themselves sitting atop a large, reliable aquifer. Water that, by reason of being buried deep, escaped the lethal taint of fallouts and other poisons that had fouled so much of the land.

As trade resumed, as it always did where humans lived, substantial routes gravitated here, and crossed.

The early barons had rebuilt their domain as best they could. The wealth from trade—and water—gave them more resources than most to do it with. They had paid handsomely to have wagloads of scavvied brick and building stone and timber brought in, gradually replacing shacks with solid, respectable structures.

It was an ongoing process, and a lot remained to be done. Most of the new buildings were relatively modest in size. Some larger old buildings remained derelict because they were too precarious, or eaten away inside, to use, and too dangerous to tear down. Over the years it had apparently been decided to leave those and let time take its course, concentrate on what could readily be done now.

The brick office building on the north side of the town square was one of those derelicts. Its stairways were alarmingly swaybacked, and creaked and groaned when walked on. Ryan, Krysty and Doc took their lives in their hands every time they went up and down.

It wasn't any novelty for them. And it wasn't as if they aimed to stay.

Sweetwater Junction itself showed a variety of tones of washed-out oranges, browns and yellows in the gradually softening afternoon light. No colors bright, no colors pure. Just a jumble.

Ryan felt Krysty come up beside him. He could detect the slight sweetness of her sweat now. She smelled good; the baron had offered them showers while her strike team got ready to go. Ryan didn't worry that Krysty might stray too close to the window, or do anything else to get spotted by their quarry. She knew this game, too.

"It's pretty in a way," she said.

In the corner, his arms wrapped around his chest for

warmth, Doc was murmuring to himself. Ryan could pick out the odd name—Emily, Jolyon, Rachel—and knew he was talking to his wife and children, his lost family, from whose arms he'd literally been snatched by the soulless whitecoats of the Totality Concept. A family that was dust long since by the time the nuke storm hit.

Ryan grunted. "You see pretty in everything."

"Guilty as charged." Krysty rested a hand lightly on his shoulder. "Too bad it's going to be painted red so soon."

"Happens to every place."

"Not *every* place," she said.

He shook his head. "Don't kid yourself. Even if we really do find a sanctuary, we'll have to be ready to fight at any moment to keep it. A man or woman doesn't own anything they're not ready to fight for, lives and loved ones included. Reading history, talking to Doc and Mildred, it's always been that way. Only, by Mildred's time most people'd convinced themselves otherwise."

"Which might account for why they were foolish enough to burn the world."

Ryan shrugged. "Mebbe."

Doc stirred from his reverie. "Friends," he said, extending a twiglike finger out the window, "something transpires outside."

Ryan swept the longeyes as far to the right as he could. He could just see the shaded porch of a store or shop that had been shuttered since the late baron's decline had split the ville violently in two. Three figures crouched there, as furtive as mice.

"What's this?" he asked.

"Water run," Krysty said grimly.

Two of the people darted out into the slanting yellow sunlight. One held a cluster of canteens by cloth straps. The other carried a net full of ceramic jugs over her back. They were swaddled in rags against the chill and questing wind.

They'd made it halfway to the wide fountain when a volley of blaster shots broke out. Ryan lowered the long-eyes to look across at the sniper tower. The two men on station were cranking shots from their lever-action long-blasters, one a carbine, one a full-barreled rifle. He could hear their hoots of triumphant bloodlust over the bangs of their weapons.

The woman bent under the clay jugs dropped onto her face. Her companion darted a few steps more toward the brick-walled fountain. Then he hesitated, with bullets kicking up puffs of dust around his rag-wrapped feet. He took a step back toward his fallen companion, then one toward the fountain.

Ryan didn't know whether the bastards in the tower were such bad shots or just playing with their victim. Likely both, he decided.

"Triple-stupe," he said, "to make a run like that in daylight."

"Triple-desperate," Krysty said. "Jacks and the baron issue water chits only to people whose loyalty they're sure of. Others, and those they want to punish, don't get any. That leaves a lot of people mighty thirsty."

"And thirst makes you desperate quicker than anything, shy of being on fire or short on air," Ryan said.

The dithering man finally ran back to his companion and began to tug at her. She wasn't moving at all. He was barely able to budge her deadweight, furiously though he heaved.

The third water-runner dashed out to help. As he reached them a bullet pierced his gut. He fell into a flailing, bawling ball of intolerable pain.

"Ryan," Krysty said urgently, "you have to *do* something."

He shook his head. "We wait," he said. "For the go signal. This has nothing to do with us."

"Oh!" She spun away, careful to get clear of the window before straightening, to stand by the wall with arms crossed under her breasts.

Ryan watched, his lone blue eye as cold and impassive as the sky, as the drama played out. Eventually the man trying to drag his female comrade to safety was hit. He continued to try to help her until he was shot at least twice more, that Ryan could see, in leg and body. The man fell, but kept trying to crawl back to the shelter of the porch, dragging his friend by her belt. Ryan saw the impacts of more bullets hitting his back, raising little wisps of dust. Eventually he collapsed on his face and didn't move anymore.

The last wounded man continued to writhe and howl. Gut-shot, he could keep it up all day and all night. Ryan knew.

For a few minutes the blaster-storm ceased. Perhaps the coldhearts in the tower were enjoying their victim's suffering, or perhaps they were just reloading. Likely both, Ryan decided.

After a while, though, screams like that got on your nerves no matter how cruel a bastard you were. They started shooting at the wounded man again. Bullets hit his legs. An arm.

"Why do they keep firing?" Krysty asked, her voice vibrating with pain.

"Mebbe they're trying to see how often they can shoot him without killing him," Ryan said.

He saw the gut-shot man's head jerk. Dark fluid sprayed from it. His legs straightened and he rolled on his back, drumming his heels on the densely packed earth. Then he went still.

"Show's over," Ryan said.

From the depths of his waking dream Doc stirred and said in a clear voice, "The stairs. Someone is coming."

Krysty, whose hearing was better than Ryan's—she hadn't spent as much of her life with blasters going off right in her ears—was already turning, drawing her snubby revolver.

"Cocker," a child's voice said timidly from the darkness outside the open door.

"Spaniel," Krysty said. "It's Luke. The runner I sent to tell Miranda's assault team we were ready."

"Took them long enough," Ryan said.

Luke appeared in the door, a boy of about eight or nine, bundled up in a coat and shawl and knit cap so that little more than wide blue eyes were visible.

"Captain J-Jenkins says he's ready," the kid stammered. "He—he wants you to get a move on."

"'Captain,' he calls himself," Doc said with amusement. He was clearly back in the here and now, scenting action and livening up like an old coon hound. "Wonder if the baron knows that."

Ryan had set down the longeyes and shifted his chair behind his waiting longblaster. He had only to get his eye close enough to the scope to see through, without getting close enough for recoil to stamp it into his face, then lift the rifle butt and snug its cold steel plate to his shoulder.

When he did, the post-shaped reticule was already fixed on the distant tower. The two snipers held their pieces by the forestocks, obviously talking to each other, high from the chilling. And the long-distance torture.

"Hope you boys enjoyed the show," Ryan said.

He set the post so that its pointed tip had the shaved

temple of one of Jack's sec men right on it. Ryan finished drawing a deep breath, let half of it out, cut it off. *Squeezed.*

He was prepared, so the rifle's smashing roar and accompanying hard kick didn't catch him by surprise. With practiced ease he worked the bolt as the long barrel rose off-line, carrying the scope momentarily off target.

When it came back the coldheart he'd targeted was nowhere to be seen. His companion was staring at his feet openmouthed. Blood painted his features, shockingly bright red in the afternoon sun.

"Target down," Krysty said. She had slid to Ryan's side and picked up the longeyes to spot.

Ryan targeted the remaining man's left eye, then fired once more.

He was racking the bolt again when Krysty said, "Second target down."

"Let's roll," he said, standing. He slung his longblaster and reached for the duffel bag they'd brought the cushions and their water in.

"Do you not even want to see what happens, my dear Ryan?" Doc asked.

From below came war whoops and shots as the Sharp assault team charged to the attack.

"Nope," Ryan said. "Our job here is done."

Chapter Thirteen

"You're either the bravest man alive, Geither Jacks," the bearded black man said, "or the stupidest." Skinny as a power pole, he was dressed in a white shirt and canvas drawers.

The man in the barber chair, his cheeks and chin covered in fluffy white soap lather, took a cigar from his mouth. "Why can't I be both, Coffin? 'I'm large. I encompass infinities.'"

He had a long narrow face that seemed to consist of nothing but folds and seams, and a finger-length shock of dust-colored hair up top. He knew he wasn't lovely, and he made sure nobody mentioned that fact twice.

The early morning light was bright enough to fill the room, despite the filmy curtain that covered the window. Not even this deep into his realm did Geither Jacks feel cocky enough to give would-be assassins a free shot at him from outdoors. Especially since evidence suggested rumors that that witch-slut Miranda had hired herself a longblaster chiller were the straight goods, after all.

"Your pardon, Senor Jacks," the bearded, roly-poly little barber said. "It is 'contain.' 'I *contain* multitudes.'"

"See?" Coffin said. "Not only does he have a blade to your fool throat, the prick is sassing you back. You're about eight ounces of pressure from a second smile, my friend."

Jacks laughed, although not too enthusiastically. He didn't want to cut his own throat.

French doors with fancy cut-glass panes in their tops separated the parlor from the great room, where until recently Sinorice's entertainers had sat or promenaded to show off the wares to prospective customers. Through the doors came the sounds of low-level roistering: low voices, laughter, glasses tinkling. Jacks's top lieutenant, Hapgood, was kicking back in there with a few of the boys. They were drinking a little. Why not? Let them enjoy the fruits of picking the ultimate winning side. They still knew to keep it down.

The parlor itself was a wonderland of red-flocked and gilt wallpaper. It smelled of pomander and ointments the little barber used, as well as the residues of the flower essences and scavvied perfumes the sluts had doused themselves with to cover less pleasant odors—although some of the ancient perfumes seemed to have gone a bit off, and smelled mostly like paint thinner. They were still pricey and much in demand, reeking of ancient decadence as they did, or were thought to.

Jacks liked it all. He felt at home here.

But he'd never truly be at home ever again until he had the palace back, and with it all of Sweetwater Junction. Then he could rule from wherever he pleased, as befit a benevolent despot.

"But García here's got family," he said. "And he knows I know where to lay hands on them. He doesn't want his fat wife, Maria, and their two adorable little girls hung up on hooks for Levon to work his wizardry on. Do you, García?"

Levon was the three-armed mutie who was Jacks's master torturer.

"Oh, no, Senor Jacks," the barber said fervently.

"You're slack!" an age-cracked voice screeched. Jacks flinched in his chair.

"Aw, Jesus shit howdy," he muttered. "Not now, Grammaw."

"You sit here chewing the fat with your little playmates." The old woman hit the parlor like a dust devil on jolt. She was shriveled down to nothing but whalebone and meanness. You'd think to look at her that a good puff of wind could knock her down and bust her hip. You'd think wrong. "No wonder the witch snatched a vital position right out from under your nose yesterday, Geither!"

"It wasn't that key a position, Grammaw," he said. "Anyway, we'll get it back. I'll send Hapgood out to see to it tomorrow."

Hapgood had been Jacks's chief coconspirator in the failed coup that had ended the life of Baron Jeb but, sadly, not the rest of his tainted lineage.

"Miranda hasn't got the people to hold it when we surround the buildings on three sides."

"Your father never would've lost it in the first place!"

"My father's dead, so I don't hardly see how that's relevant."

"He got slack!" she screeched. "That's why you done right to chill him and take his place. He warn't fit to serve Baron Jeb no more. And now you're going slack."

"What am I supposed to do?"

"Make examples, like a man!" Very few sentences came out of Grammaw Lynndey Jacks's withered, near-toothless mouth that didn't begin in sprays of spittle and end in exclamation marks.

"You could have Levon work over one or two of the sec men who survived getting run out of the tower yesterday," Coffin said. "Encourage the others, like."

"That mutie is an abomination!" Grammaw exclaimed. "He'll corrupt the pure blood of this ville and bring ruin to us all, sure as shit's brown!"

"Levon's an artist, Grammaw. That extra arm gives more scope to his work. Especially that pincer."

"Not much chance he's gonna do much reproducing here in the ville, Grammaw Lynndey," Coffin said. "Not if the prospective mama got anything to say about it."

"Anyway, I got few enough shooters as it is," Jacks said.

"You could recruit more people from the ville," Grammaw declared, "if you hadn't let them get slack!"

Gate to Hell Jacks sighed. Not for the first time he reckoned he was the wrong member of the line, not to mention gender and generation, to bear that nickname. Much as he liked it.

What was worse, the old lady had a point. She often did, if you could find it in among all the "slacks" and exclamation marks.

He had recruited new sec men from his side of Sweetwater Junction. But they seemed more interested in sucking up his booze and beating on their fellow citizens than in serious fighting. They didn't show the proper sort of spirit that was going to take him back to the palace, where he'd slit open that little prick Colt's fish-colored belly and strangle him with his living guts before his mother's eyes. Right before he raped Miranda, then had her whipped and burned at the stake like the witch she was.

"We got people coming through town," he said.

"Merchants!"

You'd also think it was hard to tell when Grammaw wrinkled up her face, since wrinkles were mostly what it consisted of, along with the odd mole sprouting astonishingly long tufts of hair, white to match that tight bun on her head. You'd be wrong there, too. There was no mistaking it: her face folded in on itself until it seemed likely to implode.

"They got no spirit! They're slack!"

"Now, don't be hasty, there, Grammaw Lynndey," Coffin said. "Takes some sack to be a merchant. Especially on the long hard roads that meet in the Junction."

"There's other people," Jacks pointed out. "Travelers. Mercies and such. They—"

The French doors opened. A recently recruited sec man with his hair just coming back in from the ritual head-shaving stood there.

"Sorry to bother you, Baron Jacks, but some newcomers just come barging in—"

"Can't Hapgood deal with it?" Jacks asked.

His answer was a brain-smashing sound and a flash from the parlor. The young sec man jumped like a startled cat and spun.

The wedge-shaped back of Hapgood himself came through the door. He turned to show bloodhound eyes rolled up in his long balding head, and a red-rimmed black hole as big around as a shot glass through the front of his frilled white shirt. He flopped down face-first right at his boss's feet, clearly already on his way to room temperature.

"Now whoever did that ain't slack!" Grammaw crowed.

"COAST CLEAR," Jak said from the top of the concrete ramp. Overhead the sky was finally turning daylight blue, though still streaked with apricot and apple-green remnants of sunup.

J.B. waited at the bottom of the short flight of stairs, with a concrete retaining wall and a round steel rail on his right side and the footing of a building on the left. Mildred crouched on the steps between the two men, her blocky black wheel gun in her hand.

"What now, John?" she asked.

"We walk toward the gaudy house where Jacks is holed up as if we owned the place," he said.

"What?" she squeaked. He was pleased to see she had presence of mind to keep it nearly inaudible. Also nearly supersonic, but at least no unwanted ears were likely to overhear. "After we went to all the trouble of sneaking into town before the sun even came up?"

"That's right," he said. "Past patrols like as not to shoot on sight. Now, here in the middle of the ville, people who see us are going to at least wonder if we belong before reaching for their blasters."

"And if you're wrong?"

"Then we wind up staring at the sky a little sooner than anticipated," he said calmly. "Comes to everybody, sooner or later."

"Less talk, more walk," Jak said under his breath.

"Roll on, Jak," J.B. said. "We're right behind you."

He sent a meaningful look to Mildred, who sighed theatrically.

"You boys'll be the death of me," she said. "And here all I ever wanted to do was achieve immortality by not dying!"

"Here come," Jak said.

"Okay, brace it up," J.B. said. "You know the plan."

"Ace on the line," Mildred said.

"That's the spirit," J.B. replied.

He walked point down the dirt street. There was still nobody abroad between the buildings here, which were mostly one-story and obviously built since skydark, if better built than most villes could boast. Mildred walked slightly behind him at his right, while Jak slinked at his left. Their hands were empty; J.B. carried his shotgun slung muzzle-down behind his right shoulder. They wanted to show peaceable intent.

If somebody still wanted to shake it up—well, the three could accommodate them.

'Course, he thought as half a dozen sec men in green Jakes armbands spilled out of a nearby building clutching an assortment of weapons as varied as their clothing, I'd feel a whole lot more secure, especially between the shoulder blades, if I knew Ryan was out there somewhere keeping close eye through the scope of his longblaster. But thoughts like that wouldn't load any magazines for him.

"So what the fuck do you think you're doing?" demanded the tall, skinny kid whose bluster and cocky body language marked him as leader. There wasn't a scrap of rank insignia to this patch.

The sec men winged out to flank them. From the corner of his eye J.B. saw Mildred's face crease in concern. The Armorer wasn't worried much. Let the coldhearts think they held the winning hand. The shock when they learned different might keep them from acting for a few more seconds. And time, J.B. knew, was blood.

"Mornin'," he said cheerfully. "We're new in town. We'd like to talk to your boss. We're looking for mercie work."

The leader showed him a grin whose intent was clearly as nasty as his yellow teeth.

"The boss ain't looking to hire sorry-ass outlanders. But you will get to meet him. Also like as not Levon. That's his head torturer. A three-armed mutie. Third arm lets him do tricks you never dreamed of."

"I think we should just leave that to your boss to decide, don't you?" J.B. asked. He was becoming aware of a triple-nasty cesspit stench.

Dark night, he thought, if Jacks lets his men patrol the streets in shit trousers, it's a wonder plague hasn't chilled the bunch of 'em long since.

"Chris," said a burly guy with bulgy eyes, loose purple lips and blond hair, "shouldn't we oughta just take 'em to talk to Hapgood? Let the big guys decide?"

"Sure, Morris, you and Rigger and Blackie take these two pencil dicks, the sawed-off one and the white-haired mutie. The woman can stay with the rest of us. She's got big titties and plenty of meat to go around."

As he drew close to Mildred, her face clenched in disgust. J.B. recognized the stench had to be coming from the one called Chris. It took a lot to make a former medical physician make a face like that, even if she'd been mostly into research back before the days of the smoke clouds.

"You'll like us triple-fine, baby," Chris said, grabbing hold of Mildred's left breast and squeezing. She winced and her shoulders hunched. He looked around at the others.

"See? I went and found you boys some nice cunny!"

A gunshot shattered the morning calm.

Chapter Fourteen

Grabbing at himself, sec leader Chris went to his knees, letting loose a scream of pain.

"You shot my dick off! You slut!"

Mildred already had her ZKR 551 handblaster up and pointing over the wounded man at the round, dark-bearded face of one of his men.

"If you move, you die," she said. "I don't give a fuck about you."

The guy dropped his bolt-action .22 rifle and held up his hands. "Lady, I believe you," he said fervently.

J.B. had his shotgun up. He stood back to back with Jak, who'd drawn his huge Colt handblaster.

"Any of the rest of you bored with living?" J.B. asked matter-of-factly. "We can fix that for you."

Weapons clattered to the street. Hands went up. Faces were pale and covered with sweat despite the cold of the morning air.

Jak stepped close to where Chris was kneeling, doubled over and sobbing, and extended his Python. The Colt bellowed as he delivered a mercy round.

J.B. winced at the noise and side blast. There were handblasters more powerful than a .357 wheel gun, but not a one he knew of more triple-unpleasant to stand next to when they got lit off. A .44 Mag made a louder noise but it wasn't as high-pitched and piercing. The .357 Magnum was peculiar that way.

Chris's head exploded. Chunks of scalp flew in all directions, drawing crazy spirals of smoke behind them. The muzzle-flame had set his hair alight. It smelled almost as bad as he did.

"Now that that's finished," J.B. said, as the headless corpse did its final headless-chicken flopping bit, "take us to your leader."

AS GAUDIES WENT, Sinorice's Royal Flush was a big one, J.B. thought, as they strolled up, herding the five surviving members of the sec patrol before them like geese. It was four yellow-stone stories tall and covered a lot of ground. J.B. paused in front of double doors, gold, with a namesake hand in hearts painted on the left one and spades on the right, and fancy cut-glass panes above.

"You boys can run along," he said. "Take my advice and head west, and keep right on going. Things're fixing to heat this town up nuke-red even if Jacks decides not to make examples of you."

They set off at a scrambling run down the street, west as he'd suggested. From their loose-jointed stumbling, like a man who'd tripped and was hurtling forward, trying to keep moving rather than land on his face, the Armorer guessed some of them smelled like fresh dreck just as their unlamented leader had.

"Stow the blasters, people," he told Mildred and Jak. "We want this to be a friendly social call."

"What if they don't want to be friendly?" Mildred asked.

"Fix like you fixed bastard with fast hands," Jak said

with a grin. Mildred couldn't stop herself from grinning back.

"That's my girl," J.B. said, briefly squeezing her shoulder.

"What about the shotgun?" she asked. "That's not going to look too friendly even if you keep it slung."

"I'll carry it slung low enough the butt won't show over my shoulder," he said, readjusting the sling, "and the barrel tucked down behind my leg. Nobody'll notice it until introductions are made. You'll see."

"If you say so."

He pushed through the doors and led his companions in off the street. They walked into a corridor where the red-and-gold-papered walls held large framed oil paintings of women in various stages of undress and types of display. Some of which left little to the imagination.

"Wonder if this is the current staff?" Mildred said, looking left and right as they walked down the gold-edged scarlet runner. "These paintings look recent. Not too bad, really."

"You like this sort of thing?" J.B. asked.

"The technique, dummy."

The short hallway opened into a wide parlor with couches along the walls and another set of half-glass double doors beyond. Eight or ten men slouched on the couches or played cards at a folding table off to one side.

They looked at the intruding trio and their eyes got big. They started jumping to their feet.

A man in what appeared to be the vest and trousers of a brown three-piece suit, over a white shirt with frills down the front, and a gold cravat, stepped to bar their way. He wore two shoulder holsters, each showing the butt of a 9 mm Beretta blaster.

"What the fuck do you think you're doing, barging in

here?" he demanded. He had a hound dog face gone purple with rage clear to the roots of his receding seal-brown hair.

"We're mercies," J.B. said. "We come to offer our blasters to your boss. Judging by the fact nobody was standing guard outside the front doors, which by the way were unlocked, we reckon he's a bit short of sec muscle. Not to mention sec brains."

A young-looking sec man dashed to the rear set of doors and threw them open, yelling something. J.B.'s attention was focused on the man who blocked his path. Normally he would have fought his natural tunnel-vision tendency; it invited your target's friends to thunder on you without you being able to see them. But he trusted Mildred and Jak to have his flanks.

"Fuck you, your bitch and the mutie you dragged in with you, you sawed-off little shit," the man in the vest snarled. He snatched at his blasters.

Before they cleared leather, J.B. had swung up his M-4000 scattergun. He had in fact been holding it barrel-down behind his leg by the pistol grip. Now all he had to do was lift it. He pulled the trigger.

The guy in the snazzy clothes pulled his hands out of the X they'd been in, presenting the handblasters. J.B.'s shot column had barely begun to spread when it hit dead-center of his white-shirted chest, right above his vest.

Both handblasters dropped unfired. The tall man reeled back through the opened doors into the room beyond. Inside, J.B. heard a considerable commotion.

He tipped the muzzle of the Smith & Wesson blaster toward the white-painted ceiling as he stepped forward.

"Would one of you happen to be Geither Jacks?" he asked.

A man with hair like a handful of straw sprouting from

the top of his narrow head, and soap lather masking the lower half of his face, stepped forward.

"That'd be me," he said. He stuck an unlit stub of cigar in his teeth.

"Gate, you danged fool," said a rangy, bristling-bearded black dude in overalls, who jumped forward to interpose himself between Jacks and J.B.'s shotgun.

"Now, *that's* style!" screeched an old withered prairie chicken of a woman in a brown dress and stockings.

With his cigar, Jacks gestured at the man who lay dead at his feet. "Care to explain what this is all about?"

"We come to offer you our services," J.B. said. "We're mercies. Seems like you could use some help."

"No shit," Jacks said, "'specially since you just chilled my main man all over my carpet."

"He was rude," Mildred said.

"You gotta chill these bastards," the black man said. "You can't let them come here and disrespect you like this, shoot poor bastard Hapgood down right in front of you."

"Coffin," Jacks said, "listen. A major part of Hapgood's job description was keeping his own triple-stupe ass alive to be of use to me. Since he wasn't competent enough to do that, I reckon I can dispense with his services."

He turned a frown on J.B. His eyes vanished into slits.

"That said," the renegade sec boss said, "it seems to me you owe me, since you did just chill one of my bodyguards."

"Two," Mildred said. "The other was even less of a loss."

Jacks's eyes reappeared. They were a murky green, like a chem-tainted pond. They all but stood out from his khaki face on stalks.

"Consider it a free demo of what we bring to the party," Mildred said. J.B. had to struggle considerably to keep his own eyes from bugging behind his glasses, and keep his face immobile. He knew Mildred could be triple-sparky, but he didn't think she had that in her.

"Call it even," J.B. said. "You've seen what we bring. What will you pay us to bring it for you?"

"Gate," Coffin said, speaking as if J.B. and friends weren't there, "you listen to me. You can't hire people who just stroll in out of the wasteland and into your parlor, shoot up your sec chief right before your eyes. I tell you true, if you trust them you're a fool. A *triple*-fool!"

"He's more a fool for not chilling you on account of your lip, Coffin!" squalled the old lady, coming forward with the quick short steps of a sparrow hopping after crumbs. "That's where he's slack!"

"If you two are going to discuss my shortcomings," Jacks said, "why don't you take it somewhere else? These folks and I got some business to discuss."

He looked the newcomers over again. "A little guy in a hat who's handy with a scattergun. A black woman built like a brick…wall. And a, uhh—red eyes. Right. You're an albino, aren't you, Whitey?"

"Right first time," Jak said. "Only name not Whitey. Name Jak!"

"Jak." Jacks nodded. "And the rest of you are?"

"I'm Mildred. This is J.B., the finest armorer in the Deathlands!"

"Ace. Now to keep this on a business footing, can I get you to maybe put away the big blaster?"

"I reckon your remaining sec boys're pointing blasters at the backs of our heads right now," J.B. said with a smile. "So—you know."

"Yeah. Pack 'em up, boys. Our new friends here are too polite and cagey to come out and say they got me hostage. But I know which end of the blaster the fucking bullet comes out of."

"Gate," the black man said urgently.

Jacks held up two fingers by his counselor's face. "Enough, Coffin. If they wanted to chill me, you and I would be staring at the ceiling right now, without ever being able to look away. And they impress me, for a fact."

He smiled around the stump of his cigar. "Enough to hire them for one special gig. You people pull it off, then we'll talk, you know...long term."

Chapter Fifteen

The sentry stiffened. Too late. J.B. had already grabbed his chin, yanked his head back and punched the two-edged blade of his knife through the right side of his neck.

J.B. pushed outward with the knife's pierced hilt, which was cut from a single piece of steel. The blade cut through the cartilage box of larynx and through the tough skin of the sentry's throat in a gush of blood, black in the starlit street, from both jugular veins. The hot copper tang of blood joined the sour stink of the sec man's clothing.

"Relax," J.B. murmured in the shuddering man's ear. "It'll all be over soon."

The blood that jetted over the Armorer's hand on the sentry's chin felt hot in the cold, unusually still night. It congealed quickly to a sort of film over warm liquid.

None of which was new to J.B.

He walked his rapidly weakening victim back into a shadowed gap between the tower and the building next to it. From high overhead drifted the sounds of voices arguing. Though he couldn't hear the words, J.B. recognized the sound of bored men running their jaws to have something to do.

Jacks's sentry's body jerked hard and became limp weight and J.B. knew life had fled from him. There was no mistaking it if you'd felt it before. He eased the man to the alley grit, wiped the knife on his jacket and resheathed it.

Few lights showed in either half of the contested ville.

Overhead a single lantern seemed to blaze from the top of the tower's windows, the ville was so dark. Looking southward, J.B. could see the glow from the lights of Sinorice's Royal Flush, and perhaps a few hints in the northern sky from Miranda's palace. At night the ville folk hunkered down and mostly tried not to attract attention. Same as in daytime.

Two soft owl hoots came from the tower's far side. J.B. cupped hands to mouth and responded in kind to acknowledge Jak's message received. There had been a second sentry at the tower's foot. Emphasis on had been.

J.B. turned to Mildred, who lurked deeper in the alley with her handblaster ready. Her face was a little ashen in the incidental light from the window overhead, but her jaw was firmly set and the hand that held her blaster was rock-steady.

He gave her an approving nod. She had some odd scruples by his reckoning, such that on rare occasions he marveled at how impractical the world she grew up in had to have been. And look what happened to it.

Mildred gave a little frown as she moved past him into South Street, and he read it plainly: she found it difficult to believe that, having just grabbed a major toehold in enemy territory, the baron's men weren't guarding it up the wazoo.

If the three needed it, it was triple-locked confirmation that their companions weren't inside, or involved in any way with securing the structure Ryan's rifle had been key in capturing.

"I can't believe they're this lax," Mildred whispered.

"Nobody's eager to have dirt hitting them in the eye," J.B. whispered back. "No matter how het up their bosses are."

The same half-assed attitude toward sec had made it unexpectedly easy for them to get here. While the objective lay on their own side's turf, they hadn't wanted any run-ins with the renegade sec boss's patrols any more than the enemy's. As they'd seen, Jacks's street-level sec had your basic chill first, ask questions never mentality.

Both sides' patrols turned out to be loud, not subtle. The sec men were clearly bent on intimidating the populace, but at the same time didn't seem double-eager to encounter any.

Jak waited on the other side of the open door at the tower's base. J.B. and Mildred saw him because he sensed their approach and let them. As white as his hair and skin were, he could dissolve into the night like a drop of milk in a gallon of coffee, quickly and completely. He nodded at J.B. and slipped through the door, little knives gleaming in each pale hand.

A moment later he popped his head out and nodded to signal the all clear.

No clouds hung overhead to trap such heat as the faint southerly sun lent the day. It was cold enough to chill you in more than temperature terms if you got careless, or nip off a finger or toe. Despite the open door and uninsulated wooden walls, the ground-floor room felt toasty warm after the street. It smelled of spoiling blood and fairly recent dreck from the dying that had happened inside.

Jak shot J.B. a quick glance. When no veto came he slipped up the stairs. They were warped and old, like the planks that made up the rest of the structure. Over the worse odors J.B. started to smell the resin of lumber cut in the none-too-distant past. As an ex-trader himself he reckoned it had cost a bundle to build this vantage point.

Jak went up the wooden steps with no more sound than a shadow. Mildred followed with exaggerated care.

Instantly, a board creaked beneath her combat boot. She froze.

J.B. squeezed her shoulder. The men up top had quit arguing. Now the sounds of harsh laughter rolled down the stairwell. There was no hitch in the noise from above to indicate anybody had heard the plank groan.

Jak poked his head up to give the second floor a quick check. Then he vanished up the stairs. He had surveyed the third floor and clearly found nothing threatening before his companions reached the second.

Their new employer had told them the ailing baron Jeb had built the structure as a watchtower. The floors between ground and top existed solely to keep the two apart. Glancing quickly around the second story, J.B. confirmed it was empty of everything but dust and darkness.

Jak waited on the stairs, poised just below the opening to the top floor. J.B. avoided looking directly at the light coming through. He didn't want to foul up his night vision.

From his pants pocket he took a compact little mechanism, a striker based on an ancient wheel lock design that he'd cobbled together himself out of scavvied gear and metal bits filed to shape and tempered. From the pocket of his leather jacket he took a bulky object whose dark surface gleamed slightly in the light of the unseen lantern. It was a glazed ceramic jug of about a pint capacity. A fused cap had been sealed into it with wax.

Seeing it, Jak slipped back down the stairs and stood to one side. He drew his big Python. His job now was guarding J.B.'s and Mildred's backs. Very soon the shattering noise the big Magnum blaster made would be the least of anybody's concerns.

J.B. went up the stairs softly, with Mildred right behind him. He didn't make much noise, he reassured himself. He wasn't that much bulkier than Jak, nor was he much taller, although he knew that to look at him, "stealth" wasn't the word that jumped into someone's mind ahead of anything else. But he had a wealth of experience creepy-crawling. He wasn't as good as Jak; only the darkness itself was.

Just shy of the rectangle of orange light in the jet-black overhead, he stopped. He stuck the fuse end into a handy little cup in his striker, which insured quick ignition even in a stiff wind. J.B. pressed the release. A soft whir, a smell of burning powder, and then the fuse was hissing and spitting out tiny sparks.

Mildred holstered her blaster and covered her ears, mouth open.

J.B. waited a beat to make sure the fuse had lit properly. Aside from being a man who believed and lived the axiom measure twice, cut once, he found there was little more embarrassing than having an enemy relight your bomb and pitch it back at you.

Well and truly lit, the fuse emitted a shower of sparks. He stuck his hand up through the opening and gave the bomb a little push, sending it rolling along the plank floor toward the middle of the room.

He ducked back down and imitated Mildred, feeling more than hearing the grumble of the pot bumping across the uneven floorboards. A young male voice said, "What the fuck is—?"

A heavy boom cut him off. It wasn't a terribly sharp sound, and seemed somehow to have more push than volume. All the same it momentarily scrambled J.B.'s hearing, despite how he clasped hands to his ears.

He knew it would. Even as a dragon's breath of hot gas rushed over them from the opening, he unlimbered his shotgun. Then, without a backward glance, he went up through the hole.

As usual Mildred was knotted with anticipation from the moment J.B. produced the little home-built hand grenade.

Her imagination started playing horribly vivid films, like those driver-safety movies they'd made her watch in driving school, of the many, many things that could go wrong. She had spent enough time as an emergency-room intern to have very explicit visions. To say nothing of the horrors she'd witnessed since reawakening.

The explosion muffled her hearing, just before J.B. hurried up the stairs. As she drew her own handgun, she felt a flash of gratitude that the ringing in her ears muted not only the roar of his burly blaster, but the screams already pealing from the tower like a warning bell.

Though inclined to describe herself as built more for comfort than speed, Mildred could move swiftly and agilely when it was called for. She popped out of the hole almost the instant the Armorer's boot soles cleared it.

He went right; she wheeled left. They both knew the drill.

She had her ZKR thrust out before her. It was a target-style weapon; she was a target shooter, an Olympic competitor in her day, which of course, here and now, was as remote as the dinosaurs. But she had forgotten nothing of her skills. In this not-so-brave new world she had learned new ones—such as close-quarters fighting.

Not that there was much threatening in the eyeless crimson mask that screamed endlessly at her, sounding faraway and almost dreamlike, from a ragged black hole. The bursting charge had been surrounded by nails and other bits and pieces of jagged metal scrap. The black powder was more likely to burn one badly than do much damage with actual blast, even in enclosed quarters. It was the little extras that made the difference.

Stepping left to clear the opening, she put a blue hole between where her assailant's eyes had been. Her hands felt numb to the ZKR's kick. Her ears barely registered the gunshot.

She was already turning to scan the rest of the room. A figure lay slumped against the wall nearest the fountain. Seeing no one else at first glance, Mildred kept him covered. He didn't stir; she judged he had been the recipient of J.B.'s first double 0 buck blast.

A table was upended against one wall, legs sticking out into the little room. From behind it reared the third man. He was screaming. He had blood flowing down his cheeks like muttonchops, Mildred saw as she swung up her handblaster. His eardrums had burst and bled. But the table evidently had shielded him from the brunt of blast and shrapnel.

The Sharp sec man held a big Peacemaker-type single-action revolver. He tried to raise it to shoot J.B., right across the table from him. With horrified certainty Mildred knew she wasn't going to get a bullet into the survivor in time to stop him from shooting her lover.

But the little man in the fedora had the reflexes of a puma. He skipped forward and smashed the butt of the Smith & Wesson shotgun into the blood-whiskered face. Mildred's slowly returning hearing caught bone crunching and the squeal of breaking teeth.

The kid toppled backward, right out the unglazed east window. Mildred heard him shout. His cries cut off abruptly, then came back two octaves higher and triple-loud as he thrashed on the dirt street in a paroxysm of torment from shattered bones.

The screams stopped again. Leaning his head out, J.B. spoke a single syllable. "Jak."

She nodded. No more need be said.

J.B. turned back and grinned at her. She gasped. He had a light spray of red across his right cheek and temple.

Seeing her reaction, he reached up, touched himself then glanced at his fingers.

"It's not mine," he said.

"Oh, John!" He allowed her to capture him in a brief, fervent embrace. Then he gently but decisively pushed her clear.

"Watch my back now. Got some work to do."

HAMMERING AT THE DOOR brought Ryan awake with his SIG-Sauer in hand.

Beside him, Krysty rolled off the bed. He leaped to his feet on the other side and stepped away, covering the door with his handblaster as Krysty, kneeling on the far side, did the same. Lying on his pallet at the foot of the bed, Doc groped for his bulky LeMat.

"What?" Ryan called. They slept in a guest room on the third floor of Miranda Sharp's palace. After the easy and showy success the friends had handed her, she was inclined to treat them double-well.

"Baron says come quick," the young sec man said through the door. What was his name?

"What is it, Hedders?" Krysty called.

"Trouble," the youth said.

Five minutes later, fully dressed and fully armed, the three were ushered into the Baron's frou-frou parlor on the bottom floor. Ryan reckoned it was a good sign nobody tried to relieve them of their weapons. Then again, it could have been fear on the part of the underlings assigned the task. Or given what he'd seen of this outfit, and Jacks's for that matter, just plain sloppiness.

While Hedders seemed afraid of them, or perhaps life in general at this point, he wasn't treating them as enemies. So there was that.

Baron Miranda was wrapped in a light blue silk gown

that didn't quite contain her. The top half of her full right breast was clearly visible when she turned to the side, as were flashes of dark bush beneath the indifferently tied belt. Nothing could contain the fury that darkened her fine features. Her unbound hair was a wild black cloud. Ryan half expected to see blue static discharges crackle through it like lightning in a thunderhead.

"The bastards!" she exclaimed when the three stepped in. "They have stolen back the tower!"

"See?" It was Jenkins, all but hopping out of his skin with eagerness, like a teen boy about to get his first blow job. "I told you they'd fuck up! You shouldn't trust these bastard outlanders!"

Colt Sharp sat on a chair behind his mother. He'd stuffed himself into a shirt and trousers and socks, but no shoes. His pudgy young face looked sleepy and concerned.

"Ma, it isn't true!" he said. "They did what you asked them to. It's not their fault your—the sec men couldn't hold the tower!"

Seeing anger flare in her face when the youth spoke, Ryan was afraid the outburst had broken it for them. He tensed.

Take out that bastard Jenkins first, he thought, snapping into contingency-planning mode. Then Hedders, though Krysty or Doc can likely handle him. Then mebbe grab Miranda for a hostage—

But the baron only stroked her son's cheek fondly. "You're right, *querido*," she said.

She turned to Jenkins, whose excitement had morphed into sullen resentment, which Ryan judged was a usual state for him.

"The outlanders have indeed done just as I asked them," she said. "*Others* have failed me in allowing the tower to fall back into Jacks's bloodstained hands. No doubt they have paid with their lives for their incompetence, which is a good thing for them."

She paused to smile, as if contemplating the awful things she would have done to the men supposed to hold the tower for her, had any of them been stupe enough to survive.

"Now, Leroy, dear boy," Miranda purred, "you have your chance to shine in your baron's eyes. Go and recapture the tower for me. Show me what you can do."

He snapped to attention and threw a sharp salute. "You got it, Baron!" he said, flashing an evil grin at Ryan and his friends.

Miranda's smile grew fangs. "And may God have mercy if you cannot hold it this time, *chico*. Because I will not!"

SMILING IN TRIUMPH, Leroy Jenkins surveyed the carnage on the top floor of the wooden sniper tower. Granted, at least half came from his own men. He'd had two killed and four wounded retaking the tower. But this was war. You didn't make omelets without breaking eggs. Even your own.

He was bare-armed and his head was wrapped with a rolled bandanna, after an old-days poster he'd seen as a kid of *Rambo*. He didn't feel the cold. He was way too hyped on blood and victory.

"Send up the flare," he ordered one of his troops. He didn't know his name. Why bother with names? They were just worms. Disposable.

That was how a real power guy thought. A baron. He practiced thinking like a baron. Because he'd be one someday. When that hot-ass bitch Miranda finally gave in all the way to his manliness. She'd marry him, and then he'd have the power.

And she better not talk to him then the way she did now. Not if she liked having teeth.

One of his wounded men was still screaming as comrades carried him back to the Sharp side of the square on a stretcher. Jenkins thought about shouting an order to chill him to shut his pussy ass up. The new order was going to need strong men, not babies. But he decided not to bother.

He drew in a deep breath instead, cold and bracing and full of the smells of spilled blood and burned powder. Well, and piss and shit, too. But a real man got used to those things.

"All right, you outland trash," he said aloud. "I showed the baron how it's really done. Your asses are next!"

"Hey, Leroy." A voice floated up from the floor below.

"It's Captain Jenkins to you, jackhole!"

"Hey, Captain, they left a crate down here. Looks like it's whiskey!"

He grinned. Nothing sweeter than drinking to their victory with their dead enemies' hooch.

"What are you waiting for? Open it up and see what's inside."

There was a bright light and a big noise.

The explosion of two pounds of predark moldable plastic explosive launched Jenkins right out through the plank roof of the tower, a moment before the overpressure blew the top two floors completely apart. When he broke free into the open air, he was measurably shorter than the six-foot-four he'd started his brief, memorable flight as, owing to the upper half of his cranium being flattened like a slug mushrooming against bone and all.

To compensate, he was dazzlingly aflame as he arched through the sky of Sweetwater Junction, to land with a hiss and a steam cloud right in the midst of the public fountain.

AT THE HARD RAP OF AN explosion Coffin jumped and went to the sitting room window. Throwing caution to the winds, he ripped open the curtain.

J.B. smiled at the glow that lit the sky to the north. He closed his hand around the fistful of jack Jacks had just pressed into it, and savored the feel.

"You were right," the rogue sec boss said around a stub of cigar. He stood beside the Armorer's chair. It was a double-comfy chair. "The stupes actually fell for your booby. Not ten minutes after they retook the damn tower."

Huddled beside J.B. in a comforter, Mildred only shook her head. Jak had headed to bed as soon as the group reported in to Jacks and his advisers. J.B. wasn't triple-thrilled about having them split up, but the albino teen could take care of himself. So could J.B. and Mildred, for that matter.

Fortunately, Jacks's grandmother had retired, too, before word came that Miranda's goons had grabbed the tower right back.

Exactly as J.B. had told Jacks they would.

"Truth is," the Armorer said, "what really surprised me was your own boys actually obeyed orders not to open the damn crate."

"You gonna let him talk to you like that in your own parlor, Gate?" Coffin asked. "Don't let yourself get played for a fool."

Jacks laughed sourly. "I was thinking that same thing, myself."

He pulled up an ottoman upholstered in red-and-gold silk and sat at J.B.'s elbow.

"We need to talk," he said.

"We're listenin'," J.B. replied.

THE RATTLE OF WINDOW GLASS from a powerful but distant blast roused Ryan from sleep. He sat up in bed, chuckling.

"My, my," Doc said from his pallet. "That was a potent explosion. Perhaps even what my captors would have termed overkill."

"Mebbe J.B. overplayed this one," Krysty said, lying on her side close to Ryan. "Won't we need that tower to fight the rotties?"

He shrugged. "If we do, we can build it up again. At least put up scaffolding. Important thing now is getting in a position where we stand a chance against the bastards."

"J.B. knows what he's doing, I guess." Krysty sounded unconvinced. "I hope we all do."

Chapter Sixteen

"So your side didn't buy it, either?" Ryan asked.

J.B. shook his head. "Not for a second."

The six of them huddled together around a lone candle burning on a crate in a root cellar beneath yet another Sweetwater Junction house abandoned during the recent troubles. This was their first reunion since splitting up days before, to make their separate ways into the ville. It was an emotional one.

Even Ryan felt relief and an effusive warmth at having the companions back again. Plus a certain ache that they'd have to split up again in a matter of minutes.

Setting up the meeting had been simple. They had used terse handwritten notes, hidden in locations revealed by simple marks cut into walls—a blaze language Jak had taught them all from his old guerrilla days in the bayou country. The marks appeared accidental, so no one else gave them a second glance. Much less understood their import if they did.

Not that anybody in Sweetwater Junction was looking too closely at marks on walls. It seemed everyone was focused on survival.

"Miranda threw one of her diva fits," Krysty said. She and Mildred sat side by side on a crate. Both of them were equally comfortable with all their companions, but after a few days apart they seemed to feel a need to assert female solidarity.

"From what I hear those're pretty spectacular," Mildred said. "Although I don't think Jacks is an unbiased witness."

"It was quite the eruption," Doc said. "The lady has a flair for the dramatic."

SHOULD HAVE KNOWN it'd turn out like this, Ryan told himself. We didn't believe a word of it, either, when that skinny kid told us at the caravanserai.

"Do you think to take advantage of me, a poor widow trying desperately to hold on to my son's inheritance?" Miranda was yelling as she rampaged back and forth across the flowery throw rug in her parlor. She was wearing tight black riding pants and boots, and a short black vest over a lavender blouse. Ryan had yet to see her ride a horse. He had to admit she looked good in the outfit.

"Miranda—Baron," Krysty said, "we're not asking for anything over this. We're telling you the truth."

"The rotties are real," Doc said. "The *change* is real. And it is terrible to behold. It is the single greatest threat you, the ville and your son face."

"It sounds cool," Colt said.

Everybody stopped and looked at the youth, who sat on a satin-upholstered footstool, eating sugar cookies from a plate on a round table beside him. Most looked shocked at his reaction.

Ryan suppressed a grin. There'd been a time, when he was a baron's privileged teenage son, that he'd have thought stories of the rotties were cool, too. Like something from the predark storybooks he'd loved to read.

"Do you have any idea what you are saying, Colt?" his mother raved, turning on him like an angry cougar. "This isn't some game or fancy story. I have seen real horrors. I watched while my father, your grandfather, was pulled apart and eaten alive by stickies. My baby brother and I hid behind a bush and looked on, helpless, as they burned our home and danced. Danced! And then, as we fled from the muties across the desert, my brother, my beloved Antonio, died of thirst before my eyes! Those are horrors enough without made-up tales of the living dead."

Colt cringed and bit his lip to keep it from quivering. He couldn't keep his eyes from growing shiny with tears.

"It's some kind of trick, Baron."

That was Stone, Miranda's new sec boss after Jenkins's demise, which not even she seemed too torn up about. The new guy was a hard case, a bit above medium height but thick, with coal-smudge brows and retreating black hair leaving a widow's peak behind on his slab of a face.

He wasn't Miranda's new plaything. That would be Chad, a former servant. He had blond hair, a wide empty face, and even emptier blue eyes, set off by the white shirt with the fancy collar she'd stuffed him into, along with too-tight denim pants. Ryan wasn't sure what Chad, who couldn't be more than a couple years older than Miranda's son, did to pack all that muscle into his skin. He was willing to bet the muscle was packed densest between his ears, though.

Right now Chad stood to one side, as if trying to hide behind a lamp with a gilt-fringed shade, proving his head did contain at least a few brains. Enough for a basic sense of self-preservation, anyway. Although even scorpions and screamwings would hide from the baron when she was in a mood like this.

Ryan stood with Krysty at his side and Doc perched on another fancy footstool, his hands knotted between his gangly legs.

"What do you even know about these mercies, Miranda?" Stone asked.

She spun to face him.

"I know they have served me well," she said tartly. Clearly, she was in a mood to snap back at any perceived challenge. Even one offered in implicit support of the rant she'd been delivering mere heartbeats before. She was full-on crazy, no doubt about it. "Not like some who claim to, who could not deal with that devil Jacks's snipers in their tower!"

To his credit Stone stood his ground.

"Why are they playing you, then?" he asked. "Why do they come in here telling a story only a total stupe would believe?"

"Yes, why?" Miranda wheeled to confront Ryan. "Why do you bring this fairy story, after you have done service to this ville?"

"Because we're trying to do you more service, Baron," Ryan said. He wasn't going to bend to her, any more than to Miranda's new sec boss, Stone. "We bring you this warning in good faith. The threat is out there. It's real."

He met her furious black eyes with an ice-cold blue one.

"If you don't reckon you can trust us anymore," he said, "we'll hit the road again. We'll head west, fast as we can. Away from the rotties."

He felt Krysty stiffen at his side. She was wondering if he'd let his own anger get the better of him. If he'd over-played his—their—hand.

But while Krysty was definitely the gentle-persuader half of their partnership, he was no beginner at hard bargaining, nor diplomacy, either. And he had noticed the baron, for all her furious whims, tended not to press too hard on those strong enough not to cower at her outbursts.

Of course, if I'm wrong, he thought, she'll happily have my guts yanked out and tied into a noose, to hang me from a windowsill.

Miranda frowned, but thoughtfully, not in anger. At least Ryan hoped that was the case.

"You asked the right question, Miranda," Krysty said.

The baron looked at her and some of her tension dissipated. That was something Ryan couldn't comprehend. By rights the baron should have been turned into a whirling ball of jealous claws by the presence of a rival so potent as Krysty, with her drop-dead looks and gentle yet Gaia-strong personality. Instead, Miranda seemed to have taken a positive shine to the redhead.

"What do you mean, *chica?*" the baron asked.

"Why would we bring you a fairy story? Why would we risk with a lie the goodwill we've earned from you?"

"There're reasons," Stone muttered. "Scammers always have their reasons."

Krysty shot him a daggered glance. "Was it a scam that took down the snipers in the tower?"

Ryan saw Stone open his mouth, no doubt to give back a "yeah, but" argument that would just lead to a chain of "and thens." Ryan had seen that cycle many times. Evidently, Stone had, too; he shut the bear trap he used for a mouth on whatever he was going to say.

Smart, Ryan thought. Hope he's not too smart for everybody's good.

A slapping sound attracted everybody's attention. Perico, Miranda's leathery old chief adviser, had brought his palms down emphatically on the thighs of his tan canvas pants. Now he rose from the overstuffed chair where he'd been sitting with his jaw shut and his ears, obviously, open.

"Isn't it clear they believe the story, Baron?"

"Yeah," Colt said. "They wouldn't lie to you, Mother!"

Fortunately for the kid, Perico had Miranda's full attention.

"It may be as Stone says," she said. "They may be seeking some advantage."

"Of course they're seeking advantage! They're alive. Every living thing seeks advantage. Your question should be, are they seeking *unfair* advantage? Where's their angle in lying to you, Baron?"

"More power," Stone growled. "More jack."

"They asked for that? Miranda, you made your terms with them after they iced the snipers. Have you heard them ask to change those terms?"

"No. But, still—"

"Yeah," Perico said. "It's a hard story to swallow. Well, don't."

"I thought you were defending them!"

"Me, too," Krysty said under her breath. She took hold of Ryan's hand.

"I'm sayin' I don't think they're consciously lying to you, Miranda. I said they seem to believe what they say, and I stick to that."

"What should I do, then?"

He shrugged. "Let them bring you evidence."

Miranda nodded. One thing you could say for the woman, Ryan thought: she wasn't big on dithering. Whether a mood swing or a decision, she got right to it.

"Very well." She turned to the trio. "I shall believe you when you bring me more evidence. Until then you would be wise not to mention the matter again. And do not let it detract from your real duties to me! We must prepare to deliver a death blow to the traitor, Jacks."

She smiled a wicked smile. "If you are telling the truth, after all—so much more important to finish him quickly, *¿qué no?*"

"Ryan."

Walking down the hallway away from the baron's parlor, Ryan stopped. And turned. It was Perico, rolling up behind him on his slightly bowed legs.

Something about the man's gait suggested to Ryan he'd spent years walking the decks of a sailing ship. He hadn't said anything about his past or how he'd wound up in Sweetwater Junction, and Ryan wasn't inclined to ask. Perico didn't seem the sort to go in for idle chitchat.

Neither was he.

Ryan waved for Krysty and Doc to walk on, which they did. Perico came up and fell into step beside him.

"Handled yourself well in there, boy," the old man said. "Not everybody's got the smarts or the stone to stand up to Miranda. Especially in one of her moods."

Ryan said nothing.

The adviser dug a finger in one hairy ear. "Here's the thing. I'm the man who keeps track of things around here for her, now that Jacks isn't exactly doing the job anymore."

By keep track of he meant spy, Ryan knew. It didn't surprise him.

"There's something in the wind that don't smell good," Perico said. "We're getting fewer travelers from out of the east. I mean, even fewer than since the dust-up happened, when Baron Jeb got chilled. Once word of that got around traffic through here dropped off major. But now it's like there's a gate slammed shut between here and parts east."

Ryan shrugged. "We spoke our piece."

"So you did. And well. I've also heard some rumors in the marketplace about strange goings-on. Things that may refer to what you were talking about."

At the hallway's end Ryan stopped and faced him. "So why didn't you back us with the baroness?"

"Because I got no evidence. No witnesses. So far it's all talk. And I need to keep credibility with her, to keep her on as even a keel as I can."

"Yeah," Ryan said. "Good luck with that."

Perico laughed. "Bring me something solid, Ryan. You know what's at stake better than I do."

"Wow, WHAT A HARPY," Mildred said. when her friends finished their tale. "Jacks isn't totally wrong about her, then."

"Not if he characterizes the baron as something of a virago," Doc said.

"She's smart," Ryan said. "Just got too short a fuse, and too many fuses sticking out of her waiting for a spark. Like a porcupine."

"That's an image I'm not going to thank you for," Mildred said.

"For what it's worth, she's no worse than plenty of barons and bosses we've bumped into," Ryan said. "Better than most, I reckon."

"She really cares about the ville," Krysty said. "Passionately. If only so her son will have something to rule over once he gets old enough."

"Think she'll be able to let go of power just because Junior's got to be a certain age?" Mildred asked.

Krysty shrugged.

"Doesn't matter," Ryan said. "Not our problem. If we're here that long, it'll be because we're wandering around with something else driving our bodies, looking for warm bodies to bite chunks off of."

"What of your experiences?" Doc asked J.B.'s group.

"Jacks just shook head," Jak said. "Laughed. Dickhead."

"His adviser, Coffin, did considerable ranting and raving about it all being nonsense he'd have to be a fool to believe," J.B. said. "Coffin's pretty shrewd, actually. But he's too in love with his own opinions."

"Who isn't?" Mildred said. "Jacks is also advised by his grandmother, who looks like a little shriveled monkey and screeches like a paranoid parrot. Mostly about what a slacker her grandson is. She wasn't having any of it, either. But Jacks is used to tuning her out."

"So, no help from that direction, either?" Ryan said.

"Jacks didn't get where he is by being stupe," J.B. said.

"Get where?" Jak said. "Run out palace, owning half ville?"

"He didn't get chilled, Jak. Old Jeb might not have been aware of what was going on, but Miranda's paranoid as a tomcat passing by a stickie nest, and as protective of her cub as a mama bear. Plus not even Jacks says she's a stupe. If she didn't twig to what he was up to, he had to be playing pretty smooth."

"So where does all this leave us?" Mildred asked.

"Boned," Jak said. "Should shake ville off boots."

"We talked this out already, Jak," Krysty said. "We agreed to do what we could to make a stand here."

"So there it is," Ryan said, "plain as a chill in a chair. We got to bring Jacks and Miranda to the table, or bring them down. And we got just about zero time to do it in."

"We still could run for it, Ryan," J.B. said. "Like Jak says."

Ryan glanced up at his best friend and right-hand man. "Really think we can run from this threat forever, J.B.?"

The Armorer looked at him for a long moment. Then he took off his glasses, pulled out a handkerchief and began polishing them.

"Naw. They aren't fast, but they're steady. And steady does the trick, every time."

"So what are we to do, with the leaders of both dominant factions in this unfortunate town so obdurate?" Doc asked.

"We could get in touch with the locals," J.B. said. "So far we been sticking with Jacks and his sec men. You?"

"Same here," Ryan said.

"The people are beat down," Mildred said. "If they were going to take a stand against their oppressors, wouldn't they have done so by now?"

"They may be waiting to see if things get better," Krysty said. "Sometimes it even works. Anyway, keeping heads down, waiting and hoping, is a lot safer than defiance."

"People fight best when fight for homes, loved ones," Jak said.

"That's true," Ryan said. "And the sec men on both sides are mostly stupes. Miranda's got loyalists with more heart than use. Plus a core of coldhearts, like her new sec boss, Stone."

"Jacks has a bunch of bullies and assholes," Mildred said with surprising venom.

"We had a bit of a run-in on the way to talk to Jacks," J.B. said. "Somebody decided to fondle Mildred's boob."

"He live?" Ryan asked.

"She shot his dick off."

Ryan arched a brow.

"She's dead-center on Jacks's men, though," J.B. said. "Jacks got the coldest of the coldhearts. Most seasoned and best trained. Sounds like Miranda's people are better motivated. Jacks's are driven purely by greed and ambition. But bottom line—both sides' goons are better at thumping unarmed civilian heads than actual fighting."

"Gotta fix soon," Jak warned.

"He's right," Krysty said.

"You got some kinda feeling here, Krysty?" Ryan asked.

She shook her head. Her scarlet hair was stirring nervously about her shoulders of its own volition.

"Call it an intuition, lover."

"All right," Ryan said. "I've been calculating this. So here's what we do."

He quickly sketched the plan he'd been forming in his mind.

"Won't that weaken both sides?" Mildred asked when he was done.

"Only if it works."

"But why? Won't that make it harder to fight the horde when it comes?"

"If the ville's still split down the middle and fighting against itself when the rotties show," J.B. said, "the place'll fall over like a twig tepee."

"We weaken them enough so they *have* to sit down and patch things up," Ryan said. "They won't do that, then we've weakened them so we can topple them first, and get the ville ready to fight ourselves. Like Jak says, the locals'll fight just fine when there's a changed horde staring them in the face, and nobody above them to beat them down."

"You sure that'll work, my dear Ryan?" Doc asked.

"Only thing I'm sure of is that one day we'll all end up with dirt hitting us in the eyes, Doc," Ryan said, standing. "Now, unless we want that to happen sooner rather than later, it's time we all blew out of here."

Chapter Seventeen

Reed Wallen stuck close behind the big wedge-shaped back of Brick Finneran, Geither Jacks's new sec boss to replace Bill Hapgood, recently deceased. His sturdy Savage 110 bolt-action longblaster felt as light as a feather in his hands.

He had been chosen to make history in the ville of Sweetwater Junction this day.

They had infiltrated deep into the northern half of the ville. Enemy territory since the night Reed, like so many of his sec brothers, had joined their beloved leader in an attempt to seize power from the failing baron Jeb before his crazy, corrupt slut of a wife and her weakling son could grab command.

White clouds feathered high across a wintry blue sky. A stiff morning breeze blew a breath of ice from the east. It whistled in the eaves of the brick houses as the ten-man team crept along an alley. It didn't drown out crowd noises from ahead, or the cawing of the ever-present crows.

Jacks's team had the enemy streets to themselves. Thinking about why excited Reed all to pieces. He knew where most people of the witch Miranda's half of the ville were right now, making all that ruction. Same place all the taints that passed for her sec men now would be: in front of the old palace, at a ceremony in which Colton Sharp was being officially invested as heir to the ville.

When the wind shifted briefly Reed could even smell Sweetwater Junction's signature delicacy: roast prairie dog on a stick, coated in a sweetish dough, deep-frying in grease.

Reed's stomach rumbled. They'd got no breakfast that morning. Instead, Brick had led off before dawn with his picked team of chillers.

They'd made it without incident across the no-man's land of the road that ran east-west through the ville. Then they'd holed up in an empty house to wait for the locals to head north to the open space in front of the palace for the show. They knew most of Miranda's subjects would be there. She had made it triple-clear in official proclamations that not turning up would be taken as evidence of shaky loyalty. Since nobody wanted to have their bones broken with wrecking bars, and then be hung up, still alive, on one of the scaffolds outside town, attendance would be good.

And they had no idea what kind of a show they were in for.

It CAME TOGETHER FAST, because Finneran was a real go-getter. He should've been Jacks's main man from the outset, but Hapgood happened to be senior. Reed knew that the sawed-off little shit of an outlander, Dix, had done Jacks a favor by chilling Hapgood.

Reed had been on guard duty in Jacks's sitting room the previous night when it all went down. Strike for him.

Jacks and his big brass were discussing Miranda's up-coming ceremony. Finneran was talking up the need to make a decisive move, an offensive move, that could bring it all in one stroke.

The little mercie with the hat and glasses mentioned that the ceremony might look like an opportunity for a chill-shot against Miranda. He had more to say, but Brick grabbed the ball and ran with it like the warrior he was. It was just the chance they were looking for: the bitch herself, plus her useless kid coming right out in the open from behind stone palace walls and their guards. Because Brick knew, like anyone with balls, that the best defense was a good offense.

And just as Jacks was nodding and frowning and thinking it over, the black woman mercie, Mildred, who people said was a healer, but who'd signed on as a shooter, piped up. "But wouldn't it be triple-stupe to make a play at Miranda and her boy with her whole sec team drawn up tight around them and looking for trouble?"

Brick went white to the roots of the short red hair that gave him his name.

Then he jumped all over that shit. He knew an opportunity when he saw one, he all but yelled. So Miranda's cat puke so-called sec men wouldn't let anybody near her precious body? Well, her side wasn't the only one that could use a longblaster. Finneran had a man on his team who could reach out and touch them from far, far away.

Reed's ears had burned then. He'd never felt so proud. He was the best shot on Jacks's side. The best in the ville. There'd been nobody to touch him before the coup went down and Jacks went south.

He just didn't get a chance to show off his skill very often.

The outlander mercies tried to argue it down. At least the dude with the hat and the woman had. The creepy kid with the white hair and red eyes, who claimed he wasn't a mutie, though everyone knew he was, never said much. But once Finneran was on a roll he carried the boss right along with him.

Gate Jacks loved boldness. Or he never would have made his own move on the palace.

The little mercie, Dix, kept insisting it was a triple-stupe idea. The more he insisted, though, the more Jacks seemed to like it. Mebbe he was beginning to see there wasn't any point relying on mercies when you had the cream of the crop on your team already.

Jacks had one stipulation to Finneran's bold plan. The shooter would get one shot before the baron's sec men got their charges to cover. Jacks wanted Reed to take out not Miranda, but the kid. The fat little bastard, Colt, Jeb Sharp's son.

"He's the real threat, long-term," Jacks said, stabbing the air with his cigar. "Without him, Miranda's just some Mex slut who happened to catch old Jeb's attention. Colt's the heir. And he's the apple of her eye. I want her to watch him die. It'll break her mind like—" he took the cigar between his fists and snapped it "—that. After which she'll be a pushover. Too fucked up to offer real resistance when we make our move."

"Don't be a fool, Gate," Coffin started to say. But the boss wasn't listening.

"Do this for me, Finneran," he said. Then he actually laid a hand on Reed's shoulder. "Do this for me, kid, and you can write your own ticket."

So HERE REED WAS, humping his rifle and ready to go. The team made for a three-story gray stone building with a clear view of the palace steps from two hundred yards away. Reed had dropped pronghorn at three hundred. He was good for the shot.

Finneran stopped at a narrow street to look up and down. He waved to Mattox, the third man in line, to scout ahead. Holding his Winchester carbine across his chest, the slight blond Mattox trotted to the far side of the street. He waved the others to come after him.

They were now a block from their objective.

When Reed stepped from the alley, the only creatures

on the street were a couple crows strutting around half a block to his left.

Holding his longblaster diagonally across his chest, he trotted confidently forward. His heart hammered. It wasn't from fear, he told himself, but pride. Pride and exhilaration at the great service he was about to do his leader and baron-in-all-but-name.

I wonder what kind of reward Jacks will give me when—

Impact on the left side of his head filled his brain with blinding white light and the jangling of all the sounds Reed had heard in his short life.

Then blackness. It would last forever.

BRICK FINNERAN HAD a stone heart, but it landed in his boots when he saw the brains blow out the right side of his sniper's head in a gout of doughy chunks and fluid shockingly red in the morning light. A blink later a bright red spark climbed toward the sky from off to his left.

Gunfire erupted, from his left, right and out front. Muzzle-flames winked from windows across the street. Mattox did a death dance in the far alley as bullets took him from both sides point-blank. Bullets cracked past Brick's head. One struck chips off the stone edge of the building right above him.

"Fuck!" he shouted. "Take cover! It's an ambush!"

WHEN THE STEYR SETTLED back online, Ryan saw the kid with the scoped bolt gun lying on top of it in the middle of the narrow dirt street. Only half his blond head was left. His brains had spilled like clotted puke into a wide crimson pool.

Ryan allowed himself a moment's satisfaction. Gate Jacks's new sec chief had brought his hit team right to where Ryan anticipated he would.

Killzone.

Ryan sat two blocks away in the attic of a two-story house that looked right up the last street the would-be chillers had to cross.

He couldn't take much credit himself. He'd relied on J.B. and Mildred to bait the trap. And Jacks and his overaggressive head thug had gone right at it.

It took less persuasion than he'd expected to persuade the baron to go for the plan. She realized the risk in exposing herself and her beloved son to her enemy's coldhearts. Miranda Sharp had the heart of a lioness and the soul of a gambler, however crazy she was. It actively delighted her when her new mercies showed how to turn Perico's major concern, and her own greatest fear, into a lethal trap.

Pride would never allow Miranda to cancel the ceremony. But she was willing to take the risk of leaving herself and her son defended by a mere handful of men—and Chad, her current lover, who struck Ryan as about as useful in a fight as a busted bicycle inner tube—for the chance of laying some serious hurt on her foe.

As Krysty reassured the unhappy Perico, the bulk of Miranda's sec men *were* safeguarding the baron and the heir. Just from advanced positions.

Satisfied he had achieved his primary objective, which was to zero out Jacks's best henchmen, Ryan set his rifle on the floor beneath the window. He picked a homemade flare from the dusty floorboards beside it and leaned out to jam the spike of its launching tube into the sill, angling up and away from his hidey-hole. Taking out a precious butane lighter looted from a redoubt, he lit the fuse, then quickly moved away from the window and pressed his back to the wall, in case the firework simply exploded.

It didn't. The squat little rocket launched, drawing a trail of dense red smoke in a high arc over the ville.

The thunder of blasterfire rose around him as Krysty and Doc and a squad of Miranda's sec men dumped bullets at the left wing of the hit team and the backing force of more than twenty men behind. Most of the baron's refurbished sec forces were arrayed in a crescent wrapping around both flanks of the Jacks force. They opened up with everything from hunting bows and crossbows to semi-automatic rifles.

The flare had served its purpose: springing the trap, as well as reassuring Baron Miranda that things had gone as planned. There was one more objective to launching it. Only time would tell if that was accomplished.

Picking up his longblaster, Ryan headed down the stairs to help Krysty and Doc make life miserable for the invaders.

"WELL, FUCK," COFFIN SAID. "We sure been played for fools."

He and his employer and friend stood on a north-facing balcony of the former gaudy house.

For several more beats of the pulse hammering in his ears, Geither Jacks continued to grip the cold, white-painted wrought-iron railing in both hands. The green flare descended over the north half of the ville—enemy territory, which he had sworn would be his soon, possibly this day—and went out.

The crackle of gunfire reached his ears.

He pried his hands loose and used one to take his cigar out of his mouth.

"Finneran," he rasped, "you chisel-dick. Devil forgive you if you lose me half my sec force out there. Because I sure won't."

He turned and yanked open the door that led inside.

OUR EMPLOYER DOESN'T look happy, Mildred thought as she, J.B. and Jak were ushered into the parlor.

"Okay," Geither Jacks said without preamble. "You were right. As of now it appears Brick Finneran has officially got his dick stuck in a bear trap."

"He's slack!" his grandmother exclaimed. "I told you! But you were too slack to listen!"

"Can you go get him back? And, uh, as many of my men as he hasn't already managed to get chilled?"

J.B. smiled blandly. "Sure."

"What'll you give us?" Mildred demanded.

Jacks's eyebrows rose. She could almost hear J.B.'s eyeballs click as he glanced at her from behind the round lenses of his glasses.

"What's this?" Jacks said. "You work for me."

"We do, sir," she said firmly. "And you told us in no uncertain terms we weren't good enough to take part in this commando raid Finneran cooked up. Now you want us to go get his dick out of what you describe as a 'bear trap.' Which is it?"

"Which is what?" Jacks sounded really confused.

"Are we good enough or not? If we're good enough to go extracting a sec boss's dick from a bear trap, it seems to me we deserve more pay than for just sitting on our hands because we weren't good enough to go get trapped with him."

Everybody stared at her for a moment. She tried to keep her face impassive.

Grammaw cawed with laughter. "The girl's not slack! You got to give her that!"

"Gate," Coffin began, "don't be a—"

Jacks waved his cigar at him. "Don't say it," he said. "All right. I'll double your pay."

Grammaw screeched like a scorched raven.

"No, no," Jacks said, "it's no big deal. I suspect I'm going to be saving more than enough on salaries today to make up the extra. Not that you people need to go getting ideas."

"No, sir," she said. "We'll take your offer. We're on our way."

"MILLIE," J.B. SAID MILDLY, as the three of them trotted along narrow, deserted streets, "weren't you worried about mebbe overplaying our hand a little, back there?"

"We're playing mercies, John," she said. "We need to act like mercies. And mercies are avaricious. To sort of extend his metaphor, Jacks's nuts were in a nutcracker. It was natural to apply leverage. And right now we *are* mercies. As Ryan always likes to remind me, we don't work out of the goodness of our hearts. Not that 'goodness of heart' and 'working for Geither Jacks' belong within twenty miles of each other."

J.B. chuckled. "Said a true thing there, girl."

"And finally," she said, "he really pissed me off, giving in so easily when Brick the Prick said he didn't want us along. Even if that was the plan all along."

"FINNERAN."

The sec man's green eyes showed whites all around as he turned his head to look back over his shoulder.

The situation was what J.B. had expected to find, and exactly as Jacks had summed it up.

One dead kid with half a head was sprawled out in the middle of the street. Another slumped against a wall on the far side, leaking from too many holes to be among the living. The casualty in the rotting-garbage-reeking alley with Finneran was a guy sitting with his back to a filth-smudged wall, looking pale and clutching a sleeve whose olive-drab had been dyed dark brown by blood.

The baron's men weren't pressing their advantage. They

made a lot of noise, but that was just busting caps. It didn't mean all those bullets were hitting anybody.

"Dix," the strike-team leader all but gasped.

J.B. didn't spend much time trying to read people. He didn't have a knack for it. Unlike blasters or gears, human beings didn't have to make sense.

But even the Armorer could see that Finneran was a beaten man. It was plain as the often-squashed nose on his face.

"Listen up," Dix said. "Jacks sent us. We're here to get you out. We can distract them long enough for you people to pull back. But you got to move right away. No telling how long we can hold 'em."

Fortunately, J.B. was a good poker player, because he had a hard time saying that with a straight face despite the practice. If the Sharp troops weren't doing such a fine job holding themselves, Finneran's command would be history already.

"Jacks is ordering us to pull back?"

"Yeah, yeah. That's what I said. He sent us, didn't he? Only, you've got to move right now, or..." He ended in a shrug of leather-jacketed shoulders.

For a moment the big man just stared at J.B. His Adam's apple worked up and down in his thick neck.

Probably he's more afraid of what Jacks'll do to him if he loses half his sec force for him, than he is of just dying, J.B. thought.

"Right," Finneran said. "Right. Orders. Orders are orders. Gotta be obeyed."

He grabbed his nearest sec man. "Pass the word. We're pulling back. Go!"

He turned back to J.B. "Go do what you can. Buy us time!"

"I'll do that," the Armorer said.

He drew a silver whistle from one of his pants pockets. Putting it to his lips, he blew a single long blast.

"GUNFIRE'S PETERING OUT," Mildred said.

She could hear dogs barking in the distance now, and the bleak calling of the crows perched on the rooftops and wheeling through the sky. She held J.B.'s Smith & Wesson M-4000 combat shotgun, which he'd lent her.

"Blasters running out ammo," Jak said. The two knelt on the raw dirt of a yard, behind a four-foot-high brick wall.

The albino teen had led her to a point just across the street from a group of three Sharp sec men. Peering through a crack where mortar had fallen out of the wall Mildred had studied them. The sec men had their backs to them, intent on the main force of Jacks's men. Occasionally one popped around the corner of the house they sheltered behind, let loose a shot without seeming to aim.

Finneran's crew could've pulled back at any time, she realized. Finneran had to have believed his force was already surrounded. Or maybe he was afraid to withdraw without Jacks's permission, yet unable or unwilling to drive his men forward against such strong opposition.

A police whistle shrilled from somewhere down the street ahead and a block or so over. It was the sort of sound that pierced and carried. It might even have been audible over the height of the firefight, which was why J.B. had picked it for a signal.

She drew in a deep breath and looked at Jak. He nodded.

"Sorry, guys," she muttered beneath her breath. "It's you or us." Then she popped up over the wall, laid the scattergun's ghost-ring sight beneath the right armpit of a towheaded man and pulled the trigger.

Chapter Eighteen

"Grip it tight," Ryan said. "Not quite that tight. Not so much your hands shake. Just shy of that."

Colt's plump young face was fixed in concentration. A quartet of his mother's sec men in their black armbands stood by on the bank of the shallow gully, holding the horses and watching with interest as Ryan helped the youth find the proper hold on the handblaster's grip.

"All right, good," Ryan said. "Rest your thumb on the safety, there. Finger off the trigger. Keep it outside on the guard until you've got sights on target and you're ready to shoot."

It was a 1911 Colt .45ACP. At some point in its long history somebody had put a decent pair of sights on the weapon.

"Ain't that too much gun to start a beginner on?" asked Kowalski, the tallest of the four sec men.

"No," Ryan said, not looking around. "Anybody can shoot a .45 if they know how to do it right. And no point teaching a person not to do it right."

It was the morning after the battle in north Sweetwater Junction. Ryan and his team officially walked on water now. He knew better than to expect it to last. A baron's gratitude was legendary. Because, as Doc liked to say, nobody would ever believe such a thing was for real.

There was a risk in standing in a gully under this kind of sky. A flash flood could wipe them out in a heartbeat.

But the locals didn't seem concerned, and Ryan didn't know anything that was totally safe to do.

Colt licked his lips and looked toward Ryan as the tall man gave a last adjustment to the youth's soft hands.

"These blasters're supposed to kick triple-hard," Colt said. "Are you sure—?"

"Yeah. Just breathe deep. Relax everything but your grip. Ace. Now push your arms out in front of you, far as they'll go."

He stepped away and back so that he was a yard from Colt Sharp's shoulder and a step behind.

"Focus your eyes on the front sight."

"Not the target?" A cracked, thus unusable whiskey bottle stood on a mound of sand against the far bank, twenty feet away.

"No. Not the rear sight, either. Front sight. Target should be a blur. Then you just rest it on top of the front sight like an apple on a post."

"All right."

The quivering boy was swinging the blaster in little figure eights. Ryan remembered he hadn't been any better when his father's men first tried to teach him how to fire a handblaster back at Front Royal. Of course, he'd been half this kid's age.

"Draw in a deep breath. Try to bring the sight up to the target. When you got it, let out half a breath, firm up your grip and squeeze the trigger gently."

The gun roared and kicked up. Colt jumped in alarm. The bullet knocked dust from the face of the cut two feet left of the bottle, which Ryan saw from the corner of his eye. He was focused on the boy.

Ignoring a repressed snicker from one of the sec men, he said, "Good job, kid."

"But I missed!" he exclaimed. His cheeks were flushed and his voice vibrated with half-controlled excitement.

"Everybody misses," Ryan said, "until they learn to hit. You kept your arms straight, didn't let your elbows bend so you were whacked in the face with your blaster. Just let the piece ride up natural and fall back down."

"So why'd I miss?"

"Pulled off," Ryan said. "Squeezed the trigger a bit too hard. Didn't jerk it—then you'd have missed low."

"Ooh." The boy's face fell like aging pudding. "So I screwed up."

"Nobody's born knowing this shit, kid. Truth is, trigger control's the hardest thing about handblaster shooting to get right. For your very first shot you did good."

It was true. Ryan wasn't in the habit of flattering barons, much less their pups. He wasn't intending to start with this one—even if the kid amounted to their fallback plan for defending against the rottie horde that Ryan knew in his gut was out there, coming nearer every day.

"Try it again. You know now the recoil won't kill you, so try not to flinch so much. And keep both eyes open."

"There's so much to remember," Colt whined.

Ryan's surge of disgust was following by a vivid memory of himself saying the same thing to his father's armorer. In an even more sniveling tone of voice.

"Not really," he said. "Just seems like it at first. Same thing with everything new you try. Just forget it and do."

Despite the snivel, Colt Sharp was visibly more confident as he pushed the big angular blaster out into the isosceles position Ryan had taught him as the easiest stance to learn, and an effective one. He even remembered to breathe in, let some air out, catch it before he fired.

This time the shot hit right in front of the bottle and threw dust over it.

"What'd I do wrong?" Colt keened. "I didn't think I jerked it like you said."

"Think it through, kid. Remember what you did."

"Well, the gun was moving around a lot. I thought I had the bottle all lined up right. But it seemed like it moved off just as I pulled—uh, squeezed—the trigger."

Ryan nodded. "That's it, for a fact. See, nobody's perfectly steady, 'less they're really living steel. Your arms and hands are going to move. The key is to work out your own body's rhythms, work out when to shoot. And yeah, you can learn to control the swaying better. Just not perfectly."

Colt sighed. "It all seems so hard to put together."

"Is anything worthwhile easy to come by?"

"Mebbe too easy, if you're a baron's son," Colt said.

Ryan repressed a grin. He knew that, of course, but he sure wasn't about to let on how.

"I wish… I wish my mother'd let me learn more things earlier. Like this. This is great! But mebbe I'm starting too late."

He ended on a defeated note.

"No such thing," Ryan said. "Fact is, you don't have to be able to shoot a horsefly out from between his wings at fifty paces to defend yourself with a handblaster. They're almost always used inside the distance of a good spit. You just got to hit a coldheart somewhere around the middle of the body to put him down, generally. It's not hard. Of course, the better you get at shooting a handblaster, the more you'll be able to use it for. But if you keep doing what I tell you, you'll be able to keep yourself alive in most situations with a handblaster after mebbe two more hours."

"Really?"

"Really. Now try again."

The youth controlled his rising excitement with visible

effort. The idea of being able to do anything for himself seemed to thrill him.

He took aim again, carefully following the steps Ryan had taught him. Keeping both eyes open, he lined up the heavy piece and fired.

The bottle flew in two, shattered in the middle.

"I hit it! I hit it!" The kid began to dance in triumph.

Ryan grabbed his arm. "Mind where you aim that, boy. Never point it at anything you don't want a hole in."

As the echoes of the gunshot died away down the arroyo, Ryan heard the sound of velvet-gloved hands clapping from the bank behind them. He looked around in time to see the four sec men jump in alarm and stare up at their baron, who sat silhouetted against a bullet-colored sky, on the back of a shiny black stallion. At her right side, Chad, her current golden boy, was mounted on a palomino gelding. Flanking Miranda were Krysty, Doc and sec boss Stone, all on horseback.

"Didn't you boys hear them ride up?" Ryan asked Colt's guards. "I did."

He had. A quick glance had told him who was approaching. A couple guards looked a bit mulish, but under the eyes of their baron and their immediate boss they had the sense not to talk back.

"I'm sure I can find ways to sharpen their situational awareness, Ryan," Stone said drily. He was never going to love mercies, or be best buds with Ryan, but after yesterday he seemed to accept the three outlanders as valuable assets.

Ryan hoped that would be enough to help him convince Miranda of the reality of the rottie threat soon.

"You've done well, Colt," the baron said. Chad had hopped off his golden horse. She allowed him to help her dismount. Her long legs were encased in black trousers and black boots. A black jacket and flat-brimmed black hat topped the outfit.

Miranda lightly jumped down to the sand of the gully floor. Ignoring the moves of the sec men to give her a hand, she walked toward her son. She hugged and kissed him, making him squirm just a bit.

"You've instructed my son well, Ryan," she said.

To Colt she said, "May I?"

She held out a black-gloved hand. He flicked a quick glance at Ryan and handed the piece over. Miranda held it up and expertly pulled the slide back a fraction, cracking the chamber to confirm there was a cartridge up the spout. She does seem to know her way around a blaster, Ryan thought.

"I used to be a pretty fair shot myself," she said. At her direction, Kowalski and one of his pals hurried to set up four bottles in a row along the foot of the far bank, while Miranda loaded a fresh magazine into the .45.

Barely allowing her sec men to jump out of the line of fire, she stepped into a modified Weaver stance: left foot advanced, hips turned slightly toward the target, left elbow down and fingers wrapped tightly over the shooting hand. Ryan grinned at the realization that of course the baron would favor that stance. It would make her look much more elegant than the isosceles.

She rapped off four quick shots. The fragments of the first bottle were still in the air when the fourth shattered.

Krysty clapped her hands. "Great shooting, Miranda!" she exclaimed.

The baron had started buddying up to the statuesque redhead even before yesterday's triumph. For her part Krysty was no more likely to suck up to a baron than Ryan himself was. She was a warmhearted person, though, and genuinely seemed to find something likable in the beautiful, sexy and rattlesnake-dangerous baron. Now she was telling no more than the truth.

Colt, of course, looked completely deflated. Your mother really has a knack for cutting your balls off, doesn't she, boy? Ryan thought.

"Practice like I showed you, kid," he called, "and you can learn to do that, too."

Miranda's olive cheeks were flushed. "I'm not so rusty, then, yes? Chad, darling, come here."

The muscular young man trotted up like an eager pup. At the baron's direction a sec man went to her stallion, which had his head down to munch at the winter-dry grass along the cut, and rummaged quickly in her saddlebag. He came back carrying a silver hip flask.

She handed it to Chad. "Go stand by the bank," she said, "and put this on your head. I'll shoot it off."

The youth's beefy cheeks lost some of their lusty pink. From some reason he cut his blue eyes in a murderous side glance at Ryan.

"That's kinda risky, don't you think, Baron?" Ryan asked.

For that matter the flask looked like predark scavvie. Very valuable. Too valuable, you'd think, to punch a hole through with a bullet. Then again, as Ryan knew too well, some barons were all about waste as a means of displaying their power.

"Oh, poor dear," Miranda cooed to Chad. "If you're afraid—"

She didn't have to finish. All the remaining color left his face, but he almost sprinted to the bank. Turning to face her, he balanced the flask atop his head of wavy, white-blond locks. Then, crossing his arms without dislodging the flask, showing more body control than Ryan would've given him credit for, he smiled broadly at his baronial lover.

For this shot Miranda didn't use a combat stance. She turned right side to the youth, left hand stylishly on her hip, heavy pistol extended confidently in a slender hand. It was a target pose, the way Mildred stood when she needed to make a precise shot and had the time. It had been double-tough to teach her not to try it in the average firefight, where it would likely get her chilled in a hurry.

With professional assurance Miranda lined up the sights. Her breasts rose and fell as she breathed in and partially out. She squeezed the trigger.

Pale yellow flame spurted from the handblaster's blocky muzzle. A black hole appeared in the middle of the smiling Chad's forehead. His brains blew out in a black cloud behind. He was still smiling as he folded to the soft sand like a suddenly empty suit of clothes.

Miranda stalked over to stand above his corpse. She tipped the Colt's muzzle up and blew away a wisp of gray-green smoke.

"If you had to fuck one of my maids," she said casually, "you should at least have had the sense not to try to flatter her by telling her how sweet it was to fuck a nice, juicy pussy instead of a withered-up old prune."

Dropping the handblaster on the chill's chest, she turned and strode back toward the bank. A pair of ashen-faced sec men almost bowled each other over to lock hands to provide a step for the baron out of the wash.

Everybody said lots of nothing.

As Miranda mounted her stallion, Ryan told Colt, "I guess that wraps it up here for today."

The youth was scrutinizing the toes of his boots. "Can we come out again soon?" he asked shyly, without raising his head.

"Reckon so," Ryan said.

He heard hooves drum on hard dirt again. This time

they rapped faster than when Miranda and her party had arrived. He walked quickly toward the bank himself, passing close to Krysty. And wasn't surprised when she fell in beside him. Nor when she gripped his hand until they reached the bank and scrambled up, with Doc close behind.

Stone had heard the hoofbeats, too. The sec men hustled to get up the bank themselves and put themselves between the baron and the new arrival.

It was a kid of mebbe ten, a stable boy, Ryan guessed, riding a big bay bareback.

"Perico sent me, Baron," the boy shouted, reining in. Ryan changed his first assessment: stable girl. Although with bobbed brown hair and a stick figure, she wasn't easy to identify as such until she opened her mouth.

"What is it, Sandy?" Miranda asked. Her voice held surprising gentleness, for a woman who had just chilled a faithless lover in cold blood.

And would of course get away with it, since she was the law in Sweetwater Junction. The north half, anyway.

"He says to come quick, please. Been a wag train attacked at the ten-mile marker east of town. Only two survived!"

Chapter Nineteen

"Survivors said that they came out of everywhere," the young man said, "all at once. Dozens of them. Mebbe hundreds. Just attacked without warning."

He wasn't a sec man, but a local from the north half of the ville. One loyal to Miranda, it would seem, since he had come forward voluntarily. Ryan wasn't sure that was wise, from the standpoint of continued survival. It seemed to him that the safest way to deal with Baron Miranda was not to be noticed by her. Admittedly, he might have been jaundiced by recent events. Then again, that was how it ran with most barons.

Krysty gave his hand a squeeze. He sat on a chair, and she on a fancy footstool beside him in the parlor, where Miranda liked to hold audiences. Doc stood by the fireplace in his shirtsleeves, his bright blue eyes blinking as if he was befuddled.

"So, what did they say attacked them again?" Perico asked.

The witness shook his shock of brown hair. He was sturdily built, with the big callused hands of a craftsman.

"It was all crazy, what they were saying," he said. "It was like—like chills had risen up to attack. Like they were all rotting and everything, but still could walk. You could shoot them again and again, cut them, beat them down. But they just kept coming."

"Were they after the cargo?" Miranda asked. She still

wore her riding pants and boots, although she'd doffed her jacket to show the pink silk blouse she had worn beneath. She carried a riding crop, which she ticked incessantly against the gray slate of the mantelpiece.

"No. Didn't seem interested in no wags. Or anything that was in them. Just people."

"You said some traders rode horses," Stone said. He was scowling so hard he looked as if his harsh face was going to implode. "Did these creatures show any interest in them?"

"If they did, the traders didn't say nothin' about it. The monsters just zeroed in on them."

"What did these—*things*—do to the merchants?" Miranda asked.

"Et 'em alive," he said, "ma'am."

For a moment there was no sound except the popping of the fire. The imported firewood smelled like piñon pine from parts far west.

Colt Sharp sat perched on the front of a chair, twisting his hands together between his knees. He still looked green around the gills. Apparently the night of blood and fire when his father had died and Gate Jacks and his traitorous accomplices were chased from the palace hadn't accustomed him to seeing people get chilled up close and personal. Then again, Chad's death had caught Ryan by surprise, too.

"So our new friends were right about the rotties all along?" Colt asked.

His mother scowled.

"Mebbe," Perico said quickly.

"Not proved," Miranda snapped. "Where are these traders? I want to talk to them now, Stone."

The witness turned wide brown eyes to the sec chief. "Tell her," Stone said.

"They came riding in on their horses like they had

screamwings on their tails," the witness said. "Threw some jack at the guards for water chits. Let their horses drink from the trough, drank like a day's ration themselves, and filled their canteens. They just babbled their story to anyone who'd listen. Then when their horses had drunk and caught their breaths, they jumped back on, said they was riding west fast as they could. They said ever'body else should, too, if they liked living."

"Send four men, Stone," Miranda said. "Give them fast horses. Tell them to ride hard to Ten Mile and find out what really happened. Tell them to be careful."

"I'll tell them to do their best, Baron," Stone said drily.

He left. As usual, Miranda had come to a decision quickly. She liked them carried out the same way.

"What do we do now?" Colt asked.

"Wait," Perico said. "Your mother's right. We can't go running off in all directions until we got a better idea what we're up against."

The baron looked to the townie, still standing by and looking nervous.

"You may go," she said.

"Did I do well, Baron?"

"Yes. You have served your ville well. Your family shall have a week's extra water ration chits as reward. See to it, Perico?"

The man jabbered his thanks to Miranda for her generosity as the grizzled adviser led him out.

Ryan gave Krysty's hand a last squeeze and stood. "I'd like to go out, cruise around the ville some. See if I can pick up anything more. Doc, you come with me. Krysty, why don't you stay here."

Miranda nodded. "She can lighten the hours for me with stories of her adventures."

"It'd be my pleasure," Krysty said.

She gave Ryan a "be careful" look as he gathered up Doc and headed out. He just grinned back.

Yeah, he thought. As if.

THE TRADERS' HORROR TALE had gotten the people of Sweetwater Junction stirred up. They stood in little groups on street corners or talked across fences, and even forgot to duck and scurry when Ryan and Doc swung by with their black sec man armbands. The two men garnered no more than increasingly wild rumors about the attack. The stories got stranger every time they heard them.

Almost strange enough to approach the truth.

Some spoke in favor of fleeing west into the wasteland straightaway. Others spoke of getting ready and fighting for their homes, their loved ones, their lives. Still others observed that'd just get them chilled by one faction or another. Neither would-be baron of Sweetwater Junction brooked anything resembling rivalry from anywhere else.

Still, the talk of fighting back made Ryan and Doc exchange a knowing look and furtive smile.

Mebbe there's hope, after all, Ryan thought.

STONE'S INVESTIGATIVE PATROL came back at sunset. One lone man rode up to the palace, swaying in the saddle of a horse that blew froth and rolled its eyes in terror. Palace servants ran out to help the injured sec man gently from his saddle.

The horse uttered a mighty grunt, shuddered and dropped dead.

The baron's personal healer, Lamellar, raced out, with Ryan, Krysty and Doc right behind. The wounded man was moaning. His clothes were ripped into ribbons and blotched with blood like a paint horse's rump.

Lamellar, who had a black comb-over of prodigious length that was always coming loose, knelt by the injured man's side. On cue, the comb-over fell down so it was almost tickling the sec man's cheek.

"He's been severely scratched and bitten," the healer said. "He's lost a substantial amount of blood. But unless he's bleeding internally he seems to have no major trauma. We'll have to get him inside and examine him carefully to tell."

"Wait, Miranda," Krysty said urgently. "If he's bitten, he's a danger to everybody. He'll *change*."

"If that's true," Perico said, "best for all concerned to just chill him."

"There is no 'maybe' about it, my friend," Doc said. "Unless you think the prospect of becoming a mindless monster with an insatiable appetite for human flesh and brains might appeal to him? I did not know him well."

Perico looked hard at Doc.

"When you get him inside you need to strap him down tight," Ryan said to Lamellar. "Before you even examine him. And you need to keep him that way. You can work around the restraints."

"Why, that's barbaric!" the healer said, turning his head toward Ryan so that the strayed combover fell to his shoulder.

"'Barbaric' does not even begin to describe the nature and conduct of the creature he is turning into," Doc said. "'Diabolical' would be closer."

"Baron—"

Miranda's brows were pulled together thoughtfully. "Do as they say," she said. "If these people are telling the truth about the monsters that did this to him, we don't dare take the slightest risk."

She swept Ryan, Doc and Krysty with her dark and searching gaze.

"It would appear you were telling the truth," she said.

Stone appeared. His long, heavy face hardened as he saw the wounded man.

"He's the only one back?" he asked.

"He's it," Ryan said.

He was about to say something else, something urgent, but Miranda preempted him.

"We must seal the entrances to the ville," she snapped. "Not just the main gates. There are ways through the perimeter fence. Everybody knows. They must be sealed or guarded."

Stone's coal-smudge eyebrows squashed even closer together. "What about the other half of the ville?" he asked, with the air of a man who knew the risks he ran in mentioning that the baron was in reality only half a ruler.

But she was focused. As with Doc's spells, so it seemed with Miranda's rages: real danger flatlined everything else.

"Seal the streets and secure the buildings along the square and the east and west roads," she ordered. "We'll deal with the traitor's side...later."

"That'll take a lot of men, baron."

"Use them all if you have to. Arm trustworthy servants. Impress citizens if that's what it takes."

She looked at Ryan and his companions.

"We have to at least act as if the whole story the outlanders told us is true. If even one of these horrors gets into my ville undetected..."

She shook her head. Miranda didn't strike Ryan as the sort to shrink from much. But even she couldn't face the consequences of the change sickness taking a foothold in Sweetwater Junction.

Two servants rushed up carrying a blue tarp. Lamellar directed them to transfer the wounded man onto it as gently as possible. Then, by unspoken consent, Ryan and Doc took the corners of the tarp by the sec man's feet, leaving the ones by his head to the servants.

"One, two, three, heave," Lamellar chanted. The four men rose, picking up the injured man. His deadweight, distributed among the four of them, was bearable.

"You're still here?" Miranda said to Stone. He moved off with alacrity surprising in a man so solidly built.

The rest of them followed the healer into the big house. He led them to a flight of stairs to the basement. Navigating the wooden steps with what amounted to a swaying bag of 170-pound man, with nothing but lantern light to guide them, was tricky, but they got him down without incident.

An oil lantern burned on a rickety table on the packed-dirt floor of a hallway. The basement was cold and smelled of cool earth and vinegar. At Lamellar's direction they carried the victim through the first door on the right.

It was lit by what milky light made its way through long, narrow, glass-block windows near the ceiling. Sudden garish white light flooded the room as the healer flipped a switch. It came from an incandescent bulb in a flattened-cone reflector hanging from the scavvied acoustic-tile ceiling.

"On-demand alcohol-fueled generator," he explained. "The late baron's father didn't fancy having his wounds tended to by someone with a squint."

It told Ryan something about the barons of Sweetwater Junction, that they had the capacity for electric power, and kept it reserved solely for emergencies. Most would've used it extravagantly, to show off their own power if nothing else.

A gleaming stainless-steel surgical table dominated the medical room. Leather straps dangled from brackets above a white tile floor that sloped subtly toward a brass drain in its center.

Ryan and Doc helped hoist the moaning man onto the table, then they stepped aside.

"I mislike the look of that table, my dear Ryan," Doc murmured, as they found themselves in front of white enameled-metal cabinets and a counter of what seemed to be poured and smoothed concrete.

"I hear you," Ryan replied.

Fussing like a mother duck, Lamellar supervised the servants transferring the patient from tarp to table safely, then he shooed them out.

"I know what you're thinking," he said to Ryan and Doc as he fastened straps over the wounded man's ankles. "This is my domain. Upstairs in the palace, Miranda rules. In the ville her word is law—or at least in the north half. Down here I'm king, and I would never condone torture."

Ryan wasn't especially reassured by the way the stooped old man emphasized the last by gesticulating with a razor-edged scalpel.

"Besides," the healer said, slicing bootlaces stiff and crusty with half-dried blood and muck, "Miranda isn't much given to private torture. If she's going to inflict pain, she likes to make a public example of it."

He didn't seem at all abashed by the fact that scarcely were the words out of his mouth than the woman herself blew in, still smelling of the outdoors and glowering like a thunderhead. She was followed closely by Krysty and Perico.

With a pealing scream that rang off the walls and ceiling tiles, the wounded man sat bolt upright even as Lamellar cinched his waist. The doctor leaped back with his comb-over flapping in alarm.

"They're coming!" the sec man shrieked. "Nothing stops them! Blasters can't stop them! Can't chill the dead. The eyes—"

He flopped back, his own eyes staring unblinking at the ceiling.

With a sigh, Lamellar straightened. "That's that, then. It's over." He reached to shut the man's open eyes.

Ryan grabbed his wrist. "Fireblast, it is!" he snapped. "You get right back there and fasten up all those straps now, or I'll chill you where you stand!"

Dark eyes saucer wide, Lamellar turned a colorless face to the baron.

"Do as he tells you," she ordered, "or I'll let him do as he said."

"And by the Three Kennedys, man, make sure the straps are tight!" Doc proclaimed in a voice that quavered with passion. "Because now is when the *real* danger starts!"

Chapter Twenty

Knuckles rattling the bedroom door snapped Ryan awake as he lay in the warm circle of Krysty's arms. Her soft silken nakedness was hot against his bare back and buttocks.

"What?" he barked hoarsely.

"Baron says come quick," a male voice called through the door.

"Come where?"

"Basement," the man said. "The chill just woke up!"

Ryan bothered to pull on only his jeans and boots. He tucked his SIG-Sauer handblaster inside the waistband, just in case. It wasn't an ideal way to carry the weapon, but these weren't ideal circumstances.

Krysty followed in bare feet and a thigh-length scavvied Tennessee University sweatshirt she used as a nightgown.

Shrieks of pain and terror blew out of the stairwell when Ryan pulled the door open.

"That doesn't sound like a dead person," Krysty said.

"Not yet," he said grimly.

In the medical room they found Miranda wrapped in what looked to be a brown bearskin, scowling furiously. Beside her Lamellar wrung his hands in distress, his comb-over hanging down the right side of his face like a peeled-off scalp. A pair of sec men, presumably the baron's bedroom-door guard detail, hovered in the background, looking as if they were trying not to freak out completely.

Another stick-skinny, middle-aged guy in a white lab coat liberally spattered with gore and muck had his arm clamped in the jaws of the dead sec man. He was the one making most of the noise.

The chill growled and rolled eyes glazed over with a milky film as he shook his prize with bloody teeth.

"It's impossible, Baron," Lamellar was saying. Evidently on behalf of his man, who finally left off howling and thrashing to try gingerly to dislodge the chill's teeth from his bare forearm. From the looks of things he'd given violent tugging a try and failed. "This man died hours ago. He has no heartbeat nor apparent respiration even now. Morris was trying to monitor his state of decomposition when... when this happened. There's no blame, surely."

Points to the old bastard for having the stone to take the sec man's pulse while he was struggling to get loose, with his jaws clamped on the med tech's arm, Ryan thought.

"It's clearly *not* impossible, Lamellar," Miranda said. "It happens, *sí?* The dead man moves. It's not as if you weren't warned of this. It's precisely why you were directed to secure him firmly. I am *not* pleased."

The healer's doleful face went even grayer. Clearly, as terrors went, chills returning to a ghastly parody of life to attack the living paled beside the wrath of Baron Miranda.

The baron looked at Ryan. "You and our friends are vindicated," she said. "I was double-stupe to doubt you and not act before. I can only act decisively now, and hope it's not too late."

"I don't believe it is, Miranda," Krysty said. "But the ville needs to be roused. The rotties could arrive at any time. And despite the fact they seem mindless, they've shown flashes of cleverness. Even tactical sense."

"How is that even possible?"

"We have no idea," Ryan said. "All we know is that we can't underestimate the bastards."

"Help me," moaned Morris the med tech. He now had hold of his own arm above where the rottie's mouth gripped it, as if hoping to keep the unnatural creature from swallowing it whole.

"Right," Miranda said. Her right hand whipped out from her bulky robe toward Morris's head. Before even Ryan could grasp what she was doing, a yellow light flashed and a painful sound shattered the air inside the little room like glass.

Morris slumped down behind the table, shot in the face and dead at once. Miranda pivoted back to Ryan. The front of her bare robe fell open, revealing the olive contours of her body. What really distracted Ryan was the P08 Luger she held tipped toward the acoustic ceiling with a thin string of smoke coming from its muzzle.

"You killed him!" Lamellar screeched. His voice was like fingernails on a chalkboard. Ryan half hoped the baron would chill him next. Just to shut his pie hole.

"You display a firm grasp of the obvious, Lamellar," Miranda said. "I commend you. May I recall to your razor-keen mind what happens to those who are bitten by the creatures who have—what did you say, Ryan? Changed."

"But...but...how do we know it happens in every case, Baron?"

"It has happened in every case I have direct knowledge of," she said crisply. "In fact, did not this whole unpleasant scene arise from doubting that very fact? As I said before, we can take no chances."

Lamellar's purple lips sagged. He was breathing so quickly Ryan thought he might be hyperventilating, and waited with a certain interest to see if he keeled over.

"Now get a grip on yourself," Miranda told the healer. "Clean up this mess."

She turned to Ryan again. "I have a risky mission for you."

He shrugged. "You pay, I play."

A sudden movement from the chill made everybody jump. Ryan saw the corpse's head come up. The face had gone gray, and the flesh seemed to have loosened on its bones. Bruised markings discolored the skin, green and brown and yellow, reminding Ryan of somebody who'd taken a good dose of rads—not enough to chill him, but enough to make his hair fall out and have him look weird for a week or two. The skin around the eyes had shrunk and taken on a weird, scaly appearance, like chicken legs.

The thing chewed with monotonous rhythm on a chunk of skin and muscle it had ripped from the late Morris's arm.

"Have we further need of this abomination?" Miranda asked.

"No, ma'am," said Doc, who had come in late in shirt and trousers and sock feet, with his suspenders dangling behind. "Unless you wish to observe the progression of the disease, if we may call the change that. Which, though it might be of academic interest, I am forced to admit is unlikely to confer any benefit to us in a useful period of time."

"To translate," Ryan said, "no, we don't need it anymore."

"Good." The Luger flared and barked again. The bullet hit the former sec man above the left eye and blew a divot out of the rear of his skull. The body bowed upward against the leather restraints. The heels drummed the shiny steel tabletop. For an instant Ryan feared that the change had changed itself: that even a brain shot no longer stopped the horrors. But it was only the last gasp of the monster's stolen central nervous system. The rottie went limp with finality.

"You should tell your assistants to exercise the utmost care in cleaning up the detritus, Dr. Lamellar," Doc said, giving the healer a courtesy title he probably didn't merit. "We don't yet understand all the possible means by which the sickness is transmitted. But we know saliva's involved, at least."

"About that mission, Baron," Ryan said.

"Geither Jacks must be made aware of the gravity of this situation," she said.

Her two sec men actually gasped at that. She ignored them. They quickly got busy trying to cover their obvious relief that she didn't seem inclined to send them.

Ryan's unscarred right eyebrow rose. Her response surprised him, in a good way.

"Smart," he said. "Your usual baron might think, if the change were to get loose in a rival's part of town, he could mebbe exploit the chaos to smash that rival. Be triple-stupe here. Self-death sure. But most wouldn't see it."

"I'm not having *that* get loose in my ville," she said. "I see too clearly what hell there would be eradicating it. If we even could."

"So you're willing to negotiate a settlement with Jacks?" Krysty asked.

Miranda shook her head firmly. "Never. This ville is mine—is my son's. Jacks is a traitor and usurper. I'll never rest until he is spinning slowly in the wind, and what is mine by right is mine once again. But I will not tolerate his fouling the nest through inaction!"

Ryan nodded. It was a start.

"I'll do it," he said. "Doc, finish getting dressed. Krysty, why don't you stay here, keep the baron company—"

Green fury flared in Krysty's eyes. Her scarlet hair whipped around her shoulders like a nest of angry snakes.

"Don't even say it, Ryan! Don't you *dare* try to leave me behind!"

Ryan sighed. "All right. We'll all get dressed while the baron writes her note to Jacks. Then we'll deliver it."

"But it's suicide!" Lamellar choked out. "He'll kill you all!"

"Then we won't end up like that poor bastard, will we?"

LOUD MALE VOICES and wavering torchlight carried on up the street.

"Whistling past the grave," Doc remarked. The three had hidden behind some crates and assorted trash in a side yard to allow the Jacks sec patrol to pass. As usual, they had experienced no trouble slipping past each faction's foot patrols. Even crossing no-man's-land had been a breeze.

"Do they think that by waving torches and talking loudly they'll keep the rotties from jumping out at them?" Krysty asked.

"Mebbe," Ryan said. "They're on edge. Not thinking clear."

He shook his head. "Well, things won't get better if we just stand here."

When they were within a couple blocks of the former gaudy house that served Gate Jacks as a palace-in-exile, they stepped out and boldly strode up the street. Ryan carried a white flag consisting of a bleached linen pillowcase on a broomstick, prominently displayed.

Almost at once a four-man sec patrol challenged them.

"What have we got here?" The obvious leader was a big man with the sides of his head shaved, leaving a shock of wavy brown hair on top. He planted his burly form directly in Ryan's path, with cantaloupe-size fists on his hips.

"Looks like some of Miranda's bitches done jumped the fence and strayed over here," a skinny guy with unshaved jaws and a rat's nest of dark hair said. One of his eyes shone dead white in the gleam of stars from above. It reminded Ryan eerily of the changed sec man's eyes.

"Can we chill 'em, Lou?" asked a third, as tall as the leader but a real string bean, with an Adam's apple as large as, well, an apple. "Can we, huh?"

"After we play with the big-tit bitch," Dead-Eye said hurriedly.

"We're here under a flag of truce," Ryan said, shaking his stick to call attention to the fact. "We're bringing Jacks a message from Miranda."

"Well, just hand that bad boy on over," Lou said, extending a hand the size of a paving stone. "We'll see Gate gets it, nice and safe."

"We're supposed to deliver it to Jacks's own hand," Krysty said. "And we claim right of passage."

"Well, whoop-de-do, Sandbag Boobs," Lou said. "I wasn't *asking*. Boys, take 'em—"

A loud noise interrupted him. Also a bright yellow flash that illuminated the big man collapsing on himself. Black fluid squirted out of his ears as he went down.

His LeMat handblaster held at the end of his extended arm, Doc let the huge weapon's muzzle wander back and forth across the three surviving sec men as if at random. "That is no way to talk to a lady," he said in tones of mild reproof. "Now, you gentlemen will be good enough to escort us to Mr. Jacks without further ado."

He didn't phrase it as a request. The patrol didn't take it that way. They did as he said.

Blasterfire in his own street was apparently enough to rouse the man himself. By the time they'd covered the block and a half remaining, Jacks was standing on the stoop. He wore a robe—maroon silk, judging by the yellow light spilling out the windows and open double doors—over pale pajamas. He puffed at a lit cigar.

"So you're the bitch's new outlander mercies," he said, when Ryan, Krysty and Doc walked up to him with their captive escort. "I got me some, too. Mebbe we should get you and them to square off."

Three figures emerged from the French doors behind Jacks, looking grim as rad death: J.B., Mildred and Jak.

"Another time," Ryan said. "Miranda said to give you this."

He handed over a rolled scrap of fancy stationery sealed with black wax pressed with a signet ring Miranda wore.

"She always did know how to do things in style," Jacks said, examining it. As he broke the seal he added, "So I reckon Lou got frisky with you on the way in?"

"He required instruction in the niceties of diplomacy, sir," Doc said. "Also common courtesy."

"Take it he didn't survive the lesson? No loss. A white flag's got to be respected. It's part and parcel of the accepted order. Without that we got anarchy. The rest of you assholes, take that to heart."

Ryan and his companions practiced squaring off and looking fierce at their friends as Jacks read the message Miranda had written in her looping and dramatic but clear hand. The others glared furiously back.

"So all that bull-goose crap about walking chills is true?" Jacks said. "Or at least Miranda wants me to believe it is."

"What does she have to gain by your guarding your part of the ville more closely, Mr. Jacks?" Krysty asked.

He shrugged. "Mebbe string my forces out along the perimeter so she can bust through? All right. Tell Miranda her message came through loud and clear."

"Will you prepare to defend your side?"

"I'll think about it," Jacks said. "She can stew in her juices until she finds out. You can go now. Make sure they get back all safe and sound."

"Will do!" said Dead-Eye, throwing a salute so sharp he almost coldcocked himself.

"Wasn't talking to you, cock-snot."

J.B. STOOD IN THE COLD night air, watching his friends and their three unhappy companions walk away down the street.

"You three follow 'em," Jacks growled. "Make sure they keep headed in the right direction."

"Want us to chill them?" Mildred asked.

"Didn't you hear me just now?"

"Thought it was a speech for those other numb nuts."

He laughed. "Good point. But I meant it. This time. Now move."

"What'd you go and say that for, Mildred?" J.B. asked when they were out of sight—and earshot—of their employer and his gaudy house HQ.

She grinned. "Just playing the role, J.B."

"Wonder if you aren't enjoying it a mite too much. And such a mild soul you act, most of the time. We don't want to come off too bloodthirsty."

Jak snorted. "Jacks sec boss," he pointed out. "No such thing, too bloodthirsty."

Chapter Twenty-One

"Listen to me," Reno shouted to the ville folk and traders gathered around the thirty-foot-wide fountain in Sweetwater Junction's main square. He climbed up on the red sandstone cap of its yard-high brick walls. "Listen! You're all in deadly danger!"

Nervous faces turned toward him, pinched and pale. People were queued up north and south of the big fountain along the main road, clutching chits that seemed to be written on broken pottery pieces—cheap and available. Clumps of sec men at barricades took the chits before allowing people access to the fountain. Trade wags, both gas- and horse-drawn, waited at the north and south checkpoints.

The sec men north of the east–west highway wore black armbands. The ones south wore green. They seemed to ignore one another studiously. Just as the ones manning the checkpoint where he'd entered the ville from the east had.

Reno had spent the last of his jack, plus bartered his last tin of scavvied corned beef, to buy the water chit required for entry into the ville. He wasn't concerned about that. He had ways of getting more.

And those ways entailed telling tales. True tales. Unwelcome yet necessary tales.

"There's an army of monsters headed to your ville!" he declaimed, his voice ringing back from stone-and-brick building fronts. "They're right behind me. You have to listen! They're coming to eat you—you and your children! They'll chill you all unless you get ready to fight them!"

Groups of sec men in both colors of armband stared at him in consternation. Rousing the populace of a ville to fight was a dangerous proposition for all concerned. As a rule, barons feared that if their people decided to fight, they were as likely to fight their own bosses for freedom as any external enemy.

But not this enemy. Reno knew too well. If only he could persuade enough people in time.

"They rise from the dead. They're chills, but they walk like you and me. If they bite you, you turn into one of them. If they get loose in the ville, it'll be the end of all of you."

The green armbands moved first, three burly men breaking away to run toward him. An eye blink later the black armbands reacted. But by then a blond-bearded, green-armband guy had Reno by one elbow.

"Come down from there, you stupe!"

"Listen to me!" Reno yelled. "Hear my words! You must prepare now!"

As he was dragged away, he turned his head.

"You've got to get ready. Or you're all doomed!"

"You mean you believe me?" Reno asked.

Gratefully, he accepted a mug of hot spearmint tea from a servant girl who, despite a lack of the stucco-thick paint that the kind customarily wore, put him in mind of a gaudy slut. Come to think of it, the red-velvet-and-gold decor in Boss Jacks's audience room wouldn't have been out of place in a gaudy. The whole building looked like one that had been taken over and transformed into a heavily armed headquarters.

"Not exactly the first we've heard about it," Jacks said.

He was a lanky guy with a bit of a pot and a set of wrinkles for a face, and hair the color and straightness of straw.

"We were fools not to listen," said the mournful black guy in coveralls who stood beside the boss's easy chair.

"Well," Reno said nervously, "what do you want from me, Mr. Jacks?"

"The whole story."

"From the beginning?"

Jacks nodded.

"But—I mean, why? If you've heard it all before?"

"I didn't say we've heard it *all* before. I said we heard some. I want everything you got. Leave out no detail, however minor. If we're gonna fight these things, we need every edge we can get."

"We'd be fools not to learn as much as we can," the black dude, Coffin, said.

"You think he repeats himself a lot," Jacks said, "wait'll you meet my grammaw. Go on now, son. Lay it on us."

THE TALE-TELLING STRETCHED for hours. Jacks kept asking him to go back over parts of it, try to remember more. Reno didn't mind. This was his bread and butter now. Literally. Jacks had him served grilled pronghorn with dried apple slice sandwiches while he talked. If he pleased the baron, or whatever this dude was, enough, he'd be square to stay here a spell. He'd get chow, and water and shelter.

Until the swarm came, of course. And then it'd be time to move on. Or—it wouldn't.

The sky outside the windows had darkened enough to be noticeable through the curtains when Jacks stiffened and said, "Wait. Go back."

"Huh? I mean, yes, sir, Mr. Jacks, sir. Only what part?" He'd brought them up to almost the present day with an account of his progress overland, trying to stay out of the hands, not to mention the mouths, of the changed. Of hair-raising escapes and scrapes and near misses.

"You said something about the bunch you met up with when you went to the caravanserai."

"Oh, yeah." He'd kind of glossed over that part. The narrative had been rolling, though, so they hadn't pressed him before. "They were a pretty wild crew, I got to tell you. There was the one-eyed dude, first I ever heard call these creatures rotties. And his sidekick, a short little shit with glasses and a hat. And his woman was this drop-dead gorgeous redhead with tits out to here—

"What? Why are you staring at me like that?"

MIRANDA SHARP'S MOUTH tightened when she saw Stone come out of the sod house into the moonlight with a man even bigger than he was.

"Finneran," she said tightly.

He glared back from his meat slab face.

"Lady," Perico said at her side.

She set her jaw. It cut her like a knife to have to deal with those who had betrayed her. But the situation, the very welfare of her ville and her only child, demanded it.

Besides, the formerly low-ranked sec man wasn't the most heinous traitor she would meet with this night.

"We're good," Stone said. "No surprises."

Miranda hated surprises. She always had. She was surprised enough when she received a message requesting an urgent midnight meeting between her and her hated enemy, the vile Geither Jacks, in an abandoned farmhouse just west of the ville. She was even more surprised when Perico urged her to accept.

It had flashed into her mind that perhaps he had betrayed her, too, but she quickly saw that was unlikely.

Perico had long since had all the opportunities he could desire had he meant to turn on her.

And his quiet, earnest words had convinced her to agree.

She had also been surprised at Jacks's terms: "Leave your shiny new mercies at home. I'll do the same." But she had concurred. Reluctantly, because she had come to rely on the three. Especially Krysty, who was developing into something she'd never really had in her life before: a female confidante. And Krysty's handsome one-eyed devil of a man, of course. Even the courtly and surprisingly formidable Dr. Tanner had proved his worth, both as a tutor for Colt and as a fighter.

"What now?" she asked. The wind hissed over the plains. From the icy knife edge in it she would scarcely have known spring was coming, with its less-welcome accompaniment of occasional torrential and lethal acid-rain storms.

"We go inside, Baron," Stone said. "It's safe."

Inside, the single room was lit by two lanterns, and a fire crackled in the hearth. Three men waited. One was a stranger. The other two were all too familiar.

And hated.

"Miranda," said Geither Jacks, turning away from the fire. Stone and Finneran came in, closing the door against the chill. It had obviously been recently repaired, and actually kept most of the wind out, though it whistled in the rafters.

"You will use my proper title," she gritted.

He grinned that lopsided, trap-mouthed grin of his. "Very well. Mrs. Sharp."

She felt her face knot into a grimace of fury.

"Easy, Baron," Perico said from her elbow. "Now's the time for talk and reason."

She drew in a deep breath. "Very well. I agree. Or I

would not be here. What is so important you want me to see, Jacks?"

"Not see," he said. "Hear."

He turned to the third man, the stranger. He was a slight young man with an unruly mop of brown hair and brown eyes huge behind the lenses of his glasses.

"Go ahead, boy," Jacks said. "Talk."

The young man moistened his lips with a pink tongue. "Evening, Baron," he said. "Uh, you can call me Reno."

Chapter Twenty-Two

The instant Ryan opened the bedroom door, the steel-shod butt of a longblaster caught him hard in the face. The world spun into crazy chaos. Vaguely, he heard Krysty's scream of fear and fury, heard Doc bellow like an angry bull; a flash, the roar of a shot, and somehow over all the sound of a bullet striking something; a grunt of pain as the room filled with acrid black smoke.

Ryan was on his back on the cold hardwood floor without knowing clearly how he got there.

"Alive!" someone shouted. It sounded like Stone. "The baron wants them *alive!*"

Ryan fought to get control of his body, leap to his feet, leap into action. But his muscles refused to respond. His stomach rolled over and over inside him.

Then the boots began to thud against his ribs. It was all red and pain, until the blackness mercifully swallowed him.

"YOUR SENTRIES KEEP seeing things outside the wire, Mr. Jacks," J.B. said.

Although it was well past midnight, the boss of Sweetwater Junction's southern half sat in a dressing gown in his favorite chair, with his feet up on one of those fancy silky footstools, his inevitable cigar and a snifter of some dark liquid that might just have been scavvied brandy in hand. The room smelled of pungent imported firewood and cigar smoke.

Unusually, neither his adviser, Coffin, nor his grandmother were in attendance, although the old lady often went to bed early. J.B.'s team had encountered the withered old crone only a few times, which J.B. considered a good thing.

The heat of the fire blazing in the big fireplace seemed to sting his cheeks and hands. It was that cold outside. He could still smell the cold beating off his companions' clothing and his own from their nocturnal survey of Jacks's defensive positions.

Jacks drew on his cigar and blew out a greenish smoke ring.

"Seeing real things?" he asked. "Or seeing shadows?"

"Both," Jak said. "Some."

"That seems to be the way of it, Mr. Jacks," Mildred said. "We saw some things moving around out there, too, before the moon set. Upright things, not like coyotes."

"Are these rotties smart enough to do something like that?"

"Doesn't take a lot of smarts to walk around at night," J.B. said.

"I mean, if they're mindless and driven purely by hunger, wouldn't they just keep coming toward where the food was?"

"We don't know much about them," Mildred said. "We don't know enough. Remember how we told you that while individual ones act pretty mindless, collectively they seem to show some kind of sense?"

Jacks's smile looked a mite peculiar to J.B. He wasn't a noted connoisseur of smiles, nothing like that. But he'd learned to keep his eyes skinned for signs of odd behavior among people he dealt with. Keeping close watch on *details* was something that came easily to him.

"Yes," their employer rasped, drawing out the syllable. "You told me. So you did. And just today I got pretty solid confirmation of what you told me."

He turned his head. "You can come out."

A slight figure with wild hair and eyeglasses not that different from J.B.'s own emerged from the staircase.

"Reno?" Mildred said. "You get a different prescription? Last I saw you, you had bat-wing glasses."

He smiled shyly. "They got busted. When I'm scavvying, I keep a lookout for ones I can use. Been collecting 'em a long time."

J.B. felt the hairs at the back of his neck rise as the implications of the kid's presence trickled down his spine.

Apparently, Jak did, too. "We fucked," he said.

J.B. stuck a hand inside his jacket. He heard metal click right behind his head, and he froze.

The Armorer knew the sound of a blaster's safety coming off when he heard it.

Jacks ticked a finger back and forth at them. "Tut-tut," he said. "Don't do anything foolish, Mr. Dix, Mr. Lauren. Dr. Wyeth, a healer, I'm given to understand. My men already have the drop on you. You have no chance."

"Couldn't smell," Jak said disgustedly. "Too much fancy smoke and whore perfume inside."

Mildred cut her eyes to J.B.

"If you're thinking of making a play for me, and either blasting your way out or going down in a blaze of glory," Jacks said, "my men have orders to shoot to wound."

J.B. raised his hands, as did the others. Hard hands frisked them professionally.

Brick Finneran came out of the stairwell, smiling all over his pink adobe-block face. "You made me look triple-stupe out there, Dix," he said. "I been hoping for something like this."

"I didn't make you look stupe, Brick," J.B. said. "You did that all by your lonesome."

Still smiling, Brick stepped forward and slammed a sledgehammer fist into J.B.'s gut. The air burst out of him, and he fell to his knees, gasping and retching.

Hands yanked his jacket down behind him to bind his arms.

J.B. shook his head and looked up. Sec men held a furious-looking Mildred by the arms. A pair flanked Jak with Winchesters pointed at his head. Another was tying his hands behind his slender back. His red eyes had the blankness of an animal's.

J.B. looked at Jacks, who grinned at him.

"There's someone I'd like you folks to meet," he said. "You're going to get to know him *real* well. Levon?"

If his arms hadn't been bound behind him by his own leather jacket, J.B. would've gone for it then and there. They hadn't met Levon before, but they'd heard the name. Usually whispered in various mixtures of awe, horror and sadistic glee.

From the stairs came a thumping and a moist wheezing. The figure that descended needed to turn sideways to navigate them.

Jacks's pet mutie torturer Levon was a monster in *size,* sure enough. He had to have been six-seven, six-eight, and weighed a good four hundred pounds. His face was asymmetrical, one eye larger and higher than the other, both heavy-lidded. He didn't have a nose so much as a swelling in the middle of his face with two thumb-size holes in it, both running snot into a mouth that was a loose hole J.B. doubted could even close right, with wet lips framing a few twisted, brown teeth. His complexion suggested boiled oatmeal poured into a cheesecloth bag shaped kind of like an onion. The point was on top, with a thatch of brown hair sticking up like leaves.

Levon wore stained denim overalls above a faded orange T-shirt. His general body shape suggested a bag of boiled oatmeal, too. His vast splayed feet were bare, mottled pink and blue and white. The nails were humped, yellow and cracked. His left foot had four toes.

The most striking feature, as he jiggled and whuffled and giggled and lurched his way out onto the floral carpet in the sitting room, was his right shoulder. Or shoulders. An extra one sprouted from the armpit of the other.

J.B. felt a bit cheated. When he'd heard about Levon's three arms, he'd expected three full-size limbs, with meat hooks to match. Instead, the lower right arm was small, not much larger than a child's, sticking out through a hole in the T-shirt. Instead of a hand it had a fleshy, two-lobed claw.

The real ones were nothing to sneer at, though. Levon had arms like most men had legs. And the hands were huge even for his massive frame.

"Don't let those pincers fool you," Jacks said with satisfaction. "They got a stronger grip than you do. Stronger than Brick, even. They can give you the nastiest pinch you ever felt in your soon-to-be-ending-in-agony lives."

"Levon…play," the mutie wheezed. The noise seemed to come as much out his nose holes as through his mouth. J.B. got the notion that, while Levon likely wasn't the brightest star in Constellation Mutie, his slowness of speech was more a function of physical difficulty in speaking than any necessary slowness of thought.

"Yes," Jacks said, "Levon play. But don't do any permanent harm. And don't leave any marks."

He took a hearty puff on his stogie.

"We don't want 'em all used-up-looking when you torture them to death in the central square tomorrow, after my little rendezvous with destiny, now, do we?"

THE CAT O' NINE TAILS WHISTLED evilly in the air, to crack against Krysty's buttocks. Bright white pain flashed through her whole body. Try as she might, she couldn't stifle a cry of agony.

"You *bitch,*" Ryan shouted at her tormentor. "No way you'll survive this. No...bastard...way."

Baron Miranda Sharp trailed the knot-tipped leather thongs over a bare forearm and smiled. "Ah, the passion, the fire! The devotion! You are quite the man, Ryan."

She shook her head. "It's too bad that you came to the ville under false pretenses. To do what? Assassinate me? And your friends, to assassinate Jacks? Seize power for yourselves?"

Suspended by steel manacles cutting agonizingly into her wrists, Krysty turned slowly on chains hung from a huge iron hook in the ceiling. Ryan came into view, manacled to a heavy chair that was bolted to the floor. His face was puffy and bruised from the beating he had received. Then Doc, likewise fastened in a chair, his head down and his white hair falling lank almost to his lap.

"Never that," Doc said. He raised his head with a groan of effort. A red bib of bloodstain ran down the front of his white shirt. Black trails of drying blood ran from his nostrils over his lip. "We came here to do one thing and one thing only—to try to get the ville ready to fight the rotties!"

Miranda made a sound that was half cluck, half snort. "Perhaps. But why not come openly?"

"You didn't...believe us when we told you," Krysty said. She had mastered the pain. For the moment. She didn't want to call on Gaia for strength unless the situation got worse.

"But you deceived me, all the same. You are not to be trusted. Under the circumstances, that means you must pay the price."

Still smiling, she lashed out again. The multithonged whip licked across Krysty's buttocks like blowtorch flames. She screamed again.

Ryan roared with fury. His face went red, and the tendons stood out on his neck and jaw at his colossal struggle to get free.

"You would tear me apart with your hands if you could, Ryan," Miranda said. "That's why I torture and humiliate your woman before you. I'm pressed for time. And when I'm done meeting with Jacks, you will be promptly executed in public."

"Your healer said you were not the sort for private torture," Doc said. "Yet you had this dungeon tricked out and ready, all along."

Again she shrugged. "Normally I'm not. As for this room, it was built by a baron long ago. I have made little use of it, and that only for interrogations. But your treachery has wounded me deeply. I thought you were my friend, Krysty Wroth!"

THE DOOR TO THE CELLAR ROOM beneath the former gaudy house opened inward. A hard hand propelled a slight, stumbling figure forward.

"There," a harsh voice said. "You got 'em in here. Now why don't you keep them company? You and they should have plenty to talk about."

Raucous laughter faded down the hall and up the stairs.

With a moan, Mildred rolled over to check out the new arrival.

"So, Reno," she heard J.B. say. "How's it hanging?"

Reno had slammed face-first into the wall. Now he turned and slumped until his butt rested on the crude concrete floor. In the light streaming through the long, shallow windows up by the ceiling, far too low even for Jak to crawl through, she recognized the young man as he adjusted his glasses on his nose.

"I'm sorry," he said. "I came to warn the ville about the horde's approach. I had no idea telling my story would bring disaster on you and your friends."

"Right," Jak said.

"Let him have his say," J.B. said. He sounded marrow-weary. "Anyway, how could he have known what we were up to?"

The Armorer settled his own glasses on his face, then picked up his fedora and adjusted it on his head. He sighed. That came close to shocking Mildred. Such displays of emotion weren't like him.

Then again, she had seen what he'd been put through. She had experienced a lot of it herself. Much too much.

Jacks had been right about the brutal power in the mutie's fleshy claw.

"That's right," Reno said, with a smile that was either shy or feeble, depending on how you wanted to look at it. While, rationally, Mildred knew J.B. was right, that no way could the scavvie have wittingly blown their scheme, she was disinclined to give him the benefit of justice, much less doubt. "I mean, I didn't even know you were here. Right?"

I don't trust the little weasel, anyway, she thought.

"How come you keep turning up?" she asked. "I mean, alive. And a step or two ahead of the rotties?"

"Just lucky, I guess," he said, without apparent irony.

"Listen. There's some things I didn't tell you about how this whole shitstorm started."

"No shit," Jak said.

The young man told them how he and his friends, Drygulch and their fiery auburn-haired leader, Lariat, had descended into a broken-open redoubt. What had happened there. And afterward, at their camp at night.

"When Drygulch rose up I could see right off how he'd changed," Reno said. His voice shook like flesh expecting the kiss of a red-hot iron, and his body did likewise. "Right then, I knew what was going on. Don't know how. But I did."

"So ran off and left buddies?" Jak said with a sneer, leaning back against the wall of the basement room with a thump of his shoulders on raw concrete.

Mildred wondered if the room had been dug out and shored with cement post-nuke. She also wondered what it was meant for. It certainly *seemed* like a cell. And it had obviously been here long before Geither Jacks took up residency just a few weeks ago. Was it for gaudy house customers to play out certain dark kinks? Or did it have a more evil purpose?

Whatever its original intent, it was being used for something amply bad now.

"What could I have done? Stayed and got bit, too? Become one of them?"

"Naw, back off the trigger of the blaster, there, Jak," J.B. said. "You been there, you would have done the same thing. Have to be triple-stupe not to. Dark night, it happens to us, you run right off like a jackrabbit, never look back."

Jak appeared mulish but said no more.

"So the cabinet was labeled Prions," Mildred said.

"You know the word?" Reno asked.

She shrugged. "A bit." She didn't want to tell him too much about her actual origins. You never knew what evil uses information like that could be put to. And one thing was sure: the boy had loose lips.

"A prion is a kind of protein that seems to act in ways similar to a virus. It can spread like a virus, and cause its host to produce copies of it. But it doesn't seem to be even a little bit alive. It was implicated in a nasty sickness called mad cow disease, or Creutzfeldt-Jakob syndrome in humans, back before…before the war."

"So could something like that be causing the change?" Reno asked.

"I don't really know." Not my area of expertise, she thought, but chose not to say. "One way or another it looks as if the old-days whitecoats have a lot to answer for."

"True words," Reno said, nodding.

J.B. got up and hobbled to the door. It pained Mildred like the mutie's claw to see him move so like an oldie. He examined the keyhole of the lock beneath the knob.

"Is there a padlock or bolt on the outside, boy?" he asked, without looking back.

"We weren't in any shape to observe details like that when we were brought here," Mildred explained.

"Uh, no. Nothing like that. Just the door lock."

J.B. chuckled and stuck into the hole a pick from the compact kit he'd pulled out of the thick leather of his belt.

"Overconfident stupes," he muttered. "Be out of here like a bullet out of a blaster."

"Guards?" Jak asked.

Reno shrugged. "One or two. Geither—Mr. Jacks—is heading off to some kind of meeting with the baron. He's taking pretty much all his sec men with him."

"All?" Mildred asked in alarm. "John, what if he's pulled back the perimeter guards? What if that paranoid witch Miranda's done likewise? The rotties could be infiltrating the ville right now!"

She heard a decisive click. J.B. tested the knob gently, then turned back with a grin. He put the pick away, then stuck the kit back into its hiding place.

"We best move with purpose, then."

"What about the guards?" Reno asked in alarm. "They still got blasters and orders to shoot us all if we try anything. Isn't that kind of a problem?"

With the resiliency of youth and the intrinsic toughness of whalebone, Jak sprang to his feet. A sliver of blade gleamed in his white fist. Like the lockpick kit, it had been hidden where all but the most intensive search of their clothing would miss it.

"No problem," he said with a chilling smile.

Chapter Twenty-Three

His grizzled beard sunk in the wolf-fur collar of his heavy coat, Perico walked three paces behind his baron. He muttered complaints like water gurgling from a roof gutter in a downpour. She tuned him out.

Miranda was used to not hearing things she didn't want to hear. It was part of being a baron, although it was a skill she'd learned long, long before she ever laid eyes on Sweetwater Junction and its baron, Jeb Sharp.

It was a brisk, blustering morning. Miranda found it bracing. The sun shone from a patch of blue in the sky that dwindled rapidly as thick, evil black clouds blew in from the east. A storm was coming, although from the looks of things it would only be a thunderstorm, or perhaps a late-season blizzard. Not acid rain, yet.

Good, she thought. Things were coming to a head in the ville of Sweetwater Junction. She didn't want anything unexpected to interfere with that.

By nightfall I shall be baron in fact as well as name, she thought. Or staring at the sky with eyes that do not see.

The latter thought didn't dampen her haughty eagerness. She was used to all-or-nothing gambles. If the possibility of failure, no matter how terrible, had ever deterred her, she would've died long ago, poor and desperate.

But of course, she believed in stacking the odds on her side as much as possible. That also contributed to her still being on her legs this nippy late-winter morning.

Citizens thronged around the central plaza and its great fountain. They acted nervous and subdued, which she found appropriate. It was how the rabble *should* behave in the presence of greatness. Of great persons and great events.

"Jacks's bunch is coming from the other side," Stone said. Her sec boss strode beside her, even more monolithic than normal in his black coat and fur cap. "Per our arrangement."

Miranda smiled widely. After learning how they had been manipulated by the outside "mercies" who so fortuitously arrived within a day of one another, the respective heads of the ville's sundered halves had agreed to a public meeting to resolve their differences, in order to meet the mutie threat properly. Miranda had made her own special arrangements. No doubt Jacks had, too.

As for those strange outlanders, and how they had played both sides... Miranda felt her face tighten in a frown. She tried to force it away; frowns caused lines, especially at her age. She knew she was still beautiful. Keeping herself that way became more difficult each day.

No point in dwelling upon the ease with which you were fooled, *chica,* she assured herself. That bullet had left the blaster long since. The present was titanium hard; the future, ultimately, was impossible. Trying to manage the past was beyond even her considerable capability.

And anyway, how could they have known? Ryan, Krysty and Doc weren't the first outlanders who had wandered into the Junction seeking mercie work, nor the last. They were the most coolly competent, which had made them far more attractive than the usual.

Attractive enough, in several ways, to make it worth coddling them by housing them in her palace as her own elite.

She shook off the memory with a tight little movement of her head. *Enough.*

I wish Colt could be here to see this, she thought. But she had insisted he stay behind. Things would get dangerous soon.

If anything happened to her son, her life would have no meaning.

It didn't take Stone's glowering face to clear a path toward the townspeople who blocked the north road. Miranda strode forth with her head held high. People naturally gave way to her certainty. Her superiority. Despite the low circumstances of her birth, she had always known she was born to rule.

They came to where a cordon of sec men in her black armbands held the crowd back from the plaza. They opened up a way for their baron with eyes respectfully downcast. Across the way Jacks likewise came through his green-armbanded ranks, flanked by Coffin and his moving brick wall of a security boss, Brick Finneran.

Miranda bit down hard on her rage at seeing three arch traitors so close together. Coffin had been a personal friend and adviser to her lost Jeb. Baron Jeb had personally given Finneran his first promotion within the ranks of his sec corps. And the unspeakable Jacks...

Hold it in, she ordered herself with a savagery she didn't allow to disturb in the least her placid smile. She had much experience at swallowing her righteous rage. Now was the time to exert control to the utmost, for the sake of her son and all their ville.

By agreement, the two parties swung to meet south of the great fountain and its associated watering stations. Jacks's homely, seamed face split in a smile as the two groups grew near. He extended a hand.

"Miranda," he said. "Welcome to destiny."

Beyond him, her keen eyes spotted movement in the windows of the shops. "Now!" she shouted.

Longblasters poked out of the dark oblongs of windows along the square's south side. Miranda turned to dart for the cover of the fountain's redbrick walls. Stone shouted and pushed her to the ground. He had great strength. The baron went down painfully hard on her right knee, then onto her face.

Gunfire slammed across the square. Stone grunted. His weight slammed down on top of Miranda, crushing her breasts against the cold packed earth and driving the breath from her lungs.

The sec men she had infiltrated into the opposing structures on the square's northern side opened up a beat late. Miranda had intended the same treachery as her archenemy. But to her frustration and rage he had pulled the string first.

LYING FACEDOWN WHERE he'd dived to the ground after giving the signal—extending his hand to the witch as if he actually intended her to shake it—Geither Jacks smiled at the mounded body of his successor. His *most recent* successor, he amended mentally, recalling the explosive fate of the self-proclaimed Captain Jenkins.

Blasterfire roared behind and in front of him. Damn, she had the same idea I did! he thought. I was afraid she'd try something I *didn't* expect.

The first violent volleys from either side gave way to more sporadic crackling of gunfire as those shooters with single-shot weapons, black powder and smokeless alike, ducked into cover to frantically reload.

"Wait!" he shouted from his prone position. "It's over! The baron is dead. I saw her fall with my own eyes!"

It was half a bluff. He had seen her drop, but he hadn't with certainty seen her hit.

"Cease firing!" he yelled. The cry was echoed by Finneran, who also lay on his belly, right behind his leader.

Jacks sensed more than heard a commotion to his right. He glanced back that way. Coffin rolled around on the ground, clutching a shin shattered by a bullet, and moaning. His normally dark face was a color not that different from the clouds gathering overhead.

Jacks grimaced. The bitch had a lot to pay for. She should *hope* she was dead.

And now he decided she had to be. At the best of times her temper was like a rabid giant hound's, straining constantly to break its leash, or simply to take off, dragging its owner helplessly behind. It was that fiery Mex-land nature, mixed with a woman's inherent emotionalism. If Miranda Sharp were still alive, she'd be shrieking in fury like a wounded horse.

In response to the repeated orders to cease firing, the shooting actually died away on both sides. Jacks grinned openly as he rose to his feet. If Miranda really was chilled or badly wounded, he knew, none of her people wanted to be caught still shooting at him. With the so-called baron gone, he was unquestionably master of Sweetwater Junction. Her fat, spoiled fool of a son meant nothing.

Jacks came up holding his hands over his head in an attitude of triumph. "It's over!" he shouted, his words echoing back to him off black-eyed building faces of stone and wood and brick. "I'm your baron now! I will lead you out of the—"

He saw the quiescent, black-suited bulk of Stone shift. Then fire stabbed yellow from beneath the dead sec boss. Before Jacks could react, sledgehammer impacts took him in the gut, low down on the left, and then smashed into his short ribs on the right.

He lost control of his legs and toppled to the ground. Pain consumed him like fire even before he hit.

"DARK NIGHT!" J.B. exclaimed as shooting broke out across no-man's land.

With everybody in Sweetwater Junction either thronging the square or lying low, the three escaped prisoners had easily made their way into a potter's shop on the corner where the west road hit the square. It stood next door to the two-story stump of the sniper tower whose upper floors J.B.'s booby had vaporized.

Jacks's ambushing sec men had hidden along the square's north edge, so the one-story stone potter's shop was empty. From the south and east windows, Mildred, J.B. and Jak had a ringside view of the drama playing out around the fountain.

Wriggling out from under her dead bodyguard, as lithe as a rattler, Miranda reared up to aim what looked like a Luger at the fallen Jacks, who was clutching his belly in agony and kicking at the hard dirt with the heels of his boots. A big-shouldered guy with short grizzled hair and a beard to match darted out from behind the fountain and dragged Miranda bodily back behind it as bullets kicked craters around where she had knelt. Mildred could see her fallen bodyguard's black suit coat twitch as bullets struck it.

The front room where the escapees lurked had a stout table with a potter's wheel on it, and a big jar partially thrown still rested on it. It had gotten to the stage of a truncated cone that put Mildred in mind of a nuclear plant's cooling tower, before being abandoned during the commotion and confused street fighting that followed Jacks's abortive coup attempt. The room had the smell of clay and slip, like the soil it derived from, but slightly acrid.

"Looks as if they're settling into one of those hesitation waltzes," J.B. said, "like when we found Brick's bunch after they made their play at Miranda and her kid."

"We should move on, John," Mildred said. Her every nerve danced with urgency. "We need to rescue Ryan, Krysty and Doc."

"Naw," he said with that infuriating bland assurance of his. "We need to sit right here and keep an eye on things in case the rotties bust in. Jak, you go get Ryan and the others out."

Jak showed white teeth in his white face, bobbed his head then turned and slipped out of the room.

"We have to go with him!"

"He can get 'em out," J.B. said.

"But the baron's guards—"

"Are all here, Millie. Don't you see? Both sides pulled in everybody they could spare for this shindig, each hoping it was pullin' a fast one on the other."

"Everybody—" She felt her stomach lurch as if she'd been gut-punched. "You don't mean the ville perimeter guards?"

"I surely do."

"But that'd be—that'd be sheer lunacy! It's as good as inviting the rotties in!"

"Barons and people who want to be barons go blank when they get a whiff of more power or wealth. Can't see past the ends of their own noses."

He smiled. "Which is why we gotta stay right here and keep tabs on things."

She drew in a deep breath and opened her mouth, then said nothing.

After a moment she sighed. "You're right, John." Mildred turned to watch out the front window once more.

"Ryan! Krysty! Dr. Tanner!"

Ryan raised his head. He sat with his back against the cold outer wall of their basement cell. The warm weight of Krysty, slumped against him with his coat covering her, shifted away from him.

"Colt?" he heard her call.

He was having more trouble than usual becoming conscious and sharp. Got something to do with all those rifle butts and boots dancing on your head, mebbe, he thought muzzily.

"Are you all right?" The boy's voice was muffled by the solid wood of the door.

"Splendid, lad," he heard Doc call. The scholar's voice was more slurred than was normal. "Absolutely splendid."

They heard bolts thrown, and then a clatter from the lock.

"I'll have you out of there in a moment," Colt called.

The door swung open. What walked in first wasn't plump Sharp Jr., but a middle-aged sec man with his shirt-tail out and his sparse hair wild on his head. He looked suspiciously as if he'd been rousted from a good nap.

"You three are witnesses," he said a little more loudly than necessary. "I had no choice. Boy held a gun to my head."

In marched Colt, holding a gun to the guard's head. Actually, he had the 1911 Colt, the same as or identical to the one Ryan had been teaching him to shoot with just the day before, held out in front of him with both hands and pointed at the back of the sec man's balding head. He wore a white shirt and black leather riding pants. He might have cut a ridiculous figure without that big handblaster.

In Ryan's experience, it wasn't wise to laugh at someone holding a blaster. Especially when he held it with such authority. Ryan's teaching was either that good or the kid was a quick study.

Ryan shook his head, which made it feel as if somebody was whacking the back of his skull all over again. He got to his feet as steadily as he could. Krysty pressed her hip against him for mutual support.

"What are you doing, Colt?" Doc asked.

The old man had been lying on his back on the low bench against the wall that was the room's sole item of furniture. This wasn't the torture chamber where Miranda had whipped Krysty, but a holding cell across the hall. Now he got to his feet, a little more confidently than his companions had, or so Ryan thought. The one-eyed man suspected the professor hadn't been beaten as comprehensively as he had. Not because the vengeful baron or her loyalist sec men had any consideration for Doc's apparent age, but because they reckoned he *needed* less of a beating to be disabled.

The boy moistened his lips before defiantly announcing, "I'm getting you out of here."

Chapter Twenty-Four

"Lad," Doc said, "why would you want to go and do a thing like that? It was your own mother who put us here."

"She was wrong about you! I know it!"

"No, she wasn't," Krysty said through her teeth. She was pulling on her clothes, her jaw set against the pain.

"Krysty," Ryan said, "that might not be the best way to go about—"

She waved him off. The sight of blood dried to a brownish hue on her white hand stilled him as much as the gesture. His reflex was to jump the boy, his words—and his blaster—notwithstanding, and seize him as a hostage. He stamped it down hard. His rational mind told him that would be triple-stupe. And he trusted Krysty's intuition.

The boy's face worked like a couple of fists in a pillowcase.

"My mother," he gritted out, "is not a...stable person. She wants what's best for the ville. And me. But she gets blinded by her own anger sometimes."

"We did deceive her," Krysty said evenly.

"Yes! Because you came here to warn us about the rotties. And you knew she wouldn't believe you. But you were right! But you...you pissed her off, hotter than nuke-red. And now she's gone to do something stupe with Jacks!"

"Fireblast," Ryan said. "So beyond letting us loose, what's on your mind, Colt?"

The kid's chest swelled out past his gut as he drew in a decisive breath. "We're going to make sure the rotties don't take this ville."

"MAMA!" COLT YIPPED as blasterfire boiled up from the center of town. The fountain was still out of sight, since they didn't want to walk right down the main north–south drag in plain view of the square.

Ryan's hard grip on the youth's shoulder prevented him from rabbiting toward the sound of shooting. A vast crowd of crows circled above the square and its public fountain like a black whirlwind.

"He lacks little of courage, my dear Ryan," Doc said, "if still much of sense."

A stiffening breeze ruffled Ryan's shaggy hair. He held his head up even though the wind's icy fingers managed to probe even beneath his eyepatch and wake a dull throb of pain in the socket. The bruises and scrapes he'd suffered being battered into a stupor hurt double-bad now. But he was damned if he'd let the world—much less Miranda Sharp—see evidence of that in his face or bearing.

Well, other than the puffiness, bruising and split lip, of course. Nothing he could do there.

They had the streets to themselves this early morning. Ryan guessed most of the citizens were inside, heads down, knowing that whatever happened on the main square, all they could gain personally from any kind of involvement, or mebbe even seeing too much, was a triple-load of grief.

Floating on the wind he heard a *dee-dee-dee* like a killdeer flying nearby. It wasn't an uncommon winter sound here on the plains. Just not in the middle of a ville, with the only birds in view being crows. He grinned.

"Come on out, Jak," he called.

"Who that?" a voice asked from somewhere unseen. "Baron's son?"

"Yes," Colt said, not even slowing his stride. "I'm going to—to talk some sense into my mother."

Krysty caught Ryan's eye and shrugged, wincing as she did. Personally, Ryan wouldn't undertake to pound sense into Miranda with a nuke-powered pile driver. But plans began to coalesce from the myriad contingencies that swarmed in his mind like the crows above the firefight. The boy might yet be the key to saving the ville.

And, most importantly, the asses of Ryan and his companions. Which, after all, was the whole purpose of the enterprise.

Jak vaulted a board fence to join them. "Where're Mildred and J.B.?" Krysty asked.

"By square. Watching shitstorm come down."

"How did you come to be there?" Doc asked.

"Thrown in jail. J.B. picked lock. Chilled guards, grabbed gear, blew out." He frowned. "Glasses kid in cell with us. Told about rotties, first."

"Reno?" Krysty asked.

"Fireblast!" Ryan said. "That must be what blew our cover. He told his story to fucking Jacks, who recognized us in the tale."

"And told Miranda," Krysty said. "They must have used that as a pretext to set up their meeting today."

"Which, predictably, has ended in violence," Doc added.

The initial burst of blasterfire had died down. Now Ryan heard shouting and the fresh rippling of shots from the square.

"Come on!" Colt shouted. This time he was too far from Ryan to grab. He cut left toward the main road that ran from the palace to the square.

"Ryan?" Doc asked.

He shrugged again. "We follow. Kid's our best card right now. And he seems set on playing himself, here and now."

Colt Sharp stopped stock-still in the middle of the wide dirt road and screamed.

WATCHING FROM THE SHOP'S east window, Mildred had to give Brick Finneran credit. He was right on Jacks after Miranda shot him. He scooped his boss, groaning and doubled up around at least one gut wound, into his treetrunk arms and carried the tall straw-haired man toward cover.

The man's big body rocked as bullets slammed him from behind. He managed to make it to the shelter of a stack of barrels under the overhang of a porch fronting on the square. The wooden containers had to have been filled with something fairly solid, for Coffin had dragged himself behind them, and he and several sec men successfully sheltered there.

The black man waved an arm and shouted. Two sec men jumped out to take hold of their wounded boss. Finneran fell on his face and didn't move.

In low, quick bursts of words between high points in the shooting, Mildred reported to J.B., who was keeping an eye on Miranda's side from the south window. Despite the blasterfire, she was worried about being overheard by Jacks loyalists angling for better shots. After Jak left, she had shut the rear door and shoved the big table against it. And the front door was locked, so they'd have at least some warning if enemies tried to come into their hideout.

J.B. listened, nodding. Then Mildred saw his eyes widen behind his wire-rimmed lenses.

"Dark night, look!" he whispered. "Rotties! They're in the ville!"

Mildred saw a sudden flurry of wild action from where Miranda's people had dragged her to cover behind the fountain. Shrieks of rage that had to have come from the baron turned quickly to those of pain laced with mind-melting fear.

At first glimpse the gray figures shambling into the square from the east didn't look anything too out of the ordinary. Until you noticed some were walking obliviously into the killzone of a full-on firefight, something you'd have to be deaf *and* blind to miss.

Or dead.

The ville folk who'd been bold, or stupe, enough to turn out to watch the Great Conciliation reunite the happy ville of Sweetwater Junction had taken cover when blasters joined the negotiations. Now Mildred saw commotion and heard shrieks as the rotties found them.

Miranda erupted from her hiding place with rotties clinging to her by claws and jaws like wolves taking down a bull bison. Why they had homed so directly in on her Mildred would never learn. There was so much meat on the hoof here. Mildred would've expected the changed to focus first on the warm pumping blood of the wounded.

Men and women rotties alike beset the furiously struggling baron. In age they ranged from a twelve-year-old boy with his left arm missing from elbow on, to a white-haired granny who had the four or so teeth remaining in her head clamped firmly on Miranda's left shoulder. Some had been dead so long they had rotted almost to pieces; others displayed gaping, bloodless wounds. One thick dude had a blue-gray face whose width and impressive sagginess suggested he'd been morbidly obese. But his paunch and the entrails it had contained had been eaten away almost to the spine. Mildred wasn't sure how he managed to stay upright.

But Miranda Sharp was a strong woman, and adrenaline had turbocharged her strength and speed. The toggle action atop her antique handblaster was locked up in a little triangle, confirming it was both a Luger and out of ammo. But she lashed out ferociously with it, hammering a woman in the forehead so hard the rottie went down as if shot.

There were still too many of the changed for the baron, for all her strength and fury. With her black hair whipping out of the tight bun it had been wrapped in, she went down, screaming like a red-tailed hawk and fighting like a badger. Mildred saw the flash of a knife in her hand as they swarmed over her.

The roar of J.B.'s shotgun snapped Mildred's attention back to their hideout. She had been so focused on the baron's dramatic last stand she hadn't even noticed a rottie wandering right up the street in front of the potter's shop until J.B. blew its head off.

"Mebbe we should join the party?" he asked, racking the action.

For answer she raised the ZKR, lined up the sights and shot one of Miranda's attackers through the head from a good fifty yards off.

It wasn't so much she was trying to save Miranda—who was beyond help, anyway—as that was the first target to offer itself. But now Mildred faced a new problem: the rotties had gotten in among their intended victims so thoroughly it was hard to target one without hitting another.

J.B. saw her hesitation. "Go ahead and shoot," he said. "If people get bit, a .38 hole or two's gonna be the least of their worries!"

WITH DESPERATE ENERGY but not much skill, Colt Sharp ran toward where his mother had fallen. His arms and legs went any which way, like the limbs of a newborn moose calf, and he was slow. But he was dead set on running right into the killzone.

"Jak!" Ryan rapped. He didn't have to add a command.

Hair streaming behind like a snow-white pennon, the albino teen ran after the baron's boy, seemingly weightless. He ran him down like a coyote after a rabbit, raced past him, dropped to a crouch and tripped him with a leg sweep.

"Oh, dear," Krysty said as the chubby boy sprawled onto the hard dirt and slid four feet on his face. It still was a lot healthier than running right into a battle.

"Cover," Ryan ordered, unlimbering the Steyr from his back. Racing out of the palace with Colt as a guarantee of safe passage, the companions had left backpacks behind and just grabbed up weapons and ammo.

Krysty and Doc split to the left side of the street. Jak dragged the weeping and feebly struggling Colt Sharp the same way a mountain lion would drag a chilled pronghorn. Ryan ducked behind a pile of wood crates and aimed the longblaster over the top of them.

He laid the scope on Miranda just as she went down. There wasn't any point in trying to shoot the rotties off her. They were biting her all over. He thought briefly of putting a bullet in her brain to end it for her, but decided she hadn't exactly earned any breaks from him.

Besides, the changed still on the hunt for flesh were the real threat.

"Moving, lover!" he heard Krysty call. He took his eye from the rifle sight to look across the street. Snub-nosed revolver in hand, Krysty raced down the north road. She ducked behind the parked horse-type wag, minus horse, where Jak had pulled Colt. The albino youth had pushed the heir to the ville down on his back and was sitting on him while he looked for targets around the wag's wooden side.

Kneeling beside the youths, Krysty bent her head to speak earnestly to Colt. Her prehensile red hair writhed around her cheeks.

Ryan looked back through the sight and began popping rottie heads like blood balloons.

FRANTICALLY, MIRANDA'S sec men blasted and beat the remaining rotties off their baron. She lay rolling to and fro in pain as townspeople and sec men from both sides engaged the horrifying creatures in a brief, savage battle.

Shooting from their window into the square, Mildred and J.B. did what they could. Mildred tried to pick off rotties directly threatening the living. J.B., who was shooting buck instead of solid shot and had to contend with a wide pellet spread at this range, blasted isolated rotties.

Just as she wondered how many of the creatures had got in, Mildred saw no more targets. The people and sec men of Sweetwater Junction were tending to their wounded fellows, or just standing around staring at one another in amazed horror at the sudden invasion of their ville.

To Mildred's astonishment, Geither Jacks walked back into the square.

For a moment she thought he had to have been wearing a bulletproof vest. But no. He pressed a handkerchief against his side. Blood gleamed red on his knuckles.

Mildred was sure he'd been hit twice. Miranda's first copper-jacketed 9 mm slug might have gone through his lower torso without puncturing his peritoneum, but she doubted it. She knew Jacks had scavvied antibiotics at his headquarters; he wasn't necessarily going to die from the inevitable peritonitis if his body cavity had been penetrated. But if that had happened, he had to be in brutal pain.

Nobody said Gate to Hell Jacks wasn't hard-core, she thought. She lined her sights up on his straw-haired head.

"John," she said, "should I ice the fucker?" She could feel once again the horrific caress of Levon's meat pincer, and burned to take in the last few ounces of slack in the ZKR's finely tuned competition trigger.

"Hold off, Millie," he said softly. "Mebbe he just now turned into our best shot at staying alive. Much as I hate to say it."

"People of Sweetwater Junction!" Geither Jacks shouted. "Listen to me, your new baron!"

That stilled the hyperkinetic conversation that had replaced blasterfire in the square. Pale faces turned toward the tall man, who held one hand to his side and the other bloody palm in the air.

"I'm in command here now," Jacks declared. "You all see it. Baron Miranda is dead. I'm all that stands between you and anarchy. Between you and these terrible creatures who came to destroy us, our children, our peaceful way of life."

"Nuke take you," a hoarse male voice shouted, "the baron ain't dead! She's just wounded."

"She's been bitten by the horrors," Jacks said. "Sweetwater Junction, you need to know what that means. It's a sentence of death! She's gone."

The silence that followed the pronouncement boomed with the rising wind and crackled with the cries of crows circling overhead, impatient for the fresh feast laid out below them. Some, bolder than their already bold comrades, lighted on chills with upturned faces to pick at that greatest of delicacies, human eyeballs.

Mildred saw the ville folk turn heads toward one another, heard a mutter of consternation. She didn't doubt everyone in Sweetwater Junction had heard the story of the rotties by now, had learned of the terrible way in which Miranda's men had confirmed the unimaginable reality that such a pestilence existed, and now threatened to sweep their ville away in blood and terror.

"Baron Jacks," she heard a voice call out. The throb of agony in it only lent it strength and power. "Baron Jacks! Baron Jacks!"

"Coffin," J.B. said, feeding fresh shells, contemporary reloads with brown, waxed-paper hulls, into the M-4000's magazine. "Good man. Too bad he's got a prick for a master."

The crowd began to take up the wounded man's chant.

Mildred stared at her partner. "What do we do now, John?" she asked as the chant gained volume and conviction. "Saying those words would blister my tongue."

Maybe the people saw the ville's civil war had to end now or the rotties would end it for them, she thought. Maybe it was plain self-interest, backing a contender after the race was won. Which in the Deathlands was always by far the best time to do it.

"Do we have to acclaim the bastard, too?"

Chapter Twenty-Five

"Now," Jacks said. His voice was clear and strong, as if power was the best painkiller, which it likely was, Mildred reflected. "Some changes got to be made to combat this new and terrible menace. Gone are the days of slack. We must impose absolute discipline. Absolute—"

"No!"

The voice that pealed out from the north side of the square was that of a young male, cracking with adolescence. It matched the figure that stalked out from beside the fountain—a youth in his mid to late teens, curly blond hair tousled in the wind, wearing fine clothes that seemed mussed and soiled as if he'd been rolling recently in the dirt. He breathed heavily. His face was plump, red and twisted with passion.

In his hands he held a big angular semiauto handblaster. The 1911's squared-off muzzle was wavering badly as the youth's arms shook, with emotion or fatigue or both.

"I'm the baron of Sweetwater Junction now," the youth shouted. "I'm Colt Sharp, son of the man you treacherously murdered. Now you murdered my mother, too. I am baron here!"

"But Jacks didn't murder his mom, actually," J.B. murmured. "Close to the other way around, in fact."

"Hush, now, John. He's on a roll."

Jacks showed the youth a sneering grin. "You? Baron of Sweetwater Junction? Don't make me laugh, jelly roll.

You can't even hold that piece steady. Who's gonna believe you can strong-arm this ville?"

"I am the baron by right," Colt Sharp declared. He walked past his fallen mother toward his rival without a sideways glance that Mildred could see.

Jacks barked a laugh. "Over my chilled body."

"That's my intention!"

"You? Shoot me?"

Jacks took out a cigar and struck a match with his thumb. He puffed the cigar alight.

"You don't have the balls to pull the trigger, boy."

His answer was loud enough to make Mildred flinch. Geither Jacks took a step back. He looked down to see a dark stain spread rapidly in the middle of his blue shirt. He raised a look of ashy astonishment to the youth.

Colt Sharp fired again. Jacks jerked as another 230-grain slug rammed home in his rib cage. The chubby boy was walking forward, his face now as white as sun-bleached bone.

He pumped two more shots into the tall, lean man. Jacks fell back a step at each one. His haughtiness was long gone. He looked appalled now.

He bent over, pressing a hand to one of the new wet wounds in his chest. Colt marched right up to him.

For a moment Jacks stared down into his palm, filled to overflowing with his own bright red blood. He looked up at Colt.

"No," he said, "please. Wait—"

Colt was close enough that the muzzle-flash licked Jacks's imploring eyes with yellow fire. The bullet slammed between them. The whole back of the man's skull blew out in a spray of blood and chunks.

Gate to Hell Jacks fell down on his face. A crow immediately settled on his nape and began to eat his remaining brains like cherries from a bowl.

"Baron Sharp!" a clear, high feminine voice sang out.

"BARON SHARP!"

Ryan's single eye turned in surprise to Krysty, marching by his side. They followed the young heir by twenty paces. The redhead had her fist in the air.

"Baron Sharp!" she cried again. "Baron Sharp!"

One by one the crowd took up the cry, until it beat like the wind over the lone figure of the youth who stood staring down at the man he'd just chilled, oblivious to everything but his own thoughts.

"Baron Sharp!" It was Perico, rising from shelter behind the fountain. He tossed a single unreadable look at the three outlanders walking down the street toward him from the north. Then, squaring his wide shoulders, he marched up to the youth, grabbed his gun hand and thrust it and blaster aloft. "Baron Sharp."

"WELL, ISN'T THAT a relief," J.B. said.

The plump kid shook himself like a wet dog. The stocky gray-bearded guy let go of his arm and stepped back.

"Amnesty to all those who swear to serve me as rightful baron!" Colt cried.

"Smart move, kid," Mildred said. "You might actually pull this off. If it, you know, *can* be pulled off."

"Come on, Mildred," J.B. said, readjusting his hat on his head. "Let's go greet the new order here in Sweetwater Junction. Then we gotta get busy, unless we all want to wake up rotties tomorrow morning!"

GEITHER JACKS'S GOONS all practically jumped out of their skins, dropping weapons and throwing their fists in the air, each trying to drown out the other shouting, "Baron Sharp!"

Perico stood by his new baron's side, his head inclined and beard wagging as if he spoke urgently.

"Tryin' to get the kid to put the blaster away before he hurts someone," Ryan suggested.

But Colt Sharp refused. He turned away from his new chief adviser and marched back the way he had come.

The crowd went silent again. Entertainment wasn't easy to come by in the Deathlands. They knew impending drama when they saw it.

"Hold me, Colt," his mother said, extending an arm from where she lay.

Ryan went stiff. "If she bites him, we're fucked." He had slung his rifle, so he reached for his SIG.

Krysty gripped his arm. "Leave it," she said. "She hasn't changed yet."

It came to Ryan's tongue to ask how she knew, but he didn't voice the question. When Krysty spoke with that kind of certainty, she *did* know. That was enough for him.

Mostly.

Colt knelt and cradled his mother's head on his lap. Tears streamed down his round cheeks.

"People of Sweetwater Junction," she shouted, pulling away and rearing up slightly, then using his knee to prop herself. "Listen to me, your baron."

Little exclamations of horror burst like squibs from the crowd. Miranda was in bad shape. The rottie pack had ripped her clothes to shreds. They had raked and ripped mouthfuls from her firm olive flesh, from the muscles of arms and shoulders and the flesh of her breasts. She looked as if she had bathed in blood.

"I almost feel sorry for the bitch," Ryan rasped.

"I do feel sorry for her," Krysty said.

Ryan glanced at his woman. Even given her quick healing ability, her pale skin still bore the marks of the whipping Miranda Sharp had given her. Yet her words were
heartfelt, sincere.

Ryan put his left arm around her.

Then with his right he whipped out the SIG and fired.

Two burly men wearing green armbands were approaching Colt and his mother from the south, supporting a lean
black man between them. The left leg of the man's overalls
was soaked with dark blood from below the knee down.
Seeing Ryan's move, his eyes flew wide.

He stretched a desperate hand toward Colt and shouted,
"Baron! Look out!"

Unnoticed by everyone, a rottie who had mauled Miranda lay facedown right behind the youngster. It had once
been a gaunt, middle-aged woman. Apparently the baron's
sec men had only broken its spine.

Raising its head, opening its jaws, it had reached a bluish hand toward Colt's ankle from behind.

Ryan's shot took the rottie in the temple. The creature
dropped to the dirt.

Colt looked back at Ryan and nodded once.

"I was wrong about the outlanders, Colt, darling," his
mother said, loudly enough for a good half of the square
to hear. "Wrong about the rotties. And it's cost me everything. Everything except the thing that means most in the
world to me. You, my darling. You."

"Mother, no—"

"He is the baron now!" she cried, sweeping the crowd
with her fierce black eyes. "He will lead you through this!
Serve him well and you'll...live."

The effort drained her. Her head slumped toward her
ravaged breasts.

"Somebody bring a stretcher," Colt shouted desperately. "Get Lamellar. She needs attention, fast!"

"No!" Her head snapped up. "Didn't you learn anything here, *mijo?*"

Colt recoiled as if she'd slapped him. Miranda's voice had the same whip crack that had made her son cringe so often in Ryan's short acquaintance of the family. He frowned. If she de-nutted the poor bastard *now...*

"I've been bitten by those things," Miranda said in a voice vibrant with pain. "You know what that means. Didn't our new friends tell us?"

He shook his head. "Mother, there's got to be some other way."

"There is no other way! There is only one. Now, do what you have to do, my son. And let this be an example to everyone. Because should anyone be bitten, be it friend or loved one—there is...no other...way!"

Still he hesitated. "Give your mother a kiss, boy," Miranda said gently.

Colt bent his wet face to kiss her cheek. She grabbed him and planted a hard kiss on his face. Then with a sigh she sank back against him.

"Do it fast for Mama, Colt, dear," she said. "It hurts so. And—I can feel it coming. The change."

Colt stood up and hesitated only a few heartbeats.

Then he thrust the handblaster downward and fired a single shot.

Chapter Twenty-Six

With a screech a small pallid figure flew out of the closet as if launched on springs. A shattering shotgun blast caught it in midair. Its head blew apart.

"Don't get any of that crap in your mouth, Ryan," J.B. said, chambering a fresh shell. "Don't know what you might catch."

Black ooze spattered his own face and glasses.

Ryan grunted, his heart hammering in his chest. He kept his finger on the trigger of his SIG-Sauer handblaster.

He'd left his longblaster behind. This was close-quarters work now. A sniping longblaster was as useless in this house-to-house rottie mop-up as tits on a boar hog.

"Thought I was ready for it," he said. "But it still gave me a fright. Damn, I hate this."

The smell of mildew and unwashed human bodies in the little shack's dim interior was crowded out by the stinks of burned propellant and lubricant, and the stench of decomposing human flesh. That reek had clued them in to the rottie's presence when they'd poked their heads inside. It was their only real edge in hunting down those who somehow retained enough of a spark of self-preservation to hide from the otherwise total slaughter of the changed who had broken into Sweetwater Junction. And it only applied to those who had rotted enough to start getting ripe.

Ryan nudged the small corpse in its simple shift, which

ground-in blood and guts had turned the same decay-bluish-gray as the rottie's neck and bone-thin arms.

"Especially when it's a kid."

"Ain't half as bad as what Millie and Krysty have to do," J.B. said.

"Yeah," Ryan said. "That sucks triple-hard."

The two women were engaged in something a taut-lipped Mildred called triage. That meant examining the wounded. The ones who had received bites had to be chilled. No matter who they were.

Including children like the one J.B. had just blasted. Even before they changed.

Meanwhile Doc and Jak were teamed up, also performing the risky and grisly search-and-destroy task Ryan and the Armorer were engaged in. It might not have been the optimal pairing, especially since Jak and Doc were prone to jaw at each other. But they knew how to buckle down to the task at hand, and their strengths and weaknesses complemented each other pretty solidly.

For Ryan's part, it felt good to have J.B. watching his back again. The two men made a fast search of the shack. It was shotgun-style, and looked as if a large number of people had lived there at one point. As far as they knew, nobody had been inside when the rottie child had gotten in.

No one knew how many rotties had broken into the ville in the first place. Several dozen had promptly attacked the greatest concentration of food: the crowd in the square watching Miranda and Jacks hold their final showdown. Fortunately, the humans had fought back vigorously and effectively, putting the rotties on the ground before they got their teeth into too many folks.

Once Colt was in command—of himself as well as the ville, after shooting his own mother in the head—his first order had been to make sure of the *other* fallen rotties. The one Ryan had finished off as it was about to latch its jaws on Colt's ankle was a pretty stark example. Fortunately, the finishing-off task could be readily done by ville folk armed with clubs or axes.

Colt, along with Ryan and the companions, had meanwhile rushed to the east gate, to find the skeleton guard either eaten or gone and presumably changed. Nobody had a clue as to how they had been overwhelmed without raising enough of a fuss to attract attention even from the spectacle in the center of the ville. A single shot loosed off would have done it.

Unless, J.B. pointed out, it had happened while a lot more people were shooting at each other across the fountain. That would've covered up the sounds of even a decent-size little firefight the quarter-mile or so away.

Several rotties struggling over the wire fence were quickly dealt with. None could be seen on the flat land beyond, although in fact the horizon lay perhaps a mile away, where a small rise crested. Ryan was still glad Colt had heeded his advice to send sec teams double-quick to the other gates, as well as to patrolling the perimeter.

Miranda and Jacks had indeed drawn most of their sec forces off for their confrontation. Everyone was lucky, Ryan reckoned, that bit of classic baronial shortsightedness hadn't wound up with all of them at ambient temperature by now. Though not necessarily just lying there quietly, staring at the clouds.

Which were beginning to take on an ugly and suggestive mustard tinge. Acid rain storms on their way, the locals had muttered. Harbinger of spring in Sweetwater Junction.

The breeze outside was still cold, and stiff enough to blow away the lingering smell of long-past death, when Ryan and J.B. emerged, blinking, into the cloud-filtered sunlight. Fortunately, the wind blew from the west. Otherwise it might have brought the stink of the horde everyone now knew for sure was coming their way.

A little girl waited outside. She wore a shapeless linsey-woolsey shirt and canvas pants. The only way they could tell she was a girl was that her brown hair was done in pigtails.

"Baron Colt wants to see you down at the fountain," she said, "pronto."

THE SPORADIC POPPING of shots from the south clued them in to what was going on even before they reached Baron Sharp's command post, in Bill Itomaru's carpentry shop, where the south road entered the square.

"That'll be Jacks's grammaw forted up and defying the world," J.B. said. "Also that fat maggot mutie bastard, Levon."

He flashed a taut grin. "Wouldn't half mind settling up with that three-armed bastard."

"Yeah." Ryan had gotten a quick account of what had befallen the three friends who'd wound up in Jacks's camp. None had offered details. He hadn't asked for any.

He already knew the drill.

When they reached the carpentry shop, which was the only building fronting the square to have had its old bullet holes patched—although today's fresh crop remained open—Colt Sharp wasn't there. A sec man in a black Sharp armband told them the new baron had headed south to Jacks's former headquarters.

"Last time I saw that dude he had on a green armband," J.B. remarked as they walked toward where a heavily armed crowd had gathered near the huge gaudy house.

"Reckon a lot have made that switch today," Ryan said. "As long as they stay switched until we get the rotties squared away, that's ace with me."

The crowd, it turned out, was standing a block away from Jacks's HQ. "They keep taking potshots at us," Perico told the new arrivals.

The burly graybeard hadn't apologized for his late mistress's treatment of Ryan and company. Then again, he hadn't been present for any of it. With Miranda chilled and Colt at least onboard to fight the changed menace, Ryan was willing to let bygones be.

He'd forgiven worse in his time. Or at least agreed to let it slide.

"It's that crazy old lady, Grammaw Jacks," Perico explained. "She's holed up in there with a few diehards and Geither's freak pet torturer. Says she'll never surrender. Also, she says we've been chilling the wounded, and she's given sanctuary to some of them."

Ryan and J.B. stared at each other.

"Oh, shit," the Armorer said.

"Something's going down!" a man shouted. He showed no weapons and appeared to be a civilian, not a sec man.

Once Colt Sharp proclaimed himself baron, the ville folk had turned out in droves. Part of it, Ryan calculated, was simple ass-covering, showing visible support of the person who already had all Sweetwater Junction's sec men under his banner except the holdouts in there with Jacks's crazy grammaw. But to Ryan most people seemed genuinely enthusiastic about Colt Sharp, if for no other reason than they were sick of civil war. Not to mention Miranda Sharp and her archenemy, both of whom had the disposition of yellowjackets on Jolt.

Ryan, J.B. and Perico reached the cross street north of the Royal Flush. A few feet up the road Colt stood surrounded by four sec men, one of whom, at least, had been a Jacks man. The new baron was acting like the overexcited kid he was. The bodyguards were wisely keeping him from sticking himself in the line of fire.

When they reached the corner, J.B. strolled on into the intersection. At Ryan's grunt of caution he said, "None of those boys can shoot for sour owl-shit."

Nobody shot at him at all. "There is some kind of fuss going on," he reported. "You can see past the curtains."

Ryan shrugged and stepped out beside his friend. As he did, yellow flame flared behind a ground floor window.

"Uh-oh," he said. "Somebody busted a lantern."

A moment later a sec man staggered out. His hair had a scorched look, and Ryan thought his eyebrows were gone. His shirt was tattered and his arms ran with blood.

"The chills!" he screamed in the voice of a man whose mind has gone mad from unendurable terror. "The chills are walking! They—"

Shots cracked from windows above. Bullets kicked up dirt around the dazed man's boots. The shreds of his shirt flapping, he spun and gazed wildly up as if in confusion.

Then his head nodded violently forward, accompanied by a spray of blood. He dropped.

Ryan saw Hedders, the earnest young Miranda loyalist, lowering a lever-action carbine. "He was bit," the young man said.

Ryan's jaw tightened. Hedders had been one of those who'd beaten him and strung Krysty up for Miranda to play with. He knew it was the kid's job, which didn't matter a spent casing.

Mebbe I'll settle up with you after this rottie mayhem's behind us, he thought. If we both are still standing.

The gaudy house's first-floor interior took light pretty quickly, then flames showed on the second floor. One sec man clambered out a window there and onto the top of the ornate white portico over the entryway. A rattle of blaster-fire shot up from the street and he fell.

A couple more sec men jumped from higher windows. One rolled around screaming, with part of his thighbone sticking out a tear in his trousers like a jagged yellow spear. The other just lay on his back with eyes open, his neck or back broken. Both got shot up some until Perico shouted to the men in the street to quit wasting ammo.

A peculiar whistling roar came from the open front door. Backlit by garish fire, a vast, bulky figure appeared just inside it. It thrashed and struggled mightily.

"Levon," J.B. said, and this time his voice wasn't laid-back at all. It cracked like a blaster. "Jacks's torturer. He's so big and fat he's having trouble getting out the door."

"Especially with rotties hanging all over him," Ryan said. He saw gray hands clutching at the stocky figure.

Then a weird pale moon-face appeared in the doorway as Levon remembered to duck under the lintel. Despite Perico's earlier command, a volley of blasterfire cracked out. The three-armed mutie bellowed, staggered back, fell.

"Seems like former Jacks boys were shooting as enthusiastically as Miranda's crew," Ryan said.

Supine, the vast misshapen form thrashed on the floorboards of the gaudy house's foyer. Flames enveloped it. Levon's roars became high-pitched screams.

"Being on fire doesn't seem to dampen the rotties' appetites any," Ryan observed. He could see the changed ripping mouthfuls from the wounded mutie despite the flames that charred and melted their lifeless flesh.

"Wish Mildred could be here," J.B. said.

Ryan looked at him. "Thought she was still on the squeamish side."

"Not in this case."

At last Levon's howls and struggles subsided as the

smoke finished him. A mad screech drew Ryan's eye to the fourth and top floor of the gaudy house, where what looked like a khaki prune with a cotton ball on top was stuck out from a window right beneath the roof's white painted scrollwork.

"And there you see Geither Jacks's grammaw," the Armorer said.

"Lovely," Ryan muttered.

"You pricks!" she shrieked. "Burning an old lady out of her home!"

"It was your own fool sec men," someone shouted back, "fighting with the rotties you done brought inside, you old stupe."

"Lies! All lies! You murdered my poor boy, who was the light and only hope of this ville! And you're all going to die! All...going...to...die!"

The last syllable rose into a protracted shriek as decaying, blue-skinned arms seized her and dragged her back into the room. She screamed for about a minute as gray smoke first seeped, then boiled out the window.

As near as Ryan could make out, the rotties chilled her before the flames found her.

"Least she won't be coming back as one of *them*," he said. "Not that it wouldn't be a pleasure putting a bullet through that face."

"Still," J.B. said, cleaning his glasses with a handkerchief, "it's a bastard shame, this fire." He had slung his shotgun for the moment.

"Why's that, J.B.? You all said you got your gear out and stashed when you broke free. You got a soft spot for the place?"

An explosion sent a bright yellow fireball rolling into the sky toward the thickening clouds, riding a pillar of black smoke. Uncountable smaller secondaries rattled inside. Sparks danced white in the flames that now fully involved all four floors.

"Nope," J.B. said calmly, putting his specs back on. "But all the ammo and blasters Jacks had stored in there might have come in handy in another hour or so. Guess it really is the gate to hell, now."

"My gaudy!" a short man with a potbelly and a pencil-thin mustache said over and over nearby. He clutched his bald head. "My beautiful gaudy house! How will I live?"

"Your girls'll still need to work," a bystander said helpfully. "Leastwise, the ones that didn't go up with that crazy old Grammaw Jacks. Course, they might wanna take up with somebody who can better keep hold of his property."

"Move in with your pal Itomaru," another said. "Go work for him. Be plenty call for coffins now."

"Specially ones with locked lids," a third man said. The listeners laughed.

Having watched the whole bizarre show slack-jawed, Colt came suddenly to life. He began gesticulating and shouting about keeping the fire from spreading. Perico hustled over and tried to calm him down. Because the gaudy took up a large area, there were no other structures in the immediate vicinity, he pointed out. Figures were already visible on the rooftops of the buildings nearest, poised to douse any wayward sparks with buckets of sand or dirt in lieu of precious water.

Then from behind Ryan and J.B. came the wild cry, "Rotties! They're hittin' the east gate! Must be a million of 'em!"

Chapter Twenty-Seven

"It was a complete exaggeration to say there were 'a million' of them," Doc declared. "Why, that's three whole orders of magnitude off!"

"And what does that mean, exactly, Doc?" Ryan asked.

"Why, plainly, my dear Ryan, there's only a few hundred of them advancing on the town."

The six companions were reunited at the gate that closed the eastern road into town. A mob of ville residents and sec men gathered around them, all staring slack-jawed to the east.

A wave of blue-and-gray-faced human figures came shambling toward them down the long, sloping road.

"Ryan," Krysty said, "shouldn't you be doing something?"

"Like blasting some heads with that nice scoped rifle of yours?" Mildred suggested. "They're in range, aren't they?"

"Nearer ones are. For me. But if I start blasting, it's going to be hard to keep everybody else from cutting loose and shooting a lot of holes in the air. We're going to get tight on ammo here, directly."

He shook his head. "The few I can take down at long range aren't going to be a raindrop in a lake, anyway."

"Actually, I meant shouldn't you be setting up the defenses, lover?" Krysty said.

Again Ryan shook his head. "No. I'm not the man in charge."

"I am not sure this is the occasion for such niceties," said Doc. He held his big LeMat in one hand and his sword-stick, still sheathed, in the other.

"It's not that, Doc. We've gone to some trouble to get the ville calmed down to where it'll stand a chance."

He nodded to where Colt Sharp stood apart from the crowd, a little ways north along the perimeter. Some of the older sec men clustered around, jawing at him, as were Perico and Jacks's former chief adviser, Coffin. The black man's wound had been cleaned and his shin splinted by Mildred. He now was piled atop some pillows in a hand-cart.

"If I go giving orders, the new baron might not be happy. All we need is more wrangling right now."

People were yammering at one another, scared and un-certain what to do. Some cried. Some screamed. Others told them harshly to shut their holes.

"It won't matter if we don't do something soon," Mil-dred said. "Ryan."

He just raised his head and gazed out at the horde. The nearest were still about five hundred yards away. Too close for comfort.

"Mr. Cawdor," Colt called. "Uh, Ryan."

Ryan looked around to see the freshly minted baron ap-proaching, trailing advisers. A quartet of sec men took it upon themselves to thrust a path through the unquiet crowd for him. He didn't even notice.

"What can I do for you, baron?"

Colt came up close. Pitching his voice as low as he could and still have a hope of being heard above the crowd, he said, "What am I supposed to do? I mean, there are so many of them. Is there any chance we can hold them off?"

"Yes. We can, if we do everything right."

"Tell me," Colt said. *"Please."*

Ryan looked past him to where Perico stood and Coffin sat glowering at him. The sec men mostly looked uncomfortable.

"There's no time to talk things out anymore," Ryan said. "We need to just do, and do fast."

The young baron mulled that over for about five seconds. "Will you be my sec boss, then, Mr. Cawdor?"

"Yes."

The youth wavered on his feet. Krysty put up a hand to steady him. "Thank you," he breathed.

Then he turned to address the crowd and the ville in general. "Everyone, listen up! I, Baron Colt Sharp, hereby appoint Ryan Cawdor my head of sec! And his friends are all appointed as my personal bodyguards."

Ryan doubted that would settle well in every growling stomach out there, which didn't bother him a bit. He wasn't here to make friends.

"All right, people," he said, pitching his voice to carry over the wind without shouting. The crowd clamor died out.

"We need to conserve ammo. Head shots are the only things that'll drop these creatures anyway. Most important thing is *do not* get bit. Anybody who does will become the enemy, in any amount of time from hours to right nuking now."

"So how do we stop the bastards biting us?" somebody shouted. He sounded not sarcastic but frantic, his voice throbbing on the verge of tears.

"Sticks, clubs, long poles, axes. Axe handles. Shovels, hoes, rakes. Things to push them off you. Anything. Push them away, knock them down, smash their heads. And stay away from their jaws. If you don't have something to poke or hit or cut with, go find it. Now. And get back pronto!"

People scattered in all directions. About half the crowd stayed put. Some hefted blasters, smokeless or black powder. A few held crossbows or conventional bows. At least half the remaining defenders were already armed with melee weapons.

"Will they all come back?" Perico asked sourly.

"If they won't turn out to defend themselves and their families from something like that," J.B. said, nodding toward the slowly advancing swarm, "do we *want* them fighting next to us?"

"Now, you sec men," Ryan directed, "start getting people spread out along the fence. Tell them not to shoot unless they're sure of a head shot. Go."

That was something the sec men from both factions knew how to do: push ville folk around. Of course, these people were all armed and ready to fight, but that wasn't Ryan's problem. Most would work it out themselves. He and his friends could pick up the slack.

"What about cover?" Colt asked.

"Don't sweat it," Ryan said. "These things don't use blasters. Or even throw rocks, as far as we know."

"If they start using missiles," Doc said, "may heaven help us all."

"What do I do, Ryan?" the young baron said.

"Stay out of the way. Mebbe get on a roof where you can shoot with less danger of blasting your own side. Matter of fact, why don't we start getting shooters up to the roofs right now?"

Colt nodded and went away. Perico and Coffin started shouting orders, which people mostly followed.

"Ryan, sec boss," Jak said in a mixture of disbelief and amusement.

"Not like it's a job I aim to keep," he growled.

"What about us?" J.B. asked. "What do you want us to do?"

"You take Mildred and Krysty up on a roof and shoot heads. Jak and Doc, stay with me. We'll shoot while we can, then fight them hand-to-hand when they get inside."

"When?" Mildred asked in alarm.

"When. Move."

Ville folk were already filtering back, armed with a variety of long-hafted weapons, as per Ryan's instruction. Some carried bundles of poles, boards and tools, which they handed out to those who lacked close-combat weapons.

A few shots went off, then a quick ripple. "Off the triggers!" Ryan yelled. "Cease firing!"

A rottie went down, still a good two hundred yards off. Too far for any but the best marksman to hit with a non-scoped rifle except by sheer luck. The crowd cheered. A few opened fire again in defiance of Ryan's shouted command.

The rottie clambered back to his feet and lumbered on again as if nothing had happened.

"That's" what we're up against," Ryan said in the sudden silence. "Just shooting them does jackshit. So hold your fire until it counts."

Bracing his legs, taking a quick turn of his sling around his left forearm, he shouldered the Steyr and sighted on the rottie that had been shot. Ryan was good at picking up a target in the scope right off—a tougher trick than most people realized.

He almost wished he hadn't. The rottie's face had shrunk, or been gnawed on, until it was little more than a greasy-looking skull with two shrunken gray eyes staring out of it. It also lacked a lower jaw. Ryan had no idea how the bastard ate.

He had already drawn a deep breath. He let part of it out, held it, and as the field of vision briefly stabilized, squeezed off a shot.

Ryan saw the skull-head snap back before recoil kicked it out of his view. When he brought the longblaster back down online the rottie lay in a heap on the short sere grass. A changed woman following behind tripped over the corpse and fell on her face. When she got up on all fours to crawl, an eyeball was bouncing around on her bluish cheek by its optic nerve.

With more than a little relief Ryan lowered his blaster. People stared at him with new respect.

"Pick your shots and aim," he commanded. "Waste a bullet, you risk wasting your life. Or your wife's or your husband's or your kid's." Unsurprisingly, a number of woman had joined the defenders.

"One thing we can say in our opponents' favor," Doc said, standing at Ryan's side. "Their deliberate approach gives us ample time to prepare and even adjust our defenses for the onslaught."

"Yeah." The former sec men were doing a pretty good job of herding the ville folk into a fairly spread-out line. "I admit I'm kinda surprised by how many ville folk've turned out for this," Ryan said.

"Is it not likely that, after weeks of fear and frustration as they suffered the effects of the power struggle within Sweetwater Junction, they are eager for an opportunity to take action—even if it is against their worst nightmares made of decomposing flesh?" Doc murmured.

"Talk less," Jak said peevishly from Ryan's other side. "Not helping."

When the rotties had closed to about a hundred yards, an arrow arced toward them from somewhere to Ryan's left. He frowned, but by either luck or amazing skill—likely both—it struck a swag-bellied male rottie in the right eye. He pitched forward onto his blue face.

A cheer rose from the Sweetwater Junction ranks. Gunshots began to break out.

There was no point trying to make the crowd hold fire any longer. Ryan knelt and started aiming shots with his Steyr between the horizontal panels of the old steel cattle gate that blocked the east road. The changed made easy targets. They moved slowly, and pretty much straight ahead.

Then he heard screams of alarm and pulled his head back from the sight. One rottie, who had been a gaunt young woman in a tattered gingham dress, suddenly darted forward at sprinter speed. She hit the perimeter fence of scavvied chain link in a jump like a monkey and started over, oblivious to the dully gleaming knife-wire spirals that cut her arms bloodlessly to the bone.

So shocking and abrupt was her onslaught that defenders ran in terror from her.

A single shot broke the brief lull the astonishing charge had brought to the shooting. The resurrected woman's head snapped back, and then her decaying face dropped forward into the wire. She hung on the fence, truly lifeless, as if she'd been cruelly and crudely crucified.

On the nearest flat rooftop, Colt Sharp stood holding his big pistol in the isosceles stance Ryan had taught him. His guards and advisers were slapping him on the back, praising his shot, which for a fact had been pretty good; a twenty-yard head shot with a handblaster was no downhill slide, even at a fairly stationary target.

"For a fact the lad has a gift," said Doc, who was methodically reloading his LeMat. "Or he's lucky, which is almost as good."

"I'd rather be good," Ryan said. "Skill lasts. Luck doesn't."

Whether lucky or good, the youthful baron's shot had a tonic effect on the defenders, who had recoiled from the rottie's lunge like sheep from a wolf. They slunk shame-facedly back into position—so close Ryan had to shout, "Not too near the fence, dammit! Stay out of reaching range!"

The defenders started shooting hard and fast. Ryan's jaw muscles knotted at the rate that ammo was being burned, but he remembered Trader's wise words: never die with rounds in your mag.

He slung his longblaster. Even though Miranda had replenished their stocks as part of their contract, the big 7.62 mm rounds were hard to come by.

Not all the hits were head shots. While mere bullets couldn't actually knock a normal human down, they pre-sumably wouldn't even have the system-shock effects on the rotties that often resulted in shot humans falling. Still, Ryan saw good leg or torso hits drop some of the shambling horrors. The rotties behind tripped over them or trampled them. It made little difference. Those who could get up did; the rest crawled relentlessly on. As long as a rottie could move a single limb, it kept dragging itself toward living flesh.

Bluish bodies pressed against the gate and the wire. De-spite having the breeze at their backs, the defenders began getting the full whiff of decomposing flesh. Some gagged. Others puked their guts up.

One youth wielding a pocketknife thought it would be fun to race right up to the wire and stab at the bodies seem-ingly immobilized against it. His buddies cheered him on.

Then a blue arm showing yellow bone between wrist and elbow snaked through and caught his shirt.

Chapter Twenty-Eight

The rottie yanked the youth against the wire. Other arms reached out to entangle him. Their blackened nails clawed at his flesh.

Despite frenzied screams and thrashing, he couldn't break free. Several ville folk darted forward to try to help him.

"Don't get close!" Ryan shouted. "Chop their arms off!"

His friends tried pulling him away. It did no good. Then the youth screamed, and blood spurted from the side of his head as a rottie bit into his ear.

Standing now, Ryan stepped into a Weaver stance with left foot and shoulder advanced and left elbow crooked to support his blaster hand. Taking a flash sight picture, he fired. The trapped boy's head jerked and he slumped.

His friends stared at Ryan with shock and fury mingled on their faces.

"If you're bit, you're one of them!" Ryan shouted. "Now learn from that stupe, and *stay back*."

Then he had to partially disregard his own words. Because despite the way the original cattle fence had been built up to a taller height with metal-scrap makeshifts, and was topped by razor wire, the rotties were scaling it.

He, Doc and Jak moved in to show the people of Sweetwater Junction how hand-to-hand rottie fighting was done. Doc holstered his reloaded blaster and drew his sword from its sheath. Using the sheath to swat away hands that snatched at him, he started stabbing rottie faces. Doc kept the tip of his sword well sharpened, and it was well reinforced for thrusting. He could even ram it through a forehead or temple.

From somewhere Jak had turned up two hatchets, predark, and each drop-forged from a single piece of steel. He waded in like a fury, hacking off hands, breaking arms so that they flopped uselessly, closing in to split heads. Then, like a white flame, he danced back out of harm's way, only to pick a new angle, attack again.

Ryan did much the same thing with his panga. Of course, not even his panther agility and speed could come close to Jak's. Fortunately, it beat even the spriest rottie by a Grand Canyon margin.

When he stepped back for a moment to breathe and wipe sweat from his eye with the back of one hand, Ryan saw the ville defenders battling hard to either side of him. They seemed to be getting the hang of it. Those with poles or long-handled tools poked at the shrunken bellies of the rotties climbing the mesh, knocking them back into their comrades behind. That thinned the numbers making it to the top, made them easier to manage. It also made it less likely the monsters would bring the fence down from sheer weight.

"You've left a smear of something unspeakable over your eye," Doc said, falling back beside him.

"Thanks for the good news."

"I certainly hope the change cannot be transmitted by this ooze we're inevitably drenching ourselves in."

Ryan could find nothing to say to that better than "Me, too."

He glanced up at Colt on his rooftop. Either out of ammo or having heeded advisers telling him to save his shots, the young baron stood looking worried. He clearly wanted to be down there fighting, yet understood why that was at best a last-ditch measure.

"Colt!" Ryan shouted, trying to make himself heard over the yells and screams of the defenders. This close, the rotties' strange muttering sounded as loud as ocean surf. "Yo, Baron!"

He waved his arms. Colt looked at him.

"Check for places the fence is giving way!" Ryan yelled. "Send reinforcements!"

For an instant the pudgy, smudged face crumpled in incomprehension. Ryan realized the kid still had his own mother's blood and brains dried on his face. Well, it was a triple-tough day for everybody.

Then Colt jerked his head up as the import of Ryan's words hit him. He turned, looked around, started waving his arms and shouting.

"What can we do?" Mildred asked from Ryan's elbow.

He spun like a cat hit with a static spark. "What the fireblast are you doing here?" he demanded of his three companions.

"Lookin' to do some good, Ryan," J.B. said. "Our ammo won't last forever."

Ryan glared at them. His main intention, though he would never say so, was to keep the women, especially Krysty, out of rottie reach. He'd been willing to do without the Armorer fighting at his side to help justify that.

"What about doctoring up the wounded?" Ryan demanded.

"Right," Mildred said. "Most who get injured are bitten. That means the indicated treatment is a bullet in the head. Screw that."

"The fight's here," Krysty said. "Our place is with you." She held a double-bitted ax. Somewhere Mildred had scored herself an aluminum baseball bat, and J.B. held a pool cue.

"What the fuck, J.B.?" Ryan said.

The Armorer shrugged and twirled the long, tapered stick. "Just feels natural in my hands, Ryan."

Before they could say anything else, screams rang out from their left. Forty yards or so north a thirty-foot-wide section of fence bowed inward under the weight of the invaders' bodies. So hard did the rotties behind press the ones in front in their mindless, unswerving hunger, that they were pushing bits of their fellows' bodies through the heavy-gauge wire mesh as if it were some kind of rotting-meat strainer.

One of the high-speed rotties went capering up the mound of flesh to leap over the fence. It twisted in the midst of leaping on a knot of taken-by-surprised defenders as Ryan sent a snapshot through its body. That wasn't enough to put it down to stay, of course, but the hit made the creature miss its target. A moment later somebody had shattered its skull with an ax.

By now the east gate was mostly barricaded by a mound of rotties chilled for the second and final time. It seemed to be holding them at bay.

"Go!" Ryan shouted, leading his companions toward the breach on the run.

As more rotties surged against the fence, it fell down with a crash. Rotties rolled into the ville, in among the defenders. Those who weren't powering out of there in a panic.

A fat changed man in the stained and tattered remains of an apron struggled to his feet in front of Ryan. His jowls were dark and crusted with old gore. His eyes seemed to burn like mad white beacons in his blue-gray face.

Ryan buried the panga in the man's forehead, splitting

the bean-shaped head clear to the bridge of a squashed nose. Whatever light had gleamed in those staring eyes went out. The rottie slumped, done.

And Ryan found out he'd struck the creature *too* well. The panga blade stuck tight in its skull. The chill's bulk, which still had to be north of 250 pounds even allowing for wastage, dragged Ryan's arm inexorably down.

"Shit!" he yelped. He put a boot against the man-boobs below where the chin slumped in a pool of loose discolored skin, and pushed hard, tugging with both hands.

From the corner of his eye he saw a rottie homing in on him, not fast but almost in range to grab him. He knew those outstretched fingers contained terrible strength even though half were rotted to little more than bone and brown sinew.

With a wild cry Mildred skipped past him. Her avenging baseball bat whistled through the air and struck the rottie attacking Ryan with a ringing thump. The skull caved in.

At last Ryan's panga came free. "Thanks," he breathed to Mildred. He gave the blade a quick double swipe on the fat chill and stuck it in his belt.

"Don't mention it," Mildred said. "Aiieeee!"

The latter cry was addressed to a skeleton-lean female rottie with wisps of long graying hair hanging from the half of the scalp that remained on her head. It wasn't a cry of dismay. Rather, Mildred had reverted to some kind of primal berserker state Ryan couldn't recall seeing before. The stocky black woman, whom he belatedly noticed had tied a red rag around her head like *Rambo* in an ancient vidposter, wound up two-handed and swung for the fences.

Her bat rang like a warning bell as it struck the changed woman's high cheekbone. The half-gnawed head snapped around 180 degrees. Her neck broke with a sound like blasterfire.

It was good enough. She dropped like a sack.

Mildred charged on in search of new heads to break.

"Fuck this," Ryan grunted. His trusty panga wasn't doing the deed. Casting about, he saw a shovel lying ten feet away, where a wounded or fled defender had dropped it.

Ace. It might not be an ideal weapon, but he'd chilled men and muties with a shovel before. Its advantage here was that it was long.

He grabbed it up, spun and swung it ball-bat style so that the shallow-angled blade smacked a rottie across the face. The changed man staggered back, but he didn't go down.

Quick balance recovery wasn't a notable strength among the changed. The creature was still trying to get into forward motion again when Krysty pounced and split its head with her ax.

"Good job," Ryan told her. She grinned at him. The ax's handle gave her leverage Ryan hadn't had when trying to pull his panga out of a rottie's head. But it still took her a moment to free it.

Tactics came easy to Ryan.

"Krysty," he yelled, "Doc. You hang back a couple steps. The rest of us will put the bastards on the ground. You finish off the ones as they need it."

Ryan saw a quick rebellious flare in Krysty's eyes. It went out at once. She had long since agreed to accept his command as iron. Plus her tactical mind was just a beat or two behind his. She saw the wisdom of his plan as clearly as he did.

He charged into the swarm of rotties battling a clot of determined ville folk in the mouth of an alley that opened on the cleared path along the inside of the perimeter. J.B. was at his right, using the pool cue more as a quarterstaff than a club, holding its middle third between his callused, sun-browned hands, jabbing and tripping with either end, pushing with the middle. The grip still allowed him to extend the weapon. As Ryan shifted his own grip on his shovel to mimic his friend's, J.B. suddenly lunged, poking the cue before him like a spear. Its narrow end went into a rottie's eye socket, squishing the already shrunken ball, punching through the thin bone backing into the fevered brain behind.

The tip came out black; the rottie went down.

"Justly struck, John Barrymore!" Doc crowed from behind.

Meanwhile Ryan sidestepped a male rottie about his own size and build. Letting the shovel handle slide through his hands to almost the end, he swung the blade edge against the back of a knee. The leg folded under the rottie. As Ryan recovered from the stroke, he saw Doc's sword dart like a steel serpent's tongue to pierce the creature's temple.

From behind him Ryan heard the crunch and squelch of Krysty's ax hacking into the skull of a rottie someone had put on the ground.

Blaster shots cracked out. And to Ryan, they had the nasty, high harmonic ring of shots aimed at *him*. He winced as a bullet sang past his left ear, then he heard Colt Sharp hollering for people to cease firing. The blasters stopped.

With Mildred batting on his left and Jak with his hatchets just past her, plus J.B. at his right, Ryan led a lopsided wedge against the rotties coming through the fallen section of fence. Krysty and Doc had their backs. The ville defenders making a stand in the alley rushed out, and they all quickly mopped up the rotties who had gotten inside the wire.

Then it was just a matter of mowing down the creatures as they came through. With six Sweetwater Junction residents to help, the companions were able to do it. Most rotties were slow, and they had to wade through their fellows who had been crushed into the fence in pushing it down. Not all of those were finished by any means. Their mindlessly clutching hands and biting jaws attacked their own kind on contact with no more hesitation than they would warm flesh.

Ryan and his companions had no trouble dealing with the occasional double-speed rottie. Even with speed they didn't exactly show finesse.

The task was more like chopping firewood than a fight. Ryan's arms quickly grew tired, grew leaden, screamed with pain and grew numb. His elbows hurt from repeated impacts. His stomach fought a constant low-level insurgency against his iron self-control, not just because of the open-grave stench of the changed, but in sheer revulsion against the ichor and grunge that coated him from his hair to his boots. It got to be like hitting thrown tomatoes with a tennis racket. Except instead of tomato pulp and juice, it was foul, rotting human flesh and skin and byproducts that splattered him.

The problem was when he inhaled, the ooze went up his nostrils, clogging them physically as well as gagging him with stench. But the triple-special horror was feeling maggots cast from the decomposing rotties by the force of his and his friends' blows writhing on the skin of his face and arms.

From the corner of his eye Ryan noticed that twenty or so Sweetwater Junction defenders had set up a similar system at the gate, where rotties were climbing up and over the fallen bodies of those who had gone before. The two ranks of defenders seemed to have little trouble finishing them when they dropped inside the gate.

It was some consolation for the fact that even Ryan, with

his iron endurance and titanium will, fast approached the point where he simply couldn't fight anymore.

"I hate to plead incapacity due to my seeming age," he heard Doc wheeze, "but I am almost done, I fear."

"Me, too," Mildred muttered from his side. The light of fury burned in her dark eyes, but her movements no longer had the wild energy she'd shown when she'd ripped into the changed mob like a living chainsaw. Even Jak's motions were labored, almost slow.

Their bodies no longer able to obey, the ville defenders had started to drop out around them. Then men and women were shoving in front of Ryan and his friends. Men and women who smelled clean, instead of like a dug-up graveyard in a heat wave.

"You've done enough," Colt shouted close to Ryan. "We'll take over now."

"You…shouldn't…be here, Baron," Ryan panted. With no mutant enemy within range, his arms had fallen of their own accord. He literally wasn't sure he could lift them again. He had to glance down to make sure he still gripped the shovel. He couldn't feel his hands anymore.

"Not…safe," he managed to mutter.

The plump young baron had his blaster in his left hand and a wrought-iron fireplace poker in the other. He jabbed it at a rottie's face, forcing the creature back a step. A sec man crushed its skull with an ax handle.

"This is where I have to be now, Ryan," Colt said.

Ryan couldn't argue. He and his friends retreated to the weathered plank front of a house and just leaned there.

"Need water," Mildred said.

"Parched as I am," Doc said, "I am not sure I could stomach water that had passed through the vileness on my lips, and even in my mouth."

"We need to wash this shit off us!" Mildred said, with

more energy than Ryan reckoned she had in her. "We don't know what it'll do."

Either on his own hook or his counselors' advice, Colt had mustered ville kids to act as runners. Most of what they were bringing was buckets and jugs of water, anyway, to rehydrate the defenders. Whatever the new baron did about controlling Sweetwater Junction's main resource in the future, rationing was off for this day.

The kids ranged in age from near-toddlers to eleven or twelve. Anybody older was either hiding out or fighting. Far from being horrified or disgusted, the children treated all this as a marvelous game.

Ace, Ryan thought, as a little girl laughingly threw a whole bucket of water in his face. They had moved back in the alley, away from where Baron Sharp and his subjects now battled the advancing horde.

Somebody brought rags. Ryan and friends scrubbed as much of the rottie ooze and chunks off them as they could.

"Not sure this cloth's very clean itself," Mildred remarked, although she didn't stop scrubbing her face with the one she held.

"They could be fresh-used ass wipes," J.B. said, "and it'd be better than *this*."

Finally, Ryan reached the point where he could think about drinking without wanting to puke. A terrible thirst promptly hit him. His lips felt like the cracked dry mudflats outside the ville, the inside of his mouth and throat like paper. He felt as if he were shriveling into a prune from the inside out, and wondered that he hadn't just sort of imploded.

"Don't drink too much too fast," Mildred cautioned.

"I know," Ryan said. He caught himself on the verge of taking a giant swallow that would have hurt like a steel fencepost going down, and might have caused massive cramps. Instead, he rinsed his mouth and spit. He could feel the water swelling his tissues back into shape.

"Be fit to fight in a little while," J.B. croaked, wringing out his well-soaked hat. "No more than, say, a week, ten days."

Ryan mustered a sound more like seeds rattling in a dried gourd than a chuckle. "Be lucky if we get ten more minutes," he said.

Then a cry went up. "They're pulling back!"

Chapter Twenty-Nine

As more voices took up the joyful cry, Ryan felt adrenaline blast through his chill-weary bones and muscles.

"Wait!" he shouted. His voice was a raven's croak and his throat hurt as if the lining was being pulled. But he managed to make himself heard. "Why are they moving back? How are they moving back? They have no bastard minds!"

It was true. The remaining rotties had turned and begun wandering away from Sweetwater Junction as if they'd all lost interest. They streamed toward the top of the distant rise, where the horizon cut the sky.

"They're not…completely mindless," a voice said. Ryan looked around to see Reno standing alone between Ryan's companions and the gate defenders. The slight young man with the unruly hair and heavy glasses had the loneliest look Ryan could ever remember seeing.

"Some show signs of something like will. Even a kind of intelligence." The kid turned and looked at Ryan. "You've seen it. The flashes of awareness. Mebbe they share a hive mind. Like an ant colony. With its queen."

He turned again to look out to the east, where storm clouds gathered in an afternoon sky. Late afternoon, Ryan was surprised to notice. The ville's angular shadows stretched well up the long swell and darkened the backs of the retreating rotties.

"Ryan, what's that?" Krysty asked, pointing.

A figure stood atop the rise, and the rotties seemed to converge on it. A little farther down the slope a second figure stood waving a hand above its head.

"I don't know."

Ryan unlimbered the Steyr, which he had slung and cinched up tight to prevent its butt banging him in the kidneys as he fought the rotties.

He saw a woman on the crest. She had a full figure, and her shoulder-length hair blew in the wind, russet rather than scarlet. The second figure seemed to be twirling something on a rope above its head.

The woman's face, and the bare upper torso and arms of the other, showed the dead blue-gray hues of the changed.

"A bullroarer," Doc said dreamily.

"Talk sense, old man," Mildred said. Exhaustion made her crabby.

Doc shook himself as if he'd caught himself nodding off.

"It's a bullroarer," he said again. "A hollowed out piece of wood...or bone. When spun around the head it makes that peculiar pulsating moan."

Now that he mentioned it, Ryan could hear the strange bass ululation.

"That's not mindless behavior," Krysty said. "Reno's right. Say, where'd he go?"

Ryan lowered the glass. For a moment he stared at the auburn-haired figure off in the distance, then he looked around.

The kid was gone.

"Ryan!"

It was Colt Sharp, walking up with a wedge of sec men trotting behind. "You did ace. It was great! You saved the ville."

Ryan just looked at him. He was too tired to make nice with a baron, even though the kid showed promise.

"But there's...there's something I need to ask you."

"What's that, Colt?" Krysty asked.

"We've got wounded. Some of them have been bitten. Others—we just don't know for sure."

He paused, blinked, worked his lips in and out. This was obviously not coming easy to him. Plus he was trying triple-hard to talk like a grown-up. Or how he reckoned grown-ups talked, anyway.

"I—I need you to take care of it for me."

It finally dawned on Ryan what the baron was asking. The one-eyed man wasn't usually this slow. Then again, most of his days didn't start with a rifle butt in the face and get hairy from there.

"Taking care of it" meant figuring out which ones had been bitten by the rotties, then chilling them before they could change. That kind of thing could cause hard feelings. Blood feuds, perhaps. Not everybody whose son or sister or father got chilled would see that it wasn't just necessary for everybody's sake, it was an act of kindness.

Naturally, Colt would want his out-of-town mercies to see to it.

"Yeah," Ryan said.

Relief made Colt nearly weepy. "Thanks. I knew I could count on you, Ryan!"

He hurried away.

J.B. pushed up his hat to scratch the front of his head. "Boy's starting to think like a baron already."

"Yeah," Ryan said. "And here I was just startin' to like him."

"AT LEAST THERE AREN'T any little kids," Mildred said with a sigh.

But that was a relative thing. A boy leaned against the wall of the large shed where the dozen or so questionable wounded had been locked on the baron's orders. His black hair hung in his fever-flushed face. He couldn't have been much more than fifteen. Sixteen max.

"Stay away from my son!" his mother screamed. She knelt protectively between him and the door. Then, she contradictorily added, "He's bad hurt. He needs attention."

The woman was as wasted as the empty lands around Sweetwater Junction by the burdens of her life. The bun her brown hair was wound into was threaded with gray. Her face might've been handsome once, if she'd ever had a square meal and enough water to drink. But labor and privation had shrunk her skin to the harsh bones of her face, which was twisted in a grimace of confusion, rage and terror. She held a hand spread, callused palm outward, to ward off Ryan and the companions as they came in.

"Ma'am," Krysty said softly, "come away now, please. You can't do him any good."

"He's hurt! He needs help." A sob racked her skinny body in its too-big cotton dress. "You want to chill him. But he's just a boy."

"He's been bit," Ryan said. "He'll change. He's becoming one of them, and there's nothing you or we or anybody can do to stop it."

"No! He ain't been bit! He's just hurt!"

"We can see the bite mark on his cheek from here plain as day," J.B. said.

"No! You can't! I won't—"

The flash dazzled Ryan's eye in the gloom of the shed. The gunshot threatened to bust his eardrums. Dust and mold filtered down from the rafters like khaki sleet.

The bitten boy lay with his head slumped against a dark blood-splash on the splintery wood. One eye had rolled unseeing up in his head.

Jak lowered his handblaster. A thread of gray smoke

trailed upward from its muzzle. The dead boy's mother shrieked and jumped at him. Ryan and Mildred caught her by the arms.

"It doesn't get easier talking about it," Mildred said. Her face was frozen in a grim mask. "Now get out of here, lady. We have work to do."

COMPLETELY DRAINED, physically and otherwise, and once again covered in stinking sludge, the six friends returned to the baron's palace not long before sundown.

Some of the bitten had begged and pleaded to be allowed to live. Some had asked to die as quickly and painlessly as possible. Both sets got the same treatment. One got what it asked for.

The good news was that only one of the six questionable wounded showed definite signs of being bitten. But Mildred remained unsure about the rest.

J.B. and Jak were for going ahead and chilling them. Mildred wanted them tied up and locked away where they could be watched. If they didn't change in a day or so, they were probably not going to. Krysty and Doc backed her.

In the end Ryan opted to give them the chance. It wasn't any skin off his ass one way or the other; he and his people weren't going to be keeping tabs on them. And the fact was, he'd had his fill of chilling and then some.

The companions surrendered their clothes to palace servants for cleaning, and took turns at hot showers using the palace's gravity-driven system.

After a two-hour nap they were summoned downstairs to the dining room to meet with their default new employer. Colt Sharp had obviously neither slept nor cleaned up, apart from having the worst dreck wiped off his face with a wet rag. He looked as haggard as a fat kid could. His cheeks were sallow and hung. His eyes were sunk in dark circles.

"Are the rotties coming back?" Ryan asked.

He feared a night assault, but he and his companions had been running on fumes. He hoped if the horde did attack again under cover of darkness, whatever the new young baron had done while they'd napped would be adequate to stand them off for a spell. Ryan and his companions had no more to give, even if the changed were running wild in the streets.

But Colt shook his head. He was flanked by his advisers, Perico and Jacks's former man, Coffin. There seemed to be no hard feelings on either side. Ryan didn't have energy or interest to try to figure it all out.

An expensive pinewood fire blazed in the hearth. A large map of the ville, hand-drawn in ink on a big sheet of age-yellowed paper, was spread on the big table.

"No," Baron Sharp said. "But it looks as if they're spreading out to surround the ville."

"So they'll try probing attacks," J.B. said. "Or mebbe just draw everybody with a big feint one side of the ville, then steamroll in on the other."

"But that's tactics, John," Mildred protested. "These creatures are mindless. They lack volition."

"They don't always act like it," Krysty said. "Remember, they responded to the call of that bullroarer thing. And it was a rottie working the device."

"We've seen them use simple tactics before," Ryan said. "And that kid, what's his name—he said they're not all mindless. That rottie woman standing way up there watching the fight wasn't, sure as rad death's a bastard way to go."

The baron scratched the back of his neck. "Speaking of that," he said, "I've got something to show you."

He called out. A door opened, and a figure stumbled into the middle of the room, propelled by a sec man's hard hand.

"Reno," Krysty said.

The kid's hands were tied together before him. He used them to set his glasses more or less square on his nose.

"Krysty," he said. "Ryan. Everybody. Fancy meeting you here."

Ryan looked at Sharp.

"We've got patrols walking the perimeter," Perico said. "They caught him trying to slip out the west gate right after sundown."

"Lucky it was the west gate," Coffin said. "Or we would've strung the fool up already."

Colt shook his head. "We'd have talked to him awhile first."

"So what's your story, kid?" Ryan asked. It seemed appropriate. He was nominal sec boss of Sweetwater Junction, after all. In *fact,* he reckoned. For now.

Thin shoulders covered in scuffed leather shrugged. "Figured I'd warned you all. Done what I could. So I was looking to move on."

"Not looking to circle around and report what you'd spied out to that weird woman?" Ryan asked.

"Of course not! I've been trying to get away from the rotties for…well, you know. Weeks."

"You do have a tendency to turn up right before they do," Mildred said.

"Well, yeah. I want to warn people what's in store. I told you that."

"Is that it?" she said. Her eyes were hard. "Really? Or are they following you? Are you leading them to fresh meat?"

The color drained out of his already pale face, leaving it as white as clean paper. "No! I'd never do anything like that. I'm trying to get away from them!"

"Take your shirt off," Mildred said.

"Huh?"

"Take off your shirt."

He stayed pale. "No, really. No reason for that. Can't we just talk—"

"Cut it off him," Ryan told the two sec men who had delivered the prisoner.

If he needed any confirmation that he really was sec boss, instead of it all being for show, he got it when the two obeyed without hesitation. One drew a hunting knife from a sheath at his belt. Neither glanced at their young baron for confirmation.

"No! Wait!" Reno yelped, sidling away. "These're the only shirt and jacket I've got."

"Why should I care?" Ryan asked.

"Please! Let me go. I'll take them off myself." He held up his tied wrists.

"How do we know you won't make a break for it?" Mildred asked.

Jak laughed. "Hope prick tries," he said, an ugly glitter in his ruby eyes.

Ryan looked at Colt. It was his house, after all.

"You can handle him, can't you?" the boy asked.

J.B. chuckled. "You can sure say that."

"Do it."

The sec man with the knife grabbed Reno's arm and none too carefully slid the blade under the coil of rope and sliced it.

"Ouch," Reno said resentfully, cringing and rubbing one wrist. "You cut me."

The sec man laughed at him, put the knife away and went to stand with his back to the fire.

Reno ran a last desperate look around the room. Whatever he had in his mind—arguing, pleading, flight—he decided not to try it. He took off his jacket. Then, with visible reluctance, his shirt.

"Gaia!" Krysty exclaimed.

"Just as I thought," Mildred said, stepping up to grab his right wrist and holding up his skinny arm. "A human bite wound. Healing, but slowly by the looks of it."

She dropped his arm and turned to the others. "He's been bitten. Maybe a couple weeks ago."

"You mean he's a rottie?" Colt asked in alarm.

"Clearly not," Mildred said. "And the sixty-four thousand dollar question is—why not?"

Chapter Thirty

Reno's head slumped to his collarbone. His bare skin was pink-and-blue. His ribs stood out like slats on a window shade.

"I don't rightly know why I haven't changed," he said.

"Talk," Ryan said.

"All right. What I told you all—what I reckon you told these people here?"

"Yeah."

"That was the straight skinny. Mostly. Just not all the details. Nor what happened after Drygulch changed."

"We're all ears," Perico said.

Reno told again about the redoubt raid and the cabinet of prions.

"I remember a bit more about those now," Mildred said. "Back in the nineties there was debate about whether they caused mad cow disease. Also, they were blamed for a condition called kuru, which tribal people in New Guinea or somewhere like that got from eating the brains of their enemies. Like that cannie disease."

"I heard my captors mention these prions," Doc said.

"So what are they?" Colt asked.

She shrugged. "I really don't know. Supposedly they were a kind of protein that could infect a living thing and make it duplicate them. Like viruses. Except unlike viruses, they're not really alive."

She shook her head. "I don't know much about them, and I can't pretend I understand them."

"Appropriate," Doc murmured. He sat near the fire in his shirtsleeves. His chin had drooped as if he was falling asleep. For once Ryan couldn't blame him if he had.

"How so?" Mildred asked sharply.

"Prions, you say, are unliving. How like the changed. They also do not seem to live, insofar as we can tell."

"Could these pry-things cause something like this plague?" Perico asked.

"Something has," Ryan said. "Don't see anything else matters a spent round right now."

"So what really happened that night by the fire, Reno?" J.B. asked mildly.

"It was like I told you," Reno said, "up to the point Drygulch rose up and attacked. He grabbed hold of Lariat, starting biting her and growling. She screamed and tried to fight him off. I blasted him with my shotgun in the body and he went down. Blew his rib cage wide-open.

"I went to Lariat to help her. She was bit pretty bad. Bleeding heavily from the neck. I was trying to staunch the bleeding when here came Drygulch again. He knocked the shotgun clean outta my hands, bit my arm when I tried to defend myself. Hurt like nuke-red. I fell on my butt, bleeding like a stuck pig. Drygulch kept coming. I grabbed my pack and ran. Just ran till I couldn't run no more."

"You didn't fight anymore?" Ryan asked.

"I never saw my shotgun again. Mr. Cawdor, I could see one of his *lungs*. It was all pink and oozy. But it wasn't moving. And he still was. Didn't think anything could stop him, if he could survive a hit like that."

"Then what?"

"Found, like, a wolf den dug in the ground. Burrowed

right on in and huddled up for the night. Lucky for me no wolves came back while I was there.

"Next morning I just headed west. After a spell I spotted smoke rising. When I got closer, I saw it came from the chimney of a sod house.

"When I went inside there was food on the table and blood all over everywhere. Five places laid, like for a family. But nobody there. All I found was Dryglulch lying in the front room with a hole in his forehead and the back of his skull blown out."

Reno hunkered down on his haunches and let his head sink to his clavicle. "And that's how it started."

"What about your bite wound, Reno?"

"Bandaged it best I could. Sickness came over me bad— fever, chills. I stayed in the cabin two days until it passed. There was water there and food, though it took a day and a half before I could keep anything down."

"So whatever it is, some people are immune." Mildred frowned. "Hate to think we might have chilled people who were bitten but might have pulled through."

"Didn't know," Ryan said. "Couldn't take the chance if we had. Still can't."

"Honestly," Reno said, "I'm the only one I know who's been bitten who hasn't changed."

"So do you think they're following you?" Colt asked. He sounded more curious than hostile or suspicious. "Like, mebbe you have some kind of link to them? To Lariat, mebbe? She's the auburn-haired woman we saw on the rise to the east, isn't she?"

"She was," Reno said in a tiny, broken voice. "Don't know what she is now."

"Spy," Jak said. "Better chill now."

"It's possible he's played everybody for a fool," Coffin said. Some of the brandy Jeb Sharp had laid up had allayed the pain of the sec man's bullet-shattered shin. It hadn't seemed to dull his wits much, though.

"If he's a spy, why would he've stayed in the ville?" Ryan asked.

"Check defenses," Jak said. "Anyway, caught leaving."

"I was trying to get away from them!" Reno said. "They do seem to go the places I go. But it's not my fault. I swear! I don't know why."

"So mebbe this Lariat is following you," J.B. said.

"No!"

"They're predators," said Krysty, who'd been sitting quietly by the table, taking everything in with those emerald-green eyes. "They go where the food is. You've been going from outpost to outpost, haven't you? Settlement to settlement, ville to ville."

Reno gave her a wary look. "Yeah."

"You've been looking for people, right?"

"Yeah. I want to warn 'em. Well, and find shelter and a bite to eat."

"You and they are looking for the same things, then," she said. "That could be why they seem to follow you."

"Could be," Ryan said, in a tone that said he didn't wholly buy the idea.

"How do there get to be so rad-blasted many of them?" Perico asked. "There still has to be a hundred or more of the bastards left out there even though we finished off hundreds today. This is a pretty desolate area. Not much population to change. So where'd they get numbers like that?"

"Taking villes," Reno said. "Trading posts. Farms."

"There are at least one hundred people on farms around Sweetwater Junction," Coffin said. "Within, say, a twenty-mile radius. Mebbe more, come to think of it."

"They've run off or been changed," Reno said. "At least if they lived east of here."

"Sweetwater Junction's lost some people, too," Mildred said. "Refugees fleeing the civil war."

Perico and Coffin exchanged looks. For just a moment they appeared almost ashamed.

"Yes," Coffin said. "That's so."

"Any that went east," Mildred said, "have come back changed."

For a moment only the fire spoke in its crackling voice. Then Doc stirred.

"I see a germ of hope here, friends," he said. "This Lariat woman—she appears to be some kind of leader, correct?"

"Yes," Reno said. "She had the strongest will of anybody I ever knew. I guess it—that will—survived somehow. In some form. That's not Lariat out there, not the woman I knew. But it's *like* her in a lot of ways. Got a lot of her traits."

"We know there's some form of virus or bacteria that takes over running the body, and can keep it running even without most of the vital processes going," Mildred said. "Mebbe she and it came to terms."

"You were saying, Doc?" Ryan said.

"What? Oh, yes. Yes. Linear propagation is not a normal pattern for a disease to spread, is it, Mildred?"

"You know it's not, old man. Normally it spreads outward like a stain. Unless there's something that channels the vectors."

"Vectors?" Ryan asked.

"Plague carriers."

Doc was nodding and beaming. "Yet so far as we know the horde is cohesive, yes? The rotties are all moving relentlessly west together?"

"That's how it looks," Reno acknowledged.

"So the swarm somehow gathers around this changed woman companion of yours, this Lariat."

"I guess."

"How does knowing this fill any mags for us?" Ryan asked.

"It means that the plague itself is traveling in a single direction, following its leader, the erstwhile Lariat," Doc said, "instead of radiating outward to take over he world."

The Sweetwater Junction people frowned. The discussion had clearly lost them a couple turns back. But Ryan got it. He could tell his friends did, too.

"So if we can somehow stop it here—"

"We might be able to stop it for good!"

"Great! Dr. Tanner, that's great!" Colt was almost jumping up and down. He looked at Ryan. "*Can* we stop them?"

Ryan frowned. "Mebbe. We need a plan."

"I got a few ideas rattling around under my hat, Ryan," J.B. said.

"Ace," Ryan said. "I got some, too. Let's get them out in the air and figure out which give us our best shot. And we best get to it triple-fast, because whatever we come up with is going to take some doing. And only that auburn-haired rottie bitch has any idea how long we've got!"

THE PLANNING SESSION wasn't the free-for-all Ryan was afraid it might be.

It helped that Colt clearly thought Ryan walked on water. Perico and Coffin didn't think so, but they seemed pretty impressed by what the outlanders brought to the table. Neither of them exactly hated the sound of his own voice, but both knew when to buckle down and say only what needed saying. And now was such a time.

The sec men present—the most senior survivor of Miranda's crew, Morrissey; the eager-beaver loyalist, Hedders; and a burly round guy with a shaved head and a sandy spade beard named Parrack, who'd worn a green armband to start the day—seemed mostly relieved they didn't have to puzzle out how to defend the ville by themselves. Especially since reports kept filtering in from the patrols orbiting the perimeter fence, via ville-kid runners, of shadowy movements in the night. The ville was surrounded now, though the rotties still kept their distance.

In a little over an hour, a plan took shape. It wasn't a perfect one. It wasn't what Ryan would call a good plan. But it was possibly workable, and better than nothing.

He hoped.

Just as they were nailing down the last details, a young sec man raced into the room. "Come outside, quick!"

"What?" Colt asked in alarm. "Are the rotties attacking?"

"No, Colt, uh, no, Baron Sharp. It's the sky."

They all went out the door, and didn't need to be told what they'd been called out to see. It was plainly visible.

A front was rolling in from the east, but it wasn't normal white clouds lit by the stars and sinking moon and scattered lights on the ground. It glowed from within, a seething mass of orange and yellow, like sulfur heated to a yellow-hot boil.

It was a sight all too familiar to Ryan and his friends, to any survivor who crawled on the face of this world still devastated by long-ago war.

"That's a bad one coming," Krysty said.

"Acid rain," Jak said, wrinkling his nose. "Can smell."

"Now's the time we usually get hit by a nasty acid rain storm," Perico said. "We usually have two bad weeks or so. Then it tapers off again and we start to get regular rain. That's when we put the crops in."

"Oh, no," Colt said. "How can we fight in this?"

"How long we got until it cuts loose?" Ryan asked.

"We'll get hit before sundown tomorrow," Coffin said, "unless we're a luckier lot of fools than we deserve to be."

Ryan felt a smile stretch across his face. A grim smile, but a smile.

"We may just pull this off, after all," he said, "if we're triple-sharp and five times as lucky."

Chapter Thirty-One

"What in the name of the Three Kennedys does he imagine he's doing?" Doc queried.

"Betraying," Jak said.

The stinking morning wind whipped his long white hair about his head. His fine-featured face was lifted defiantly to it. Jak showed no sign of being aware of the terrible smell of death and decay, although he had a highly sensitive nose. His arms were folded across his chest, which Ryan thought was triple-ballsy, given all the nasty sharp bits of glass and metal he'd sewn into the fabric of his jacket. Then again, he knew where the pointy bits were.

"You could drop him from here with your Steyr," J.B. said from Ryan's side.

The figure trudging up the long, slow rise to the eastern horizon was already halfway there. Mebbe eight hundred yards, Ryan thought. Not much crosswind, as the rottie-swarm stench made clear.

"Long shot," he said. "Doable."

"Shouldn't we see what he's really up to first?" Colt asked. He wore pale blue pajamas with darker blue pinstripes, a royal-blue velvet robe and blue-and-pink house slippers. When word had come of Reno's successful escape from the eastern perimeter, the baron had come running, with his mercies and a drowsy, busily cussing Perico trailing after him.

Krysty laid a hand on Ryan's arm. She didn't need to

speak. He knew she'd council mercy. Or at least a degree of patience.

The sun had yet to rise. The gray false dawn wasn't yet bright enough to compete with the roiling yellow-and-orange glow from the clouds. A strange piss-colored light lay across the land and the watching faces.

"Why aren't the rotties on him like flies on shit?" Mildred asked. The horrors continued to shamble around the razor-coil-topped wire fence. But clumps of the changed wandered out on the long slope. And Ryan had an ugly feeling most of the swarm was currently out of sight beyond the horizon.

Jak held out an arm. "*She* not want."

"Jak used a *pronoun,*" Mildred said reverently. "Shit's gotten serious."

At the top of the rise a single figure appeared. Letting his longblaster hang by the sling, Ryan raised his longeyes.

He saw what he knew he'd see; the auburn-haired, blue-faced woman, Lariat.

Ryan lowered the longeyes, to find that a long line of rotties had appeared on the distant crest to either side of their leader.

"At this point, I don't know what Reno could tell them that would hurt us," Ryan said. "He doesn't know what we're planning."

He frowned. This little sideshow was preventing them from getting into position for the day's inevitable battle. Time wasted. And time was blood. Yet he felt as unwilling as the others clearly were to tear himself away.

Besides, he thought, we might learn something.

"Mebbe he's trying to talk them into sparing the ville," Krysty said.

Ryan shrugged. "No way to know." He didn't add that he wasn't sure that would even be a good thing, given the point of the whole scam they'd run here in Sweetwater Junction was to try to finish the rottie threat once and for all.

"I'm getting on a roof," he announced. "Mebbe I can drop the queen bitch."

"Will that stop them?" the baron asked in a nervous, adolescent tone.

"Only one way to find out."

By the time Ryan had settled himself on his belly on a cold flat roof with his longblaster rested on its bipod, Reno was approaching Lariat. The other changed hadn't interfered with him. Now, though, they were moving in behind him.

"Even if he's trying to screw us," Ryan muttered, bringing the scene into focus in his sight, "he's got balls, just to march in among the bastards like that."

Reno stopped about ten yards shy of the female figure. He began to gesticulate, obviously telling her something. She inclined her head forward, seeming to listen.

Then she gestured, and the rotties closed in on Reno. He kept up his arguing, or pleading, or whatever it was, until he felt a dead hand seize his shoulder.

Then it was too late. Dozens of the changed surrounded the slight figure, and Ryan saw a flurry of frenzied, futile movement.

Screams floated faintly on the wind.

"Ryan!" Krysty shouted. "Can't you help him?"

"Aren't there too many of them?" Colt asked. He was following the action through a pair of compact binocs.

But Ryan knew what Krysty meant. The only help for Reno now was a bullet through the head. Even if he was immune to the change plague, nobody was immune to being eaten alive.

Ryan was lining up a shot, though—on the auburn-haired rottie woman who seemed somehow to exert command over the horde. But it was a brutally long shot even for a marksman as ace as Ryan Cawdor, and his longblaster wasn't designed for head shots at that range, even under ideal conditions.

He didn't see where the first shot went. Even though he had the longblaster back on target with a fresh cartridge chambered before the bullet had finished its second-and-a-half flight time. Then Krysty called out that it had taken down a rottie twenty feet to the left of Lariat, out of the scope's narrow vision field. The next one showed no noticeable effect at all; possibly it had gone long.

The third shot kicked up dirt between the rottie leader's boots. Ryan's heartbeat spiked in exultation.

"Got you now, bitch," he muttered.

But Lariat simply turned and walked back down out of sight. He didn't even try a desperation shot as her auburn hair vanished.

He couldn't afford to waste the bullet.

"All right," he called to his companions, "show's over. Let's move as if we got a purpose. We have a job to do."

THE STEYR SCOUT LONGBLASTER roared and kicked toward the burning yellow sky. The target was distant enough that the bullet hadn't reached its home in a female rottie's skull before Ryan lost sight of his target. But when the long barrel came back down, he saw her going down with half her head blown away.

That was the job they had to do this day. How it began, at least.

It was nearly three hours since he'd climbed his uncertain perch and started picking off the changed as they circled and probed the ville defenses. It only seemed like a lifetime.

No doubt about it, the changed were showing crude tactics. They reminded him of a wolf pack scoping out an elk herd, looking for the weak point—the calf, the sickie, the oldie, the easy prey to cut out and take down.

But wolves were alive, no question, and they were both crafty and smart. These things overwhelmingly showed no more sign of life than a lump of clay. Yet all of them moved, all of them hungered, all of them hunted.

And some, apparently, thought.

Only twenty or so rotties were trying to claw their way over the razor wire tangles on the western gate, about six hundred yards away. A small group of sec men and ville dwellers posted there seemed to have the situation well in hand. They used the drill Ryan and friends had worked out on the spot yesterday at the opposite gate. People were stabbing the rotties who tried to scale the fence or gate, using spears improvised from long sticks and kitchen knives, awls or long nails. When some creatures managed to get inside, defenders with polearms of various sorts knocked them down or tripped them up. Others hanging back would chop open their skulls with axes, or bash them in with clubs. Some even squashed them with chunks of concrete.

Those cinder-block finishes really tickled the ville kids. Ryan had heard from the small herd of runners waiting on the second floor of his lookout that they'd already dubbed it "making jelly."

Colt Sharp, a kid himself, had hit on it yesterday: not just keeping the youngsters from underfoot but making them useful, by having them be messengers and carriers of water, meds and ammo. All through the night to this early, yellow-sky morning, small packs of children had raced tirelessly around the streets near the perimeter, keeping extra eyes on the rotties to make sure none sneaked in. With them ran some of the more manageable of the ville's canine population. Dogs went crazy, barking when a rottie came close. They were afraid to attack the changed, but sure let everybody know they were there.

Satisfied that the crew at the west gate was going to hold, Ryan swept his longblaster around, pushing with his boots and pivoting on his butt, and hoping the shaky platform he sat on wouldn't give way before the fence or a gate inevitably did. As always, he saw groups of rotties walking the perimeter. That showed him that *something* was influencing them beyond their craving.

A couple began pawing at the fence where no defenders were in view. Ryan had various means of alerting his teams, including flares and his somewhat hyper kid runners. But *this* what was he was up here for.

Fortunately, these rotties were of the low-awareness variety. When he drilled one through the head, the other didn't even flinch. It was climbing resolutely into the razor wire coil up top when Ryan shot it, too.

As his longblaster descended from the second shot's recoil, he heard a fresh spate of blasterfire break out off to his left.

An iron band clamped his chest. *Krysty.*

Cold logic demanded that he be where he was, doing this job. He was the best sniper in Sweetwater Junction, with the best sniper's tool. And as Colt's sec boss, he was tactical commander, possessed of a rough-and-ready system that actually let him exercise a modicum of command over the defenders. Ryan *had* to be here. Any other way offered more risk than reward, and they operated on the thinnest of margins already.

But this plan meant he was up here, and his friends were down there, in the thick of it. Including Krysty.

CROUCHING WHERE AN east–west street led onto the wide path that ran along the inside of the wire, Krysty aimed her Smith & Wesson 640 at the mass of rotties pressing against the fence scarcely twenty feet from her. Though she was totally safe from them—for now—the stench of death threatened to knock her to her knees, even though the breeze blew from her back, out of the northeast.

Then she lowered the blaster and put it away. One rottie more or less wasn't going to make a difference here. Better to save her bullets.

The other defenders didn't seem to agree. They kept shooting.

Half an hour earlier Ryan had spotted the rotties concentrating outside this point in the perimeter. He'd sent runners to order the reaction force waiting in the square under J.B.'s command to meet the threat. Along with the Armorer, Mildred, Doc, Jak and Krysty heeded the call, with about forty sec men and citizens. They were armed with the standard assortment of blasters and bows. Each fighter also carried some kind of hand weapon to fend off the creatures' fatal jaws at close range.

It was the third time they'd had to respond since the rotties began probing at sunup. About an hour ago there had been a breakthrough, when a weak stretch of fence gave way. Fortunately, it had been a minor attack, involving no more than about a dozen rotties. The reaction team got there in plenty of time, and since the rotties were in Ryan's field of view, they were also in his field of fire. The changed attackers were put down in a minute or two. The fence was restored and shored up by one of the work crews that also waited by the big fountain in the square.

But this assault was unmistakably more serious. The Sweetwater Junction contingent blazed away furiously from between buildings, from houses and rooftops nearby. Thick, dirty white smoke began to cover the area like a screen.

To the companions it was obvious they couldn't defend the whole perimeter. Sweetwater Junction was a substantial ville. All the able-bodied men, women and teens, ville dwellers and sec men alike, could just about encircle the town if they stood inside the fence with arms outstretched and fingertips touching.

Colt had seen it, too, right off. So had Perico and Coffin. The sec men took a while to bring around.

The idea was to dot squads of defenders around the perimeter. The kid-and-dog patrols would orbit constantly, keeping eyes, ears and noses skinned for break-in attempts. And Ryan on his precarious perch would keep watch for trouble, use flares and runners to direct reinforcements to serious threats. And, of course, pop rottie heads with his longblaster.

Even those without the ability or, frankly, the taste to fight, could still help defend the ville by tending the wounded, carting water and ammo for the children to distribute, repairing damaged sections of the fence. Baron Colt was proving clever in finding ways to use everyone. He had a kid's creativity, Krysty thought. Although she was somewhat surprised his mother hadn't squeezed it out of him with her suffocating ways.

But everybody knew that a big rottie break-in couldn't be held back forever. It was only a matter of time.

"Pheromones," Mildred said over the cracking of blasters. The stocky black woman stood on a sagging wood porch next to Krysty with her back against a wall. She held her ZKR 551 .38 revolver in both hands, barrel tipped upward for safety. Her dented baseball bat, cleaned of the congealed slime that had encrusted it the day before, rode on her back in a sling improvised from an old belt.

"What?" Krysty said.

"Maybe that's how Lariat communicates with the swarm," Mildred said. "Pheromones. Or some other kind of chemical the rottie pathogen excretes. They seem to react most when the wind comes from her to them, see?"

Krysty wasn't following most of what Mildred said, but she got the drift.

"Mebbe so," she said.

J.B.'s hat appeared around the corner of the wall Mildred stood against, hanging from his scattergun muzzle. His head followed.

"Wanted to make sure nobody blasted me," he said.

"You're clear, John," Mildred told him with a smile.

He slipped around, stuffing his hat back on his head.

"This is the big push," he said. "They're coming from all over, and the fence is starting to strain."

He turned and stepped into the street. "Cease fire, boys and girls!" he called. "We'll need the bullets for when they break in. Grab up a long sharp stick and poke some rottie eyes!"

It took a while for the firing to taper off. The nearest defenders stopped shooting at once and started yelling for their comrades to do likewise. The people of Sweetwater Junction held the Armorer in almost superstitious esteem. A lot of them, especially former sec men, seemed afraid of him, Krysty thought, despite his mild manner.

Neither Jak nor Doc were in sight, but they were in the area. As the shooting died away, Krysty heard Doc shouting for the cease-fire. She didn't expect to hear Jak. Making unnecessary noise wasn't his style. In fact, *talking* wasn't his style.

"We better get Ryan to send up the general pull-back signal," J.B. said. "The things're going to bust in here any moment."

"Right," Krysty said. She turned to a runner, a little

girl with tufts of short brown hair sticking out between the top tiers of her dense bundling of cold-weather garments.

"Sandy, honey," she said, kneeling. "I need you to run a message for me. Can you do it?"

The child nodded proudly. "To Mr. Cawdor. That's what I'm here for."

From behind Krysty the desperate cry went up. "Fence is comin' down!"

"MR. DIX SAYS THEY'RE about to bust through on the southwest side, near Miller's hide warehouse," Sandy told Ryan. He recognized her as the stable girl who'd brought the first news of the Ten Mile massacre. Although the knees were out of her canvas pants and there were holes in her locally made leather shoes, she was well bundled up against the cold. "He says give the general pull-back signal."

"Right. Thanks."

Ryan shifted his weight to look that way, gingerly, because he could feel the jury-built scaffolding shift beneath his weight whenever he so much as breathed heavily. Unfortunately, the most central location for a lookout and sniper post in the whole ville was the wooden observation tower, whose top two stories had been blown into kindling—literally, in a fuel-starved ville—by J.B.'s booby trap. So the carpenter had gotten some crash business, pounding together a two-story lookout platform overnight.

It was as rushed an improvisation as the ville's other defenses for what was certainly going to be the climactic battle, win or lose. So Ryan didn't waste too much time feeling sorry for himself.

Not that he ever did.

"You got a message for me to take back, Mr. Cawdor?"

Despite the shooting and screaming and stink and general horror, the little girl seemed more excited than fearful. Most of the kids acted that way. The ville civil war between Jacks and the Sharp tribe had probably acclimated them some to fighting.

"No," Ryan said.

He got his longeyes on the red zone. Defenders battled hand-to-hand against the rotties trying to swarm through the trampled-down section of chain link. He picked up Mildred joyously knocking the decomposing head of a rottie to pieces with her bat.

He frowned. As awful as the danger Krysty and his other companions faced down there, it was nothing they weren't all going to be up against. And sooner rather than later.

"Is your family at a strong point or forted up in your house?" he asked the runner.

"We're gonna fight at home," Sandy said. "Mommy and Daddy are out helping. My brothers and sisters are still home, though."

"Good. Why don't you run along home, then? Your mom and dad'll be along soon."

"All right." She vanished down the hole in the splintery wood floor.

"Tell the rest of the kids to take off back home, too!" he called after her.

"Okay, Mr. Cawdor." Her words floated up through the floor.

The farthest shot he had from up here to anywhere along the perimeter was less than six hundred yards. And he could see most of it. He'd burned through most of the ammo he'd gotten from the palace armory, which was pretty much emptying out for the defense of Sweetwater Junction. Fortunately, Colt Sharp saw that if they didn't win this day, there was no point having ammunition or anything else in reserve.

It was Trader's old principle of never dying with bullets in your blaster, written big.

The fact the new baron *did* see that marked him as different from both his mother and Geither Jacks in a very key way. Different from most barons Ryan had encountered.

Through his longeyes Ryan saw the rotties inexorably pushing back the defenders with sheer weight as they trudged through the breach.

"All right," he said, "that's it. Time to go."

Closing his longeyes to their soup can size, he stowed them in a pocket and reached for a special flare rocket, one conveniently painted red.

As he did, a drop fell from the sky to hit the back of his bare right hand.

It tingled.

Acid rain.

Chapter Thirty-Two

"Everybody out of the pool," Mildred muttered as the red spark climbed up toward the terrible boiling, mustard-colored clouds.

"What's that, Millie?" J.B. asked.

"Time to go, John," she said. "For you in particular."

"Right," he said. Then he shouted, "Okay, everybody! Pull back! Get to a strongpoint or head to your houses, but get inside and forted up, triple-fast!"

Some with what Mildred took for relief, others with reluctance, the defenders began to back warily away from the rotties. Some took off running. Others established separation and turned to shoot whatever projectile weapons they had at the changed enemy.

"Gotta power on," J.B. said. "Hate to leave you guys like this."

"We all signed off on the plan, John," Mildred replied.

"Hurry," Krysty said. She lined up a head shot with her handblaster, then fired. "Be safe."

The Armorer threw an arm around Mildred's sturdy shoulders, hugged her close and kissed her hard. Then he was trotting off down the street on his special mission.

Mildred found herself looking after him through a screen of tears.

She blinked them quickly away when Krysty grabbed her arm and started towing her in another direction.

"He'll be fine," the redhead said. Her scarlet hair writhed

around her shoulders as she shot a female rottie, little more than a skeleton with long hair and shrunken dugs, who had gotten to within a dozen feet of them. "If anybody can pull it off, it's J.B."

"That's true," Mildred said, trying not to sniffle. While he lacked Ryan's charisma or brilliance, the Armorer was the most competent man she had ever known.

But competence could carry one only so far.

Doc and Jak came whipping around opposite corners down the street. Doc actually impaled a rottie standing on the porch in front of him through the back of the head with his sword before racing past with surprising speed. Jak blasted two shatteringly loud shots back the way he'd come, then, tucking away his Colt Python, he drew his favorite new toys, the twin steel hatchets, and hacked his way with focused savagery through to rotties to join his friends.

The four hurried toward the center of town, fast enough to distance them from the horde. The few rare, more agile rotties who sprinted after them were shot in the face for their trouble and put down to stay.

The desperate game rushed toward its climax.

Can we really do it? Mildred wondered. Or had their luck finally run out?

"ALL RIGHT," J.B. SAID when he joined the two sec men near the hastily repaired eastern gate. "Bastards've broke through the fence to the southwest. Time to get back to wherever you're planning to make your stand."

The man J.B. didn't recognize as a Jacks sec man frowned. He was youngish, with yellow hair and blue eyes.

"Look out there," he said, jerking his head toward a window of the house nearest the gate, where they were sheltering. "Most of 'em are still out that way. And they're heading here now!"

"That's why I came to fire off the claymores we set up on the gate last night," J.B. said. "Drop as many as I can. But in a few minutes the ones from the breakthrough'll be filtering through. We won't be safe hightailing it then."

"Not safe anyway," growled Higgs, the former Jacks sec man. He was a human barrel, not much taller than J.B. What hair remained on his head marched down the lines of his jowls to meet up again under his broken nose in an impressive mustache. "Why not stay here and stand these fuckers off?"

"Suit yourselves," J.B. said.

A metal box once meant to cover electrical junctions had been screwed to the wall beneath the window. A bent metal conduit ran up from it, over the sill and down to the ground.

Taking out his home-brewed fire starter, J.B. flipped open the cover. A cut end of high-speed fuse waited within.

"Wait," Higgs said. "Somethin' ain't right. I think mebbe you should step away from that thing."

He started reaching for his lever-action carbine, leaned against a side wall against a stained, framed bit of embroidery saying Bless This House.

The fuse caught. A spit and a spark, a whiff of chemical reek, and the flame was on its way along the conduit buried six inches under the ground by the work crew J.B. had supervised the previous night. It took but a second to reach the blasting caps in the charges affixed to either post of the reinforced gate.

There *were* claymores mines, of an improvised sort: two big clay jugs filled half with black powder, half with bent nails, ball bearings, cast balls for black-powder blasters, and even chunks of broken glass. Anything small, sharp and nasty that could be blown into the faces and bodies of an oncoming enemy by the low but irresistible pressure of the bursting charge. They went off with a yellow flash and single two-beat roar, quite satisfactorily. Ten or twenty rotties nearing the gate fell down. How many would *stay* down was an open question. Glancing out the unglazed window, J.B. saw freshly detached limbs flying through the air.

Then the demo charges J.B. had attached along with the improvised claymores exploded, blowing the gate right off its hinges.

"Fuck!" yelped the blond dude. "He blew up the fucking gate!"

As J.B. had been striking the flame with his left hand, his right hand hadn't been idle. It swung up his slung M-4000 by its pistol grip. The blaster roared.

The column of double 0 buck caught Higgs in his chest as he spun, bringing up his carbine. He reeled back into the wall and went down.

The blond guy whipped out a Bowie-style knife and leaped at J.B. "You bastard traitor! You killed us all!"

Slipping off the sling, J.B. slammed the shotgun butt roundhouse against his face. Bones crunched and the kid sprawled on the floor.

Although his cheekbone was dented in somewhat and his left eye above it didn't seem to track just right, the kid was game. No sooner had his tailbone stopped skidding across the warped floorboards than he gathered himself for another attack.

It didn't make a bit of difference whether he continued his attack or not. A man who valued precision, J.B. shouldered the scattergun to take steady aim.

"Sorry, boys," he said.

The shotgun bellowed again, filling the little room with brief light and the smells of burned propellant and spilled blood.

"Nothin' personal. Just has to be done."

Movement from the window caught J.B.'s eye as he

jacked the slide. He spun and blew off the top of a blue-faced head right outside.

Then he turned to run out the door.

WHEN HE CAME INTO the square and sighted the sign that read Itomaru's Wood Works, J.B. reckoned he'd made it.

Whether it was just bad luck or one of those unpredictable flashes of cunning that hit some of the rotties from time to time, he'd never know. But as J.B. crossed the street toward the shop, at least ten of the creatures rotties suddenly surrounded him.

The shells J.B. had loaded would punch through wooden walls pretty readily. He didn't want to risk shooting in the direction of the building where his friends were sheltering. Despite his lack of size, he had some speed built up, and decided to put his head down and try to power through.

He shouldered a couple of changed aside—they didn't exactly have lightning reflexes—but then he was yanked to a stop. A rottie had seized the collar of his jacket.

If the creature had the wits or the luck to yank it down over his arms and pin them, J.B. would've been chilled right there. Or worse.

Instead the Armorer used his momentum to twist in his attacker's grasp. He pivoted and slammed the shotgun's butt into the decaying face.

The rottie let go, but the others closed in on J.B., pressing in from all sides. Blue hands grabbed him.

He stuck the scattergun's muzzle up under a rottie's chin and pulled the trigger. The blast ripped the whole front of the changed man's head off, and the body dropped.

A pair of hands grabbed the barrel. J.B. struggled for control. Though she had superhuman strength, the changed woman lacked eyes. It hadn't stopped her homing in on his warm human flesh, however.

He felt the terrible nuzzle of a corroded face against his cheek. A monster behind was trying to bite him!

With a terrific adrenal surge he yanked himself away from the questing jaws. But the eyeless rottie kept bony hands clamped on the scattergun's barrel. Stinking arms as strong as barrel hoops encircled J.B.'s body. He turned his head and saw open jaws with a rotting, blue-black lump of tongue between them descending toward his face.

Blue brows and forehead suddenly blew out in a rancid black eruption. J.B. flinched, shutting tight his mouth and eyes against the reeking gobbets of cold corruption resulting.

He heard the thunder of a second longblaster shot. The rottie's hands abruptly released their death grip on his shotgun.

J.B. flailed furiously with it, not trying to bust heads, just to knock the horrors off him. He wasn't a squeamish man, nor prone to panic. But right this instant he was as close to losing his mind to sheer terror as he ever had been.

He heard a third booming blast from a high-powered longblaster. A bullet drilled the head of the rottie right in front of him crosswise. The way to the porch of the carpenter's shop, the front door, safety, lay clear.

As J.B. rabbited forward, he saw Ryan perched on the tin roof of the building just west of the shop. He had apparently hopped from roof to roof from the crudely rebuilt sniper tower. A rottie mob stood beneath him, faces eagerly raised, pawing the air like puppies standing up against a fence, begging for meat.

Ryan paid them no heed. His single blue eye was locked on his embattled friend. He held his Steyr in his left hand and his SIG in his right. The 9 mm handblaster was flashing yellow flame in J.B.'s direction.

Ryan was shouting something the Armorer couldn't hear.

Suddenly three more rotties lurched into J.B.'s path. With survival on the line right now he couldn't worry about his backstop. He poked the shotgun toward a decaying rib cage and fired, hoping the blast would take the rottie down, and that the wasted body would stop the .33 caliber pellets from traveling on to hurt one of his friends.

The creature reeled back. The other two got between J.B. and the door. Rotting fingers rasped at J.B.'s right sleeve. He was out of Ryan's line of fire now. There was no help for him. He smashed in the teeth of one of the beings blocking the way. From the corner of his eye he saw the rottie he'd blasted lunging back, to claw at J.B.'s face.

The door burst open. A double-bit ax hit the creature in the side of the head with such force that his femurs broke and speared out through decomposed and desiccated skin.

A silver flash went by J.B.'s face to the right. He heard the ringing of an aluminum bat on a rottie's skull. Then hands—warm human hands—grabbed him and yanked him into a warm room that smelled of wood chips.

From behind him he heard Doc Tanner say, "Not wanted here!" That was followed by the disproportionately huge roar of the tiny stub of shotgun beneath the main barrel of Doc's LeMat handblaster. The door squeezed the weird yellow glow from outside down to nothing and closed with a slam.

J.B. collapsed, panting, next to the heavy worktable in the middle of the room. Mildred flung her arms around his neck.

"Thanks," he wheezed, patting her arm. "Now ease up a bit before you choke me, Millie!"

A SPATE OF ACID RAIN hit Ryan as he leaped from the gutter of the tin roof he was on to the roof of the carpenter's shop. It stung the exposed backs of his hands and the tip of his left ear. He could hear his hair sizzle. Smell it, too.

Nonetheless, he managed to catch himself on the corrugations of the metal roofing sheets. The stock of the Steyr, which he had slung once he heard J.B. hustled inside, slammed him in the left butt cheek.

It didn't dislodge him. He scrambled up and over, to slide down to the porch on the south side. It was roofed in tin sheeting, as well.

Rotties milled in the street outside the shop. At least a dozen wandered across the square. Drops of acid rain sizzled and smoked on Ryan's long coat. Can't stay here long or I'll fry, he thought.

He drew his SIG with his left hand and his panga with his right, then stepped to the edge of the roof and jumped into the street.

Ryan shot a rottie in the head even before he landed. His boots hit; his legs flexed. Then rising he spun, slashing savagely with the heavy blade. The blow took the legs right out from under a rottie.

The one-eyed man got onto the porch by the main window. It was stoutly shuttered, just the way it was supposed to be. The door was blocked by a solid mass of the changed.

The ones in the street came toward him. They stared at him with their vacant, questing eyes. Hands reached; mouths opened.

He fired a couple of shots before they got too close. Then, roaring his rage, Ryan hacked at arms and blue gaping faces.

The shutter to his right slammed open. An arm snaked around his neck from inside. He froze. Had the rotties gotten in with his people? But the skin of the arm beneath his chin was smooth and warm and didn't stink of death. Instead it had a familiar, welcome smell.

Krysty hauled him in through the window as if he were a child. As his boot heels thumped on the floor, somebody yanked the shutter shut.

No sooner was it fastened than a blue fist punched through, to grope about blindly.

With a hawklike scream of fury Krysty let go of Ryan. She grabbed up her ax and, with a one-handed swing, severed the arm just this side of the elbow.

"Bill Itomaru, you should be ashamed," a voice said from under the table, beside which Ryan sprawled on his butt. "Such shoddy workmanship!"

There was a little, round-bellied guy in an undershirt and work apron stretched out beneath the worktable. He had a lantern jaw with a straggly fringe of beard.

"What are *you* staring at?" he demanded.

"Fuck you, Brad."

Ryan looked around to see a wiry little guy with long white hair pulled into a ponytail behind a dome of bare skull. He had an ax, which he used two-handed to amputate another arm that reached in through the breached shutter.

"If you don't like it here, you can go outside with them!"

A blue face appeared at the hole in the shutter. It gazed in with a blank, impassive gray eye that reminded Ryan of a shark's. Doc, stripped to his stained white shirt, lunged forward and thrust the tip of his sword through the eye.

Relentless fists hammered at the front door, the shuttered windows. Nails raked loudly on wood. Similar noises came from other rooms. Dust flew from the door. Ryan heard wood creak as it started to give way.

"This could be a problem with our plan, friends," Doc said, drawing back out of grabbing-range of the hole in the window. At once a third arm reached in to grope ineffectually. "The rotties must have been a long time without eating, I suspect. If that is so, their hunger is reaching a crescendo. It is driving them into a feeding frenzy!"

"Still rather be in here with them out there than outside with them," J.B. said.

Holding her ax in her left hand, Krysty hugged Ryan fiercely with her right arm.

She yelped and jumped back. "Gaia! That stings! You've got acid all over your coat!"

"I'll get water," Bill Itomaru said. "Sluice that stuff off you."

Ryan shrugged out of his coat and jumped to his feet. "Fireblast! The rain! Hear it?"

Downpour rattled on the metal roof like falling gravel.

"Comes down hard," Jak said.

"Hope it doesn't eat a hole in the damn roof," said Brad Sinorice, the erstwhile gaudy owner, from beneath his table.

"My roof is the least of my worries," the carpenter said. "They'll bust in soon. Five minutes, max."

"Mebbe not," Ryan said.

Another arm was stuck in the hole in the shutter. Ryan aimed a little up and right and fired a double-tap, and two more ugly, mustard light beams stabbed through the gloom of the shut-up shop when the arm slithered back out the hole.

"Ryan, what are you doing?" Krysty yelled when he jumped forward and pressed his eye to it.

He saw rotties in the street with the rain pelting down on them. As he watched, a shriveled hulk of a man rolled dead eyes up in a melting face. The decomposed flesh was sluicing off his skull and arms like melting wax. His knees gave way and he fell forward to lie on his face, smoking.

All around the rotties were sizzling, smoking, melting. *Falling.*

"Scope it out!" Ryan yelled, dancing back just in time to avoid a mostly skeletal hand slashing for his face.

He hacked the hand off with his panga. Doc moved up beside him. He shot the blue face that appeared in the window next, then risked a quick look out.

"By the Three Kennedys!" he exclaimed. "The acid rain destroys them!"

He stepped back. "I have rarely seen even the most concentrated acid rain act with anywhere near such alacrity on living tissue. Apparently their corrupted flesh is especially susceptible to it."

"English," Jak said sourly.

"He means the acid rain melts them triple-fast," Mildred said.

J.B. stepped to the other window. Despite Mildred's warning, he rose up on tiptoe to peer through where a sliver of ocher light betrayed a crack in the shutter.

"He's right," the Armorer said. "Only rotties still on their pins are the ones hammering to get in. Porch's metal roof's keeping the acid off them. All the ones in the street are down."

Ryan looked around at the others. "Everybody fit to fight?"

His friends nodded.

"What do you have in mind, young man?" the carpenter asked in alarm.

Ryan had holstered his SIG again and gone to the door. His friends formed up to flank him.

"This," he said, yanking it open.

If long-dead faces could show surprise, those of the three rotties right outside did. J.B. stepped to Ryan's right. His shotgun blast smashed into an open mouth and tore the head clean off, from the stained and jumbled teeth of the lower jaw up. To Ryan's left, Jak's Python erupted. Ryan felt the side blast of hot gas and particles hit his cheek and clatter off his eye patch.

It didn't stop him from putting the sole of his boot to the belly of the middle rottie and kicking him into the street.

Acid hissed as it took the changed man. Drying, half-decayed flesh dissolved and dripped from his hands and face as he raised them toward the tortured yellow sky. He fell over backward, wreathed in smoke.

"Time for your showers, ladies and gentlemen!" Doc shouted, stepping past Ryan as Jak slipped out the door and to the left. "Let the sky's tainted waters wash this town clean of all your evil!"

Epilogue

"I wish we had a fire," Mildred said, rubbing her arms. "It's wicked cold out here."

She squatted in such shelter as the four-foot cut offered from the nighttime prairie wind. The others hunkered around her, except for Ryan and Krysty, who stood side by side atop the bank, gazing south toward the ville they'd fled two hours before.

"Not so cold as things'd be hot in Sweetwater Junction," J.B. said.

"But we saved their asses!" Mildred exclaimed. "We could have stayed. We would've been heroes! Shoot, Ryan, you were officially sec boss and everything!"

The tall, dark figure silhouetted against the stars seemed to stiffen slightly. "Don't remind him," Krysty said. She slid her arm around his narrow waist.

The acid rainstorm had passed; the skies had cleared. Inspection had shown that if acid had fallen or flowed in this spot, it had long since sunk into the sand.

"Bound to be questions raised 'bout what happened at the east gate," J.B. said, squatting at Mildred's side.

"You mean *to* the east gate, don't you, John?"

"That, too."

Like a white wolf on its haunches, Jak hunkered not far away, content to simply sit and rest with a hunter's patience. Doc, who had drifted away from this plane of reality—not that Mildred could blame him this time—not long after they slipped away from the ville, sat on the sand humming the same tune he'd hummed the past hour.

Krysty sighed. "Couldn't we have worked something out, lover?" she asked.

"You know we couldn't," Ryan said. "We all talked this out before. Why jaw about it now?"

"Cold," Jak said by way of explanation. The others looked at him in surprise. He was the last among them to speak up at all, much less in defense of jawing.

The acid rain had washed away the entire rottie horde, leaving little more than piles of stained bones littering the streets, and the long rise east toward Ten Mile as far as the eye could see. The crazy gambit had paid off. By blowing open the gates and drawing out the bulk of the swarm, they had ensured they'd be caught in the rain, rather than remnants finding shelter somehow.

Ryan didn't know then and didn't know now where the changed might have found shelter in this treeless waste. He just knew that whatever kind of creature Lariat had turned into, he didn't want to leave her the least little slice of a chance.

Inside the ville a few rotties had managed to get in out of the rain. They'd retained sufficient wit and will to break into buildings to escape the acid bringing final death to the unquiet corpses. But they hadn't been able to hide long from the search parties that set out to hunt them once the lethal rain stopped.

Reconnaissance by Baron Sharp's horse patrols reported no sign of rotties anywhere around Sweetwater Junction. Just scoured skeletons.

The one thing they didn't find was a trace of the auburn-haired woman in her leather jacket. Mildred bought into the consensus that the woman once known as Lariat, the rottie queen, had been melted to bones out there with her ghastly flock.

The ville's mood had been madly euphoric. Everybody was utterly beaten down physically, as the companions themselves were. But they still gave themselves over to a wild celebration.

Mildred had to admit they had plenty to celebrate. Not only the victory over the changed, but an end to the civil war that had so ravaged their ville.

Somewhere out in the night a coyote yipped. A shrill chorus of barks and howls answered it. Life went on out there. Somehow knowing that reassured her.

"Never would have worked out," Ryan said. "You all know it as well as I do. All the good cheer and glorious feelings were ace. As long as they lasted. Along about the time the ville folks start feeling their hangovers they'll start remembering how many of their own we left staring at the sky. Then the bad feelings would start. And then they'd start measuring us for Miranda's old killing poles outside the ville."

He stretched, then sighed and put his arm around Krysty.

"But yeah," he said softly. "It'd be nice to kick off our boots and put our feet up for a spell. Hell, yeah."

"Did we win?" Mildred asked.

"Huh?" Ryan said.

"Alive," Jak said.

"That's not what she meant." Ryan scratched the stubble on his right cheek. "All I can say is, reckon so."

"You *reckon* so!" Mildred exclaimed. "Is that really enough? You were the one who said we absolutely had to stop the rottie plague for good and all. Did we stop it? Absolutely?"

"Like I said, I reckon so," he replied. "All we can do is all we can do. It's enough to get along with."

Gently but firmly he disengaged himself from Krysty's loving arms and turned to look down at his companions.

"Now let's get along before that Sharp kid finds more limits to a baron's gratitude and sends the cavalry after us."

Doc chortled, sprang to his feet like a much younger man and began to sing like a happy child.

"Doc," Mildred said as she winched her way painfully upright, "one thing you have to tell me before we go.

"Just where did you learn 'Singin' in the Rain'?"

* * * * *

TAKE 'EM FREE
2 action-packed novels
plus a mystery bonus

NO RISK
NO OBLIGATION TO BUY